# THE MURDERING WIVES CLUB

# THE
# MURDERING
# WIVES
# CLUB

## SHARON THOMPSON

POOLBEG

Published 2021
by Poolbeg Press Ltd.
123 Grange Hill, Baldoyle,
Dublin 13, Ireland
Email: poolbeg@poolbeg.com

A catalogue record for this book is available from the British Library.

ISBN 978178199-403-0

www.poolbeg.com

# About the Author

Sharon Thompson is a bestselling Irish author who writes historical novels and short stories. When she is not plotting gritty manuscripts like *The Abandoned*, *The Healer* and *The Quiet Truth*, Sharon enjoys conjuring up light-hearted short stories for magazines like *Woman's Way*.

A qualified copywriter, Sharon also hosts radio shows and online events. She chairs panel discussions at literary festivals and contributes to leading websites and blogs. As an avid tweeter, Sharon runs a trending tweet-chat #WritersWise, and founded her own online writing group called Indulgeinwriting.

Sharon's historical, domestic-noir novel *The Murdering Wives Club* will be the first in her Sinful Roses series.

# Acknowledgements

There's a special magic that brings me to write every day. I thank and love this magic with all of my heart.

I wish to thank and acknowledge all those who've taken me this far along the writing road – those who've pointed me in the right direction and brought me to this destination. I am grateful for every purchase, read, review, piece of advice, and kind word.

To you, the reader of this work, I hope you have escaped for a while and will want to read more of my short stories or novels. With your help there will be more.

Thank you to my agent Tracy Brennan and to the great team at Poolbeg Press, Ireland.

To all my fabulous friends, family and community who have supported me all the way.

The last mention goes to my husband Brian – thank you for encouraging me to write about murder and mayhem. But more importantly thank you for being the love of my life and my best friend.

For my husband, Brian.
(Whom I have never wanted to murder)

# Chapter 1

## Laurie Davenport
## 27th June 1944

Shadows are my world now, but shards of light dance and a precious English sun warms my knees. I don't talk about my year and four months in the Sappers, or Royal Engineers. All anyone needs to know is that I was blinded and scarred by shrapnel as we attempted to rebuild a strategically important Italian bridge. What I can recall of the brutality of war, I choose to forget. I still take a small tipple of morphine and it makes me lethargic, but it's hard to forgo that now. It's also hard to admit that I didn't want to live until I knew that my wife was trying to kill me.

The noise of the gramophone scrapes and the drawing-room door opens. I smell Norah's perfume.

"Morning, sir!" Norah Walsh, my new assistant, breezes in and lays a tray on the table. She fixes the noise, moves papers with a flourish, and then lifts the tray she was carrying again. She grunts slightly for me to sit upright in my favourite high-backed chair next to the glass doors which look out onto the gardens.

My man Giles is away visiting family, leaving Norah in charge of breakfast. The tray is placed on my lap and she brings my fingers to touch the almost-full china cup. It's all arranged in our set format, so that I can feed myself without spillages.

"It's a fine summer's morning," Norah says. "Let's ignore this flaming war and be glad that we're breathing and above ground."

She is preaching at me, but I've come to like her Irish accent. And she's terribly good-natured, even in the early morning.

That scent is definitely new. Norah is a resourceful lady who bypasses rationing.

There's an uncomfortable silence then she coughs and says, "Mrs Davenport is still away, I see."

I nod and touch my moustache.

"You look fine this morning, sir. You did very well in getting dressed without help. I'll trim your beard later if you're worried about how you look."

"There's no need. Giles will be back later today."

I listen to her move around and wonder does she mean that for a man on the cusp of forty I look all right? Or does she mean that she's become accustomed to the burn-marks on my face? I want to ask how I look to her young eyes. I presume that she's good-looking because General Freddie Ashfield, my dead brother's friend, sent her here. Freddie favours attractive ladies and has remarked on her striking red hair.

The tea from my favourite china cup is just the right temperature and strength. My moustache hairs tickle the old-gold rim and I sense that she's watching me.

"Are you still in pain since yesterday?" she asks.

If she means physical discomfort from the healing burns on my right side, then I'm at last able to say, "I'm fine."

We have discussed my need to return to normality.

"Melancholia?" she asks, coming closer.

I can make out dark and light as she blocks the window

with her slender silhouette. I've not had the heart to ask her what age she is. But by rough calculations and some amateur detective work, I surmise that she's in her early twenties.

When, at the start of May, Freddie first proposed her as a personal secretary, I thought her too young to live here at Davenport Manor – but I relented when he insisted that she would be perfect. After two days I became dependent on her. Now, she's a trusted companion.

Yet, I don't want to admit that my emotions are all still in a mess. I cry at the drop of a hat and flinch at every bang or wallop. The nightmares are still vivid as hell. I didn't see much of the real fighting, but our battalion was under severe pressure from enemy fire regularly. Someday, I might get my confidence back but it's taking a long time.

Charlotte, my wife, has been away for many months now. I've no idea where she's gone and I've been torn between missing her and being able to relax a little. I'm back alive in my childhood home, dear Davenport Manor, and today is indeed a good day. I managed to get myself dressed and downstairs to put on my favourite music. The sun is warming my knees. I'm a lucky man indeed. Then why don't I feel it?

"More music?" Norah asks. "The wireless is full of bad news. D-Day and the likes. Word is filtering through too of more captured allies in Assisi. But let's not think about that right now. How about we listen to something upbeat and cheery, eh?"

She makes me smile but I don't think that she moves to pick anything from the collection of records on the shelf.

"When you've finished your toast, what is the plan

for today?" she asks. "Will we open the General's file?"

I still don't feel up to taking on life, never mind a new task. General Freddie is convinced I can find another role for myself. If I must be productive, I want a job that doesn't involve being an officer or an architect. I have hated anything to do with construction since someone stepped on an enemy mine buried deep in the mud.

From the day and hour I set foot on the cold, icy Italian soil I'm ashamed to say that all I wanted was to be home warm in my bed, or in front of a good fire with a cigar and a nice whiskey. I never wanted to be a hero – or a cripple. But here I sit.

General Freddie gets impatient with me. He's an army man through and through. A man whose own life *is* the army cannot see that mine should be full of architectural plans and the beauty men can build instead. Explaining and finding my way out of this darkness is very difficult. But there's something motivational about Norah's enthusiasm and she's starting to wear down my determination to be miserable.

Freddie said, "Norah Walsh is one of my most highly thought-of personnel. Make use of her keen brain and abilities. Get back in the saddle, Laurie. Your country still needs you."

When I returned home on an army stretcher I made an oath to rebel for the first time in my life. Being one of the lucky ones to be repatriated home, I should have been grateful. However, I'm aggressive and angry most of the time and, although I've always been compliant, this is going to change. The dependable, solid, moral me in school and in the army is no more. My country took everything from me. My darling parents were bombed in the Blitz. Their London home levelled because father was too stubborn to return here to our country estate. My only brother blown to bits somewhere in Poland, and me, orphan Laurie, only half the man he was.

I also have a rather large dilemma. I left at the start of this wretched war as a married man. I returned a cripple to a wife who wished I had died or been captured. Once I admitted that to myself, I found convincing others was even harder.

"She really is trying to kill me," I told my trusted confidants.

Freddie was incredulous. "You cannot bandy about such things without proof. If her father hears that accusation – we're all done for! He has Churchill's ear."

"He's an arse-licker, Freddie," I said. I like to use Norah's crude Irish words.

It was after 'accident' number two that Freddie insisted that I needed a personal assistant.

"I was pushed from the top landing. It was not an accident. And the morphine overdose was not my fault. I may be blind, but I'm not losing my mind. You've known me a long time, Freddie – long before these blasted uniforms – and I'm telling you now that Charlotte has tried to do me in on more than one occasion. I don't know my wife any more and I swear to you that I would never try to take my own life. All of it is her doing. When she is here, I'm a nervous wreck. But lately she's cavorting off wherever she pleases and, although I'm not altogether sure that I should allow it, I have to. As how does a blind man stop his errant wife from doing anything?"

The General's feet shuffled. He was uncomfortable.

I was glad that I couldn't see either of their faces.

Norah sighed. "I think that you should just let Mrs Davenport go where she wants. Make it easy for her to leave."

A little piece of my heart broke. I almost felt it crack off. I stood and cried in front of them both. I loved my wife.

Norah held me close. It was comforting: soft hair on my cheek, the scent of perfume and the smooth touch of a hand on mine.

"I thought we could be happy." I blubbered like a child. "I loved the woman I left here in my home. But she's not who I thought she was. What can I do now?"

"War changes us all," the General said. "There's no going back for any of us. I'm going to suggest, yet again, that you need find a purpose, Laurie. Something to take your mind away from all of this. Top up her allowance and let her stay away. Find a challenging, new direction for yourself."

"I'm blind!"

"It might come back," he replied like it was a stray cat or something. "They said your sight could improve."

The cigar and contraband supplies that he brought were always welcome. But there was no clarity as to what I was to spend my time doing. I was no longer a man who could earn a wage, that was a certainty. Feeling sorry for myself, and others, was wearing very thin.

"What do you think, Norah? What do you make of all of this?" the General asked.

I was shocked. It was unusual for Freddie to even acknowledge a woman, never mind ask her opinion.

"Arrah now, I shouldn't judge," she said in her Irish way. "But if Mr Davenport believes this, then somebody should listen to him."

"*But you don't believe me?*" I asked in a high piercing tone.

"I haven't met Mrs Davenport," she said. "I cannot talk about another woman without knowing her ways for myself. But I think that you're a good and honest man, sir."

"Cook and Giles didn't need convincing," I sniffed, forgetting that they were staff and employed at the Manor since I was a child. Both of them never liked Charlotte. I should have listened to their murmurings, but I was blinded by love. Blinded indeed. Perhaps it was lust? Perhaps it was ambition?

Charlotte is from a well-connected family. I thought that she wasn't in need of money. She was perfect. Or so it seemed. I was in my late thirties and was told it was time for settling down. Then the war surrounded us. Marriage was both romantic and necessary.

"You're daydreaming again," Norah says, standing by the shelves in the far corner. "You tilt your head and get that faraway stare when you're doing that. What are we going to do today? We've made progress counting the steps between rooms and learning the layout of the furniture – and how to ascend and descend the stairs. But I think it is time we went out somewhere? The sun is nice. A walk around the garden would please the groundsmen and –"

"*No.*"

Silence. There's a shuffle of paper, a creak from the chair and the flip of a folder being opened.

"The General sent some more documents. I can read them to you. And – before you act like a bold child again, I think this top one might interest you."

"Could I have some more tea?" I ask, not wanting to seem too curious about what she has in front of her.

Norah ignores my request for more tea and begins to read. "'*Scotland Yard have dismissed these cases.*' The names, dates and some information have been blacked out, sir, but it says . . . um, here we are . . . it says '*despite the findings, General Ashfield fears these men were murdered and that it was perpetrated by someone close to them. It has been suggested that their wives were somehow involved*'. Well, well, well! Doesn't that sound familiar?"

I sit forward in the chair and the sun heats my reddening face.

Norah's breathing has changed. I can tell that she is excited.

"There's a note here from General Ashfield. It says: '*This is for your consideration, Laurie. If you're interested in this, I can furnish more information and get you involved. It is not an active case but I've been given clearance to have a civilian look at another angle of this intriguing mystery. I also want this to be the work that will get you back on your feet.*'"

"I don't know what to say."

Norah sighs. "I agree with him, Mr Davenport. When do we start?"

# Chapter 2

## Norah Walsh

"'*Holy Mary, Mother of God, pray for us sinners, now and at the hour of our death, Amen*'," I mutter and bless myself quietly before entering the kitchen. I've had some time off from the prying questions of Giles, Mr Davenport's butler. He's back now from a few days' leave and when he gets a chance he tries to prise more information from me. We get along well and I've missed his help, but he's rightly worried about his boss and my purpose for being here.

He perches now on the kitchen stool, peers from under those spectacles and grey eyebrows, and asks, "Family is so important. I'm sure that yours want to hear more regularly from their red-haired Irish colleen?" He has tried to pull my past out of me a few times now. "And is working here really better than working for the General?" He continues shining the silver tea service like an Aladdin's lamp. "You must find work here very different?"

"I've heard that spies in Germany are tortured during interrogation," I reply. "When will that start?"

Giles chuckles while the skinny, sullen-as-ever cook batters on at the bread dough on the large kitchen table.

If only I could tell them the truth about my past. I wish that I could confess that I'm no longer someone's mistress. I have more to me than a pretty face. And I'm content here even if everything about Davenport Manor is antique: the servants, the furniture, the gardens and the air. I like Laurie Davenport, but he is still a product of his class and the manor itself – stuck in a rut, scarred by time and terribly stuffy.

"You've been here about eight weeks now," Giles says, "and it's obvious that you will stay, so we're just being friendly." He cocks his greying hair towards Cook, who looks more wizened than any Irish witch would be.

She smiles and rolls her eyes. They work well together and it's clear that they've been friends for many years. They are kind people.

Good-natured Giles laughs and waits on me to tell him about my past. His eyes are wide and curious. The nosey git! I've told him heaps about myself but he wants more.

"I've told you lots about my family and how nanny-work took me to England. What else do you want to know?"

I look around the ordered, clean surfaces for something to eat. From the shiny pots and pans hanging neatly, to the large east-facing window, there's not a cobweb in sight down here. Cook keeps her domain spotless.

Her white apron gets a rub of floury hands. She opens the cave of an ancient oven and lets the heat out to blush our cheeks.

"There's nothing too different about me," I say. "What is it that you want to know? Spit it out, Giles. Spit it out!"

"I'd love to know more about General Ashfield. He was always Fidgeting Freddie to us and he used to ruin the roses in the garden when he was a young fellow. He played with Laurie's brother, Ian, all over the grounds and caused untold mayhem. It's hard to believe he's General material. The army must've made a man out of him." Giles peers at the cloth he's using and then buffs the tray a bit more. "I've wanted to ask you – was it Lord Wester who introduced you to him?"

"Yes. When the Wester children were sent to school and my nannying came to an end, rather than going back home to the pig farm in Meath, I asked Fredrick – I mean, the General, for a position. It was that simple."

Leaving out the part of being in Wester's bed, I watch Giles work. If I was one of those girls who liked older men, Giles would be attractive for a man in his late sixties. He's still agile, slim and well-presented.

I fix the pleat in my skirt and check my stockings are straight. "I also wanted a change. I'm used to be being the bossy one and have big notions about being a woman who can make something of herself. I suppose too I want to make a difference in this wretched war. I don't like children much and sitting behind a desk doesn't suit me at all. Are those eggs I spy in that basket?" I potter over to the worn wooden work surface next to the window. The sun is blinking through the clouds and I run a hand over the smooth brown shells in the wicker container. "Are we having these today?" My mouth waters and Cook grunts in agreement. "That lifts my spirits. This rationing is hard to take. Laurie will enjoy these."

"You're very good to Mr Davenport," Giles says. He sounds pleased.

"He's a good man," I tell Giles as reassuringly as I can, "but he's been a bit of a challenge and he's going to need lots more help to get him back on his feet." I'm always a little wary of Giles as I realise he might well be jealous of my position after all his years of service to Laurie and his parents. "We've started an assignment for Fredrick. We're working on … a secret mission, I

11

suppose you'd call it. I offered to lend a hand in the hope that the General will see that I've brains as well as beauty." I wink at Giles. "In fact, we're about to go to Northern Ireland for a few days. You'll need to pack for Mr Davenport, please. As I said – it's exciting."

"Is it dangerous?" Giles asks, sitting up on the stool and raising those thick eyebrows. "Has Mr Davenport not been in enough peril?"

"If all truth be told, he's not going to be much use," I start and then realise how I sound to the only two remaining people who consider Mr Davenport to be their family. "It's giving him a purpose though. Something else to think about. We hope that it helps."

Giles sets down the cleaned items on the tray and stands to squint at them. He examines the tea-service items from a few angles. "I see," he mutters.

"I'm here to take care of him and to get him back to his old self," I say eagerly, perhaps too eagerly. I have my own reasons for wanting to be here and my own ambitions that a British General can and *will* help with. The General wants to keep tabs on what he's doing and how he's feeling. He worries. That's why I'm here. We all want to see him get better."

"So, you're saying that you are really here to spy on poor Mr Davenport?" Giles asks, taking off his spectacles to squint closer. "Is that what you're saying, Miss Walsh?" He is teasing me as usual. He smiles.

"You're like the Gestapo, Giles," I say with a giggle. "Don't you worry. I've not been trained in espionage."

Giles' attention is taken by Cook's orders about wood for the fire and I breathe a sigh of relief. But a dread sinks in. This isn't the last time I'm going to have to lie about my real reason for being here in Davenport Manor.

# Chapter 3

## Laurie Davenport

The journey aboard the *Duke of Abercorn* steamship across the Irish Sea is rougher than forecast. Not being able to see adds to the worries of being sunk by a German U-boat. Tensions are high still about the allies' campaigns. I hate listening to the constant radio bulletins but Norah reassures me that there's "a big push on" and things are turning around for the lads I've left behind.

With even the slightest movement of the ship, I curse under my breath.

Norah is as direct as ever. "Stop fretting. It doesn't help. If we die, we die but it's unlikely we will. Your nerves won't affect the outcome one way or the other."

She booked us two cabins and hired pillows and blankets, but I doubt I'll sleep much.

"Half past nine on the dot and we're going at a good speed," she says. "Doesn't it feel like we're heading along nicely?"

We're sitting in my cabin on what feels like a very small bed and I'm wishing she was going to stay with me. I don't want to be alone and close my eyes to pray that something might make her stay on the other small single bed she has laid out my things on. It would be nice thinking of her sleeping not too far away, and she could just lie there with me in the dark. I would be gentlemanly. I would not act on my impulses.

"Did you hear me?" she asks. "Once we dock in Belfast in the morning, we'll go straight to the women's prison in Armagh and then get the hired car to our guesthouse."

At least all her instructions are taking my mind off my swirling stomach and impure thoughts about her remaining with me during the night's crossing.

"I'll read some of this file to you," she says. "Are you listening?"

I usually love her voice but now it drones on like the labouring engines. The destination is almost as unsavoury as the journey itself. We're heading to interview a convicted woman who has been sentenced to death for many crimes.

"'In 1933, Eve Good was sentenced to death for the murder of Mr Frank Hockley and Mr Cedric Fellows. She was also charged with the murder of her husband Mr John Good, but there was insufficient evidence to convict her of his murder, or for the attempted murder of Mrs Marjorie Fellows. With the lack of influential people to plead for clemency, to date she's not been granted a reprieve. A date might be set for her execution at any time.'" Norah stops. "You've got that faraway look again. Are you listening at all, sir?"

"And she's the only person to mention this Murdering Wives Club?" I ask and steady myself by gripping the mattress when there is a rather large sway of the ship. "Christ, I really feel that I might die before I meet this murderer."

Norah laughs. I like the sound even if it is at my expense. I am seriously fearful of everything these days but I've never been confident on boats or ships. I cannot swim well. Like the rest of my failings, I don't want to tell Norah this. She's accomplished and in control. I miss that feeling.

"Do you need a hand to get undressed?" she asks out of blue. "I'm just thinking I might go to bed myself. I'm tired."

My groin hardens at the thought of Norah and me in a state of undress and I feel as if I have blushed crimson. "No, thank you," I mutter and then say loudly, "I think I'll stay in my clothes. A man should die with his trousers and shoes on."

Norah is giggling and getting up to go. I want to implore her to stay here until we dock in the morning. Otherwise, it's going to be a long sleepless night for me. I want to throw my arms around her and explain that I'm afraid, but it would be improper to ask for a lady to stay in my cabin. It wouldn't be fair to her reputation. What happened to me being less compliant? I'm failing at that as well. I even allowed her to bully me into leaving my morphine, my Velvet Syrup medicine, behind.

"You could stay with me?" I say hopefully.

"You have your hipflask and you can always bang on the wall and I'll come to rescue you, sir," she says with a squeeze to my arm.

I pat my front pocket and stop myself from reaching out to hug her. "Whiskey," I confirm with as much confidence as I can muster. "Dear goodness, I've just realised that we'll have to go through this on the way back too!"

"Isn't this much better than sitting in that old dusty parlour in the manor? Mind you, I don't want to be too long in the North. An Irish Catholic needs to be careful what she says and where she says it there. But isn't it great to be on a little adventure, sir?"

"*Hmm*, and please call me Laurie," I say and stop for I sense she's gone and then there's a click of the door closing.

I lean back onto the pillows and pull the scratchy blanket up to my chin. A fumble into my breast pocket unearths my twenty-first birthday present from Freddie. I take a long swig from the hipflask and it warms my throat and soothes me slightly, but with each nod off into sleep I'm back on the transport ships that took us Sappers to Italy. It was the autumn of last year and I could see back then and I still couldn't imagine the danger ahead for me. For us all. Now, I'm fearful again – of all that I cannot see and all that I *can* imagine.

# Chapter 4

## Laurie Davenport

The ninety-minute drive to Armagh Women's Goal from the docks in Belfast is uneventful and I'm thankful for that. I haven't slept a wink and feel like death warmed up. I managed a change of shirt and a splash of water to my face but it didn't help much.

Northern Ireland is suffering with bombings, conscription and rationing but Norah says, "Armagh looks nice in the sunshine. Tulips blooming and the streets are busy. It's a pretty city."

As we wait to be let into the prison, I pull at my father's repurposed suit and fix my tie. I've lost a lot of weight and nothing fits. Norah is not good with a needle and thread, but she has reassured me twice since we got here that I look dapper. I miss the confident reflection that used to greet me whenever I found a mirror. It's difficult to go out when you don't know how you appears to others.

I should be used to confined spaces or literally be blind to them, but I sense entrapment.

As we walk through echoing corridors, Norah whispers. "What an awful place!"

We reach a room and they give me a cold chair to sit on. I try to stop my leg from shaking and place a gloved hand on my knee.

"Are you all right, Norah?" I ask the presence to my right.

"Yes, sir, I have my notepad ready to take shorthand and don't you worry about me. There's a female guard here too sitting behind us and I'm told the prisoner is fairly well behaved."

The guard makes a scoffing sound.

I smell that she's just had a smoke. She likes a cigarette. I must remember to ask Norah what kind and we'll bring some the next time we visit.

"You don't agree?" I ask the guard, half-turning in the chair.

"She's a bad egg, sir. That's all I'm going to say on the matter."

"I see."

Norah has read me the rest of the file on this woman on the way over here in the hired car. It does seem that she is more dangerous than old Freddie initially thought. She refused to talk for her trial and, although she was sentenced to death, she and the rest of us are waiting on her sentence to be commuted to life imprisonment. It's rare for a woman to be executed.

She came forward months ago talking about wives murdering their husbands, but she wasn't believed. Until now, that is.

There is an opinion in the military and society that women are not capable of heinous violence or evil. I would not have believed it possible either, but here I am in a women's prison. There is a need to lock them away for crimes, so they're not all devoted mothers or members of the Women's Institute. It's not something I've given much thought to – until now.

Norah is nervous about coming to the north of Ireland and, considering she's an immigrant from the republican and rebel south, it's interesting that she is highly thought of in the British military.

She said a few times on the car journey here, "Let's be quick about this trip, sir. Get the information from this woman and get home to Davenport as quick as we can."

At this very minute, I can think of nothing else but taking her home and escaping this prison and this terrible situation.

"Eve will like to keep you waiting, sir," the guard says in a low whisper. "This is a treat for the likes of her. She's not liked at all and we don't believe a word she says. Take none of the nonsense she'll dish out."

"Agreed." I nod even though the guard is behind me. "I would appreciate your opinion for my reports though?"

"I'm not sure I should say any more, sir. You'll see what I mean for yourself soon enough. Just don't let her shock you. She'll love that."

There is more clanking and clanging and the shout of the guards to one another about the time being ten minutes past ten. There's a turn of locks, and keys on chains dangle and rattle. Feet scuff the floor and the light changes quickly. A movement of bodies and the smell of starch. The chair on the far side of the table moves and a dark figure sits.

"Mrs Eve Good, I'm Laurie Davenport," I say and stop myself from giving her my hand to shake.

"You cannot see me?" she asks in a northern Irish accent. "How can we communicate properly?"

She's trying to sound more educated than she is. As an Irish housewife, she's also haughtier than I expected.

19

I smile. Norah told me to tell her nothing about myself. It's difficult to know what is the best way to start this conversation.

"I cannot. But –"

"Is that woman taking notes?" she interrupts.

"This is Miss Norah Walsh. She is my personal assistant. She will take down all of the information for me. I cannot do this for myself."

"I see." Eve chuckles. There's a cruelty in the laugh. "I see and you cannot see. That's funny."

I scratch my moustache. She's unlikeable. Norah shuffles uncomfortably too. We are out of our depth and we both know it.

I try to take control. "This is very unorthodox practice and I hope you realise that you're lucky to be given this time. So let's begin."

"I won't start with *her* here."

This throws me off kilter. I thought that she would respond well to other women. Unusual.

"Norah is staying. Let's begin," I say with determination.

"If I begin, do you promise that I'll be kept away from the other animals in here?"

I just nod, for I'm not totally sure what she's been told will happen for her co-operation.

"I'll be killed for talking to you. You do know that? If you want me to tell you what I know then you'll need to keep me alive."

"Of course."

"I'm valuable to you and I'm not happy about another woman being here. Not happy in the least."

My lips purse tightly together. She is taking the upper hand and I feel at a disadvantage in so many ways. Not seeing her mannerisms might be a blessing – her voice is intimidating enough – but not being able to see her is making me nervous. I'm also not experienced in talking to women, never mind criminal ones.

"You're pretending that you don't need me?" she says. "I think you do though. If I wasn't important then why would a gentleman like yourself be sent from London? I'm a person with some valuable information. Men like you think women are inferior. Well, I can tell you that we are far from that."

Norah's pencil scrapes across the paper. She sniffs.

"You've reported that you were almost killed by a group of women in Netterby, County Down, in 1933?" I'm wishing I had my notes to glance at. The exact details escape my memory.

"Yes. I was shot."

"And you claim that these women wanted you to help them and others to commit more murders?"

"That's correct. They wanted me to advise others on how to kill their husbands."

"And … you allege that they shot you because you wouldn't do their bidding?"

"In short. Yes."

"And that speaking up could get you killed. Even in prison?"

"That's right, but I'm not going to sit here and keep answering questions about things I've already told the other officers. It's wasting time. I'll be killed if they hear about this."

"I doubt *they* even know we are here."

"They will know! *They* have eyes and ears everywhere."

"Why do this then – if it is so dangerous?"

"I want to be moved to a better, more comfortable place. I'm tired of waiting on word about my fate. I've been promised. I know that women with means have been sent to nicer facilities. I want the same treatment. I need to get out of this hellhole. I've signed an agreement. I asked only to speak to a man. I'm not sure I can go on with *her* here."

"I need Norah." I tell the dark shape. "She is my eyes and she stays."

"Don't you realise she could be one of them?"

"One of what?" I ask.

"The women you want to know about. No, I'll only give my accounts to you, Mr Davenport."

"Mrs Good, that's not possible. I need Norah."

She doesn't seem to be listening because she starts muttering about her safety and then says, "She'll tie me in knots and I'll not present myself properly. I'm not on trial. That's another condition. I'll explain all freely and perhaps someday you'll see that my words bring about some good. All of the information will be the truth and from my memories. But I don't want her here at all!"

"Norah will stay. End of discussion. Let's move on. There are key things we wish to know. Who are these women? And what proof do you have about what they are doing?"

Eve ignores me and continues. "This is the way it will be. No women must know."

My mouth goes dry. She talks like a man, not in tone, but in manner. She is unapologetic, speaks without fear, is full of determination and self-belief. Eve Good formidable. I wonder what she looks like. If she is beautiful then I can understand why she went undiscovered for so long. I've met similar men in the army. They are handsome, charismatic and confident, with a lack of conscience. If this Eve Good is anything like them then I think she would be a perfect vehicle for killing.

"I'm in charge here," I say but don't sound like I am at all.

"If you need to think so," Eve purrs. "You've no idea who or what you are dealing with. I'm willing to help you. I'm prepared to put my life in danger to share everything I know. I want you to catch these women before they do any more damage. You should be grateful. But, Mr Davenport, you don't seem grateful and neither does your woman here. I've changed my mind about speaking with you. I don't want to go through with this."

"You've signed an agreement."

"I also swore to love, honour and obey." The voice is again amused by its own sound. "A woman changes her mind quite often, Mr Davenport." She pauses. "Tell me, are you one of the Davenports who socialised in County Down? We may have met before?"

I know from her files that Eve Good is middle-class and poor to boot. I doubt she socialised in my parents' circles, or my own.

She reads my mind. "You think you're above me? I can tell by your face that you think I'm not good enough for the likes of you. *Huh!*"

I'm glad that I cannot see her expression. There's a chill in the room and it's making me shiver. "No," I lie. "I'm thinking of where I might have been in County Down and where we might have met."

She stalls at that on an intake of breath.

I sense that she wants to retaliate and wait.

But she must think better of more confrontation because she sighs and says, "You, what are you called again?"

"Norah. I'm Norah."

"Irish Norah, with a southern accent, working with a British military man? I bet your people what to kill you too, Norah? We're both traitors to our kind."

Norah doesn't answer. I'm not sure of how to protect her. I don't know enough about Norah's past to be useful. I mentally kick myself.

"This is not about us, Mrs Good."

"Call me Eve. I'm not good in any way. Kanaster is my maiden name. I should never have married John and the name galls me."

"Eve it is then. You'll have our undivided attention for the next few visits. But don't waste this opportunity. I'm not a patient man."

"Let me be very clear here, Mr Davenport. I *won't* tell my story to a woman. *You* are wasting your time."

# Chapter 5

## Laurie Davenport

Our lodgings on the outskirts of Armagh are not far from the prison. Norah is very quiet on the journey back in the hired vehicle. The chatty driver tries to make conversation but both of us are dumbstruck and tired. Have we come all this blessed way for nothing?

We agree to rest for an hour and then she'll come to my room and we'll go downstairs to eat as arranged with our hostess.

Lying on the bed and staring into the dappled blackness brings no ease. Exhausted from the journey, I still cannot close an eye. I never expected Eve to be that awful. I should have realised that she would be. She's a killer and not a normal human being. Yet, in other ways she seems very ordinary.

Leaving us she was adamant that she would say very little. We have learned little about her or what is going on.

"Is this a huge club?" I asked. "Who funds and runs this organisation?"

But she didn't want to divulge that crucial piece of information.

I sit up.

Opening my briefcase is of no help. I cannot read the files or her words so cannot access the information. I fling the case off the high bed and it scatters its contents out onto the wooden floor with its fringed rug. I stand out on the floor. I feel the papers underfoot and hope I manage to pick up all of them. I might slip on them.

The window lets in the fading daylight. I can vaguely see the shards of sunlight and the dressing table's mirror is large as it reflects glimmers that make me squint.

I wish to change my socks and I have to concentrate to feel them in the suitcase. Why does everything take such effort? Giles packed well but I wish he was here. I like to be well-dressed at all times and this evening I want to look more than just presentable.

I'm as ready as I can be when there's a timid knock on the door and I hear Norah ask, "May I come in?"

A tired me opens the door and I smile. "You look lovely, Norah."

"And how do you know that?" she says with a chuckle. "But thank you. Let me look at you. You are a little dishevelled." Her breasts are right close to me as she fixes my top buttons and tie slightly. "There. Perfect, sir."

I wonder if my facial scars are as bad as they feel. The ripples are large from my forehead over my right eyebrow and they extend over my cheek right out to where my ear should be. It is a mess of flesh but I can still hear well thanks to surgery. I've lost hair from my right sideburn and I feel it might be a terrible colour or be extremely off-putting.

She links my arm.

"Lead on!" I say.


An hour or so later we return to my room to discuss strategy. Dinner was plain but good, and I feel mellow after a couple of whiskeys.

I remove my shoes with my toes and walk carefully forward, feeling my way to lie on the bed. How nice it would be if she would lie in beside me! Even on top of the covers, she could nestle into my shoulder and we could rest together.

"What the heck will we do now?" Norah asks as she sits.

Even though I don't need to, I close my eyes and listen to Norah talk on about possible solutions to the dilemma of Eve's stubbornness and paranoia.

And I fall asleep.

I'm woken by Norah's screams and the uncontrollable coughing starts. *Smoke.* I am surrounded in thick throat-clenching air. Norah has my hand and she is pulling me towards the door, shouting, *"Fire! Fire! We need to move out. Now! It's bad!"*

Nightmares aren't hot like my shoeless feet are. We reach the landing. Flames lap at my calves. I cannot burn again. The smell of my flesh on fire is not forgotten. The smell rises in my nostrils immediately but there's no burning sensation anywhere. However, fear freezes me to the spot.

*"We must move on, sir! Please! Trust me."*

The coughing is impossible to stop as Norah leads us through the darkness without hesitation. Down the stairs we fumble and falter but she never once lets go.

Suddenly, there's a man's grab at my arm and I'm tossed over shoulders with an "I got you!"

The cool air of the evening hits my feet and I'm placed on a metal garden chair.

"You're safe now," a man says and then asks, "Can you see me?"

27

I try to reply but the coughing takes over.

"He's already blind – he was damaged by shrapnel in Italy," Norah says to my left. "I'm here, sir. I'm here. All is fine. Everyone got out."

"Are you sure you're not hurt?" I asked, grabbing at the hands I know are hers and following them to her shoulders and cheeks. She seems intact and breathing calmly. I wheeze.

Her hands holds mine to her face. "All is fine. I'm not hurt. You're gasping though."

"My lungs are bad since the pneumonia in hospital."

"Of course. But don't worry, it's over now – the fire is almost out."

My knees tremble. I feel silly for being the one who is in need of the rug they bring. "I'm the pathetic victim in all of this."

"You're not alone, Laurie. And you would laugh if you could see me. I'm mortified. You're respectable – fully dressed as I just covered you with a quilt when you fell asleep on the bed. But I'm only in a flimsy nightdress. I didn't even grab my dressing gown when I smelt the smoke. But, thankfully, a very handsome young fireman gave me a coat."

"How good of him," I say and grit my teeth.

# Chapter 6

## Laurie Davenport

Back in Davenport Manor, with a stethoscope to my chest, is not where I want to be.

"In and out a few more times, Laurie, if you don't mind," the doctor says and I wheeze in time to his instructions. "That sounds all right now but, dear me, you've had a lucky escape. And it was possible arson, you say?"

"Yes."

"They have some idea who set the fire?"

"No, we don't know. There are always religious tensions to consider and then I'm British. So we were possible targets." Inwardly, I've promised myself for the fiftieth time that I will not be going back to Northern Ireland anytime soon. "Thankfully, the lady of the house was alerted by Norah and not caught up in the blaze."

"And it wasn't a cooker or stove? Could it have something to do with the owners? Could they have upset someone?" he asks.

"Possibly." I am lying. Norah and I presume it was to kill us in our rooms.

"If you've been across the sea, then I needn't ask if you are going out more often? This summer sunshine will also brighten the days." I hear him move the hanger which holds my uniform. "But why go to Armagh of all places? Is Northern Ireland not a dangerous part of the world with all those Irish rebels and whatnot? Or did you have a personal reason for taking Miss Walsh to the guesthouse?"

I ignore his tone and answer him back curtly, "It was not for pleasure. It was a private matter but I can assure you that it was not for pleasure at all."

"I see," he murmurs.

"I'm glad one of us does," I reply.

"I'm sorry. You'll need to take it easy for a few days."

Then he goes through a list of instructions for me and my medications.

"Miss Walsh is in fine health too. There's no sign of any injury."

"Good, that's the best news!"

"She's a fine woman," the doctor says, clasping his bag shut. "You are both lucky to be alive."

"Indeed. She's also very brave. She saved my life."

"The world is full of heroes," he replies, "but it's not often a woman gets to be one."

If I wasn't so angry at the world, I might agree with him that it is indeed a good thing to have a woman rescue a man. But the thought sinks me into a hole of resentment. I never wanted to be hero, until it was impossible to ever be one. I don't like being rescued over and over again.

"Our boys are turning this war around," he goes on. "News reels in the cinema are bringing us all a little hope that things will change soon. I'm sure that the reports of those missing or killed must be hard on you – but we must soldier on as they say, eh?"

"Yes."

I wish he'd shut up and leave but it seems he is assessing my state of mind. Why is it that I fear he'll be reporting everything to Norah or Freddie? I listen to him pull on a coat or jacket and decide that I can be polite for a few more arduous seconds.

"I hope that this won't bring back those nightmares?" he asks on his way to the door. "You've been improving so much. I think Miss Walsh is doing you a world of good."

"Miss Walsh is just here until I get back on my feet."

"Very good, Mr Davenport," he says from near the door. "I'll leave you now and please follow all of my instructions to the letter and all will be fine. Goodbye."

The door closes and I breathe out, lowering my hunched, tense shoulders. Thankfully Norah is unharmed and we're home safe and sound. That's all the matters right now.

The ring of the telephone shrills downstairs and I just know it is Freddie. I get up and count my steps towards the door. Opening it, I cross the landing to the top of the stairs. My home is as my parents decorated it when they themselves got married. I'm sure there are repairs to be done. The floors possibly need new carpets and the walls must require a lick of paint, but thankfully I cannot see it. There's a window open somewhere as there's a nice wash of fresh air on the landing. Norah is on the telephone at the bottom of the stairs in the main hallway.

She is listening, making short responses that don't reveal what she is being told – by Freddie, I presume.

"Yes," I hear her say at last. "Yes, of course. I'll let Laurie know."

A further long silence.

31

Then she says, "That's terrible!"

She does more listening.

"A knife! Stabbed? How is that possible in a prison? Did Eve say who attacked her? No?"

Another pause.

Then, "You want her taken to where, did you say, sir?" Silence again as she listens.

"Yes. It was definitely arson, sir. It looks like someone wants us stopped. Yes. Awful, sir. He's doing fine, thank God. The doctor has just left. But now I have to tell him all that. Most disturbing."

A silence.

Then, "Of course we need to be extra careful. I'll insist on it. Yes. The Home Guard might do a night-time patrol. I'll talk with them." A pause. "Oh, right. Yes. Yes. If you think that's necessary. Thank you, sir. Goodbye, sir."

The receiver clunks into place.

*"Can you help me come down? I'm still a little shaky!"* I call. I can manage the stairs but I want Norah close to me and any excuse will do.

I hear her climb towards me. Then there's a waft of her scent and the feel of her hand on mine. I link into her arm and purposely nestle in closer. If she senses it she doesn't flinch and we descend the stairs in silence. We are almost dancing as we cross the hall and enter the warm drawing room. She guides me to the chair next to the double doors that lead out into the garden. She helps me sit into my favourite chair which faces into the sunshine.

"That was the General. You heard?" she says.

"Yes. What has happened to Eve?"

"A knife attack. I don't know the full details. But she's been taken to the jail's infirmary and Fredrick's arranging to have her brought to England. He says it will take a while to get permission to do that. Eve will be happy though. This is what she wanted all along. She wanted out of that place and, according to Fredrick, she only has a few nasty scratches. Nothing fatal. She's like a cat with nine lives. She won't say who attacked her. Happened on the night of the fire. A clear message for us to stop with this investigation. Don't you think so?"

"Definitely. Someone want us to stop what we're doing and they want Eve silenced."

"And the General is sending men to look over the garden and the house. To assess if we need protection. Before you give out, you have responsibilities to the staff." Norah thinks she will have to convince me that we need protection but I wouldn't risk her life again. "It will only be for a short time. I'll ask the Home Guard to check on us occasionally."

"That's fine."

She seems shocked that I agree for she breathes deeply and then resumes her news. "Fredrick has insisted that Eve writes down all she knows. He has promised that they will be 'for your eyes only'. Typical Fredrick! Doesn't think about what he's saying. And she has to realise I'll have to read them for you. Or perhaps she thinks Fredrick will? Anyhow, there will be letters coming from her soon. He says that he'll send over them over as she writes them, on the promise that she will stay in the prison hospital and then be moved to safety. In time she'll probably be brought over here to Fredrick's base at Thistleforth House. I'll read the letters to you and, when she gets to Thistleforth or wherever she may be, we can question her then."

"Well, we're certainly not going back to Armagh! So, that'll have to do."

There's a pause. I sense she is hesitating.

"I'm afraid that I may have more bad news for you," she says. "I've sent for some tea."

"That's not it, I hope? Is tea bad news? When was tea ever a nasty thing in England?" I mock, trying to assess where exactly she is standing. I wish to find her shadow and look at it.

"No, silly. I'm trying to tell you some more worrying news. I'm sorry to say ... Mrs Davenport is also missing. Her car was found abandoned on some waste ground on the outskirts of London. The lights were on and the engine left running. Her handbag was on the front seat. I'm sorry, Laurie. It doesn't look good."

I hold my breath and search for an emotion. "Charlotte? Gone? Are they sure?"

"Very. She was seen driving away in that vehicle twenty minutes before. She's not been back to her hotel and her acquaintance has not seen her since."

"A man, you mean? This acquaintance? Her new lover? He's not seen her in how long?"

"She went missing late on Friday, June 30th. The day we went to Ireland. Three days ago now. Not a dicky-bird from her since."

"Why didn't Freddie tell me when it happened?"

"He thought you might want to come rushing back and they had spent time and effort getting us to Northern Ireland. You won't be allowed anywhere near that case, Laurie. And what could we have done anyway?"

"I suppose you're right. Do you think these women we are finding out about took Charlotte? This Murdering

Wives Club? Did they take my wife?" I'm thinking aloud.

"It seems they might have heard about us meeting Eve. Or, this might not be connected in the slightest. Mrs Davenport could have annoyed the wrong people. She has been gambling heavily."

"*Ah.* I've known about her addictions for quite some time. But she never came to me for money. I thought she must be quite accomplished at it. Perhaps her other men furnish her with cash and gifts?" I shudder at my indiscretion. A husband shouldn't even think such things about his wife. Since returning home from the war, tears can come easily but they don't appear now. "Isn't it odd? I don't know how I feel. I cannot cry or worry any more about her. It seems that I have reached my limit."

Norah's hand is on my shoulder. I like it there.

But then the door opens and Giles arrives with the tea tray.

"Tea," he announces in that old-fashioned manner my parents taught him.

I've heard that he's given in to needing spectacles full-time now and that his hair has turned mostly grey. I like to picture him entering the room with charm and elegance. He's always been tall and distinguished and he is loved by employer and servant alike. Giles is a great butler and I know he cares for me. This is a good thought for a tired and weary soul.

"Thank you," Norah says, and I hear her making room for the tray by moving the morning papers.

I hope she doesn't throw them away without reading some of them to me. Much as I hate the articles about the battles raging, or the beautiful buildings being blitzed in cities, it gives me time listening to Norah and I like that very much. We are usually alone when she shakes out the paper and starts her tutting. If I'm brave enough I ask her to read the headlines and first few paragraphs. I do enjoy hearing about Vera Lynn, Winston Churchill or the Royal family. I usually ask her to gloss over the other realities.

"I'm glad to see you are in one piece and that the doctor is satisfied that you are both in good health," Giles says, pouring liquid into china. "We were all happy to hear that you were travelling again – until there was that fire. Are you doing all right now, sir?"

"Yes, I'm fine, thank you, Giles. Did I ask you if all was well with your family?" I know he has a big soft spot for his many nephews and nieces. Some of his own were sent to Italy at the same time I was. Others are scattered at the whims of Monty and the other generals. There is a stirring of tea. "Has there been any word of your nephews or cousins?"

"Thankfully, all is fine for now, sir. There have been letters from them all recently. Of course a lot of what they say is censored but there's always whisperings that the allies are pushing on and doing well. I can't help but wonder if it's all true. It's so hard to tell what is happening so far away. I suppose we must have faith that things are going to be better soon. I have too many people to worry about in these sad times. And I never dreamt that you'd be in danger again, sir."

"We're home in the manor, and thankfully we're safe and sound. You can thank the good Lord and Norah for that."

"Is whatever work you're doing very dangerous?" Giles asks, a shake in his usually confident voice.

"We don't think so," Norah says. "It was a shock, but

36

we're both fine. Nothing to worry about at all."

"And Mrs Davenport's disappearance?" Giles must see my startled face because he adds, "It was in the newspapers, sir. I'm very sorry."

"Charlotte will be found soon, God willing," I reply as I wring my hands together. "She's made of strong, stern stuff. As we all know, it's not unusual for Charlotte to be absent and causing worry."

"It's all this new-found freedom the womenfolk have, sir," Giles says. "The politicians and the churches are right to fear for the moral fabric of this country."

"Arrah now, Giles, us women aren't all bad. Mrs Davenport will turn up."

Giles makes a noise in his nose. He wishes to disagree with Norah but no argument starts between them.

"There will be some men coming around the house," Norah says after a few seconds. "They are to assess if we need protection."

"Gracious!" Giles says.

"We don't want to worry you," she says. "Just, if you see strange faces at the door they are probably sent by General Ashfield. We'll introduce you and let you know what's happening."

"Thank you. Will they need beds made? I can tell Cook to do it."

"Cook would not be pleased," I say, trying to make light of the taste of danger in the room. "And we might need protecting from her."

"Let *me* deal with Cook," Giles says in that droll way of his. "How many might be here?"

"Two at least," Norah says. "But they won't be sleeping on the job, I hope."

37

"You're not to worry everyone, Giles. This is a precaution." I sound afraid and I'm angry at myself for sounding fearful. "The army has given us a little thing to do and it seems that it may have hit a nerve. Once these louts realise that I'm blind and not doing much of any consequence, they'll all go away."

"If you say so, sir."

The doorbell rings and Norah scuttles out to answer it, calling back, "That'll be a delivery from Fredrick of Eve's first letter. He said it was on its way."

Giles hands me the cup and steadies it in my grasp. "I'm worried for you, sir," he says. "You must confide in me if you need to. I have a pistol under my pillow and I've no fear of using it."

"A pistol?" I whisper.

"There's not many good men left to serve. But I've been in this household since you were a lad and I aim to keep you safe when you are under my care. I promised your parents that I'd do my duty."

A lump rises in my throat. "Dear Giles. I know that you are just the best sort. I'll be fine. But might I ask a favour of you?"

"Anything, sir."

"You might keep a special eye on Miss Walsh. She's a woman after all."

"Of course, sir. Of course. But she's more than capable. I've seen her tackle Cook and the groundsmen together."

"Formidable!" I chuckle.

"She has a very steady manner. We all respect her."

"That's good to know, Giles. And very much appreciated. I wouldn't like any harm to come to her under my roof."

"I understand completely," he says. "We all wish only the best for your future now, sir. You mustn't put yourself in any more danger. You've given enough for this country. Too many families have given more than their fair share."

"I went to Armagh for selfish reasons, Giles. Very selfish reasons. I never expected us to be in any danger at all. If I had known I might not have moved from this chair. I do feel a little shaky. Mrs Davenport's disappearance has been a terrible shock."

"I hope they find her, sir."

"Yes."

The tea is as only Giles can make it: never too hot or too cold. I drink it and think of Charlotte and I listen to Giles tidy the room. If she is found, do I want her back here in my home? Do I know my wife at all? Why did I think she would be a good wife? What did I love about her? She liked to travel and that was something I used to enjoy. Egypt, India and Africa were all on the agenda. Now, there is a war and I can hardly face leaving my house. Could I possibly still love Charlotte after all we've been through? My heart beats in my chest and I heave air into battered lungs and know that I'm glad to be alive. She tried to stop all of that. Would I be sad if Charlotte stopped breathing? What has happened to her? Do I want to find out?

The clip-clop of Norah's heels return and I picture Charlotte coming though that door instead.

"It's what I thought it was," Norah says. "I'll read it to you now. Apparently Eve tried to make out that she couldn't write. She was told that she'd be sent back to the general prison from the infirmary until she was able to … and suddenly this first instalment was handed over. Fredrick said that the guards saw her sit up all through Sunday night writing. Thinks herself a novelist!"

My fist curls into a tight ball and my heart hurts with the thought that the woman with me might be my wife and not Norah. I have answered my own fears. As Norah starts to read, I decide that I never want my wife back. Never.

# Chapter 7

## Eve Good

### 2nd July 1944, Sunday

*Death is the only reason for being a Sinful Rose and it is the only way you can leave.*

There is much debate about when, where and how the Sinful Roses came to be. Yet, in 1944 the Sinful Roses survive and thrive. They talk a lot about how somewhere in the annals of history, women became tired of being victims and decided that they wished to create victims instead.

Since this time, every effort has been made by powerful men to slash and burn the Sinful Roses. They say that every male-dominated structure works on the basis of the principle of working together: settlement, farming, masonry, armies, politics, capitalism or socialism. Yet, the true nature of man is to hunt alone, and it is believed that really it was the female of the species who harnessed the art of co-operation. It was the female gender who sculpted history but also the one buried by those who rose to write it.

The Sinful Roses blame historians for obliterating the innate power wielded by women. They believe that the act of female solidarity was labelled sinful and criminal. This ethos of co-operation then needed to evolve to become immoral, as nothing is as effective, or as powerful as murder. Naturally, when threatened, man wished to stamp out the Sinful Roses.

Each Sinful Rose knows her true purpose. The need to remove tyranny is thrust upon her. Once she makes the decision to rise above her situation, she contacts those she heard of at her mother's breast. To even whisper the Sinful Roses' name makes you a dangerous woman, and there is no greater honour than to be accepted into the fold. As a Sinful Rose, a beleaguered woman becomes a weapon. She joins a coven of her own kind. She thrives and blossoms and is no longer alone. A Sinful Rose will always be a Sinful Rose and they must support others who wish to join. The price is simply to honour and help other Sinful Roses.

With all of this in mind let me begin my story.

It was the autumn of 1932 when it all started. I wrote and they replied, inviting me into her den of sin. I strode through the mounds of dried oak leaves and the arched veranda's paint peeled under my gloves. I summoned the courage to use the brass knocker of the house.

The door opened.

A distinguished woman stood there, perhaps about fifteen years older than me.

"Welcome, Eve. I'm Lydia."

I stepped in.

She shut the door, turned and walked into a large parlour. I followed.

The curtains were drawn across the bay windows and the room was as dark as the furniture. There was one other woman in the room, and she was sitting there scowling at me.

A portrait of an elderly woman loomed from over the marble fireplace and she wasn't smiling either.

I perched on the edge of an uncomfortable chair.

"What a beautiful room," I lied, smiling at the two women.

The second woman, around my own age – twenty-five – snapped, "Hullo. I'm Alice Longmire." She struck a match and lit a long cigarette.

I nodded a greeting. I knew that in her haughty opinion I was not worthy of being there. But these were the women I'd fantasised about meeting. These were leaders in the female army who would brighten up boring days. They were going to understand my needs and take me into their club. Finally, I had found an affinity with others.

Alice's dark curls and high cheekbones were beautiful. Despite her being fairly young, there was a life lived in those piercing dark eyes and I wondered how someone like her was involved in all of it. I was annoyed that her opinion mattered to me. I presumed that these women would support me but it was obvious that Alice did not to want to bother. She smoked and wouldn't look at me.

I slipped off my gloves and hat and placed them on my lap.

Lydia stared and I found the sweat rise on my temples despite the autumnal crispness in the house. I am ashamed now to admit that I was afraid then. Fearful of what was beginning and that I had simply walked into such trouble.

"To your good health!" Lydia said. She sipped from the crystal glass and a hand touched grey hair that swept back into a tight bun.

The walls felt like they were closing in. I was out of my depth. While mending my life – and my dresses – my cousin Tilly had made it all sound much more glamorous and salacious. Joining the Sinful Roses was to be an adventure. But it was more like a ghoulish wake. My cousin Tilly also made going there sound scandalous. It had raised the adrenalin and moulded dreams, but now it all just seemed like a stupid notion. For the women before me seemed strange and I sensed that they meant business. Whereas I was there for the excitement. It was far from the glamour I was expecting or the welcome I presumed I'd be greeted with. In truth, the disappointment was fierce.

"Should I go?" I said. "Thank you for giving me an appointment, Lydia, but perhaps I should go?"

"You're here now, and you cannot just leave," Alice muttered and puffed on her cigarette, "Lydia wants to look after you."

"I need to go," I told them. It was so cold my breath made a frosty cloud. I had made a huge mistake coming here and I wanted to retreat. I knew immediately that was not possible. My eyes filled with tears. These women were strong, I could tell that my weakness would make them mock me, or worse it would make them angry.

Lydia coughed. "We know why you are here and you are welcome."

"I don't think this is a good idea at all," Alice Longmire said. "Being barren is the only thing in her favour."

"The Sinful Roses will not deprive very young children of a father," Lydia explained.

Of course. I had mentioned I had no children in my 'application'.

"You're plain. But there's more to you than meets the eye." Alice stared at me. "I've done some digging about you and I don't trust you one little bit. Lydia, I would do anything for you but this is too much." She tied a silk scarf high and tight under her chin. "Lydia feels that you're a woman of substance, who needs our help. But I'm not convinced. I sense you're not what you seem. Mark my words." She pointed her long nail at me. "You'd better not cause any heartache. I'm leaving now – but be in no doubt that I'll take no nonsense from the likes of you."

"Alice, if you want to go, then just go," Lydia said calmly. "We all know what it's like to be downtrodden for so long that you don't know your own mind. We've all made a promise that, if we can, we will help others. The time has come for us to fulfil that promise. Talking and advising is all we are doing here."

"*Pah!*" Alice left the room in a swish of red material, a coat she pulled from somewhere. It almost hit my face in her twirl of temper.

"If she didn't agree to me being here, then why was I allowed to come?" I ask then.

Lydia leaned her bun against the high-backed chair, sighed and closed her eyes. "Alice forgets what it's like to be scared. It's been a long time for her and she doesn't think we need to keep revisiting our sins. Unlike me, she doesn't feel the need to atone."

"I'm sorry that she doesn't like me," I told her. "I hate to admit it but I cannot go on the way that I am. But … I shouldn't have come."

Lydia's knuckles went white on the arm of the chair.

She sat forward, her eyebrows high and questioning.

"But you did come here, Eve Good," she stated. "This is the beginning. You're now involved. There's no turning back of the clock."

Going home to Newburn Crescent felt strange. The bus trundled back to where I came from. But nothing was the same any more. People chatted about the weather and about their children. I knew some of their faces, but I couldn't bring myself to speak.

Alice's words were ringing in my ears. *"You're plain."* The cheek of her!

I knew my husband John would agree. I could hear him spitting and saying, *"What good are you?"*

To him, I was not a car or something useful or terribly pretty. All of his pursuits were ones I cared very little about. Thanks to him, bearing children was top of my hate list. Mr John Good was a policeman who thought that he was part of the old money. He convinced my parents of his nonsense.

"Your father was tired of trying to find a match for his plain daughter. Now I'm stuck with you and have nothing to show for my bother."

The blister on my heel must've bled. I could feel a trickle and a burning as I moved in my strapped shoes. The shoes were new and were far too tight on my feet.

It was my cousin Tilly who mentioned the Lydia woman to me. We were in her house, called Glensmal, in Inishowen. She dropped her into the conversation, nice as you like, when we were having a cup of tea.

"You must go to visit the infamous Lydia. Her women's

group are the talk of the country! She's out of prison but she murdered her husband, you know."

Tilly pressed her elegant hand on mine and I thought she must've been joking, but she wasn't.

"People love a scandal, don't they? They say that she killed her husband for the money!" She breathed in delight and then whispered, "Her husband was a policeman, but still she got a reprieve and only served some of her sentence."

"I've got my reputation to consider," I said.

Fantasies of my own rose to greet me. The excitement of actually being able to discuss the undiscussable gave me heart palpations. It sustained me for days and the thought of it I suppose still does. I know from being here in this prison that certain men find evil women exciting. Some come to visit the most hardened of us. I find that fascinating. An odd one comes to save our souls, but many find us sexually enticing! I laugh at that fact a lot. But back then I was an innocent in every way.

"I couldn't possibly be seen with the likes of those criminals," I said to Tilly, knowing full well I'd soon be on the next bus to the murderer's address.

"But John might harm you badly," Tilly warned. "No children . . . Eve, you need to do something. They say that Lydia talks about how she did it all the time. And that her patron, married to the rich Yank, left her that beautiful house. Imagine doing what she did and getting away scot free and inheriting a place like that to boot? Is there any justice in the world? You must go see what she's like, Eve, and then write to me here and tell me every sordid detail. You just have to go see what all the fuss is about!"

47

* * *

Some weeks after my visit to Tilly in Inishowen, my parents went and died within weeks of each other. They were managing fine alone in the terraced house in Belfast, until Daddy took sick with consumption and then Mammy took to her bed with exhaustion and hysteria. So, I forgot all about Tilly's naughty chat. "Lost without their love for each other," someone mentioned at my mother's funeral and my heart throbbed in agony that I was lost without love too. I slunk about the house for months, sometimes not bothering to wash or even to get out of bed. There was no point to anything. John said that I was "losing myself". He encouraged it. Left whiskey out, bought cigarettes and suggested when we were in company that I was very melancholic and in need of doctors. I lost even more weight, which made my clothes hang oddly. I didn't care.

Then John was inexplicably moved to Newburn. I was to be a new person in strange surroundings. I was interesting to the church ladies, until they realised I could only bake scones and had little to offer in the way of gossip. It was tiring.

Six months later, while picking daffodils in the grounds of the churchyard, I realised the unusual house next door to the church, with the name on the gatepost, was the one Tilly mentioned to me.

Immediately I felt a rush of excitement. *This is the place Tilly told me to visit.* It was the house which hosted the organisation we all called the Sinful Roses. It was very grand compared to our home. Our Number 5,

Newburn Crescent, sat on the end of a cul-de-sac and was on the main Belfast to Whinpark road. And our Number 5 was modest compared to Number 4 next door. However, we had three storeys, with an attic on top that was the whole width of the house. It was an old building that needed work which John refused to recognise.

I opened my front door with the key and pushed the shiny, brass knob and felt content. John wouldn't be home and I was glad of the space that gave my head and heart for a few hours. I loved the quietness, the stillness of the dust gathering on the few pieces of old furniture. Sometimes I even sat and watched it. Even though our main road was on a bus route, no-one called to us all the way out there. I was glad of that. The days were my own and the evenings usually free of him too. Aside from the odd snore in the other single bed, I was not lumbered with him heaving and panting on top of me any more. For warmth, I heated the small front parlour with an open fire and brought a hot bottle to bed to curl my toes around. The stairs needed a new carpet. The bare threads were always catching in my heels.

However, now I clipped up those steps like a young girl with purpose. Further on up, the wooden attic stairs were worn smooth. I hated everything in the early days in the house and the attic had become my own hidden fortress at the top of it. John never went up that far, and it was where I spend much of my time. When I was not under the slanting roof or watching the trees swaying down below in the garden, I was up in the attic in my mind.

I've always been a naughty girl and I'm bad inside. I must have been this way all my life. Why else would I thrive on the worst of daydreams? Why else does my heart pound with the joy of you now knowing the truth about me? Why would a woman like me need to be a Sinful Rose, unless I was made incorrectly from the beginning?

Like Lydia said, I'm Eve Good and I *am* bad.

She did say that I was bad, didn't she? Yes, she did. And Lydia is a woman who sees the real woman within us all. Lydia could immediately see and understand my predicament.

She told me when I was leaving, "We'll make it all better, Eve. I promise."

I might be plain-looking but when I climbed those attic stairs, I was the most beautiful, sensual woman in the country. Alice might have thought that she was above me, but up there and in my own space and time, I was a queen.

"I know you're here!" I said and opened the small attic door.

And there he was on the mattress on the floor. My young Tim.

He was pretending to be reading and not waiting on me at all.

"I'm sorry that I'm late, but I had things to do."

His handsome eyes met mine and his dimples sank into those smooth cheeks. "I'd wait forever. You know that."

His need of me was nothing to the want I had for him. I found when he was not filling me I was lost in long daydreams of the times that he was.

I still cannot believe that it actually happened. It was a mystery to me how I couldn't get enough of him.

But the other side of my life was John.

Later I watched as he slurped at the vegetable soup I made. I knew by the way he held the spoon that he was in a foul humour. The house groaned and the draughty corridors allowed doors left ajar to creak and bang all by themselves, but every so often even John noticed an odd presence in his house.

"Don't you feel watched here?" he asked, not for the first time. "And I don't mean the nosey neighbour overlooking our every move. I get a constant feeling of someone else being here though. Don't you get it too? You used to hate this place. And why lock the doors upstairs? I hope you have the keys? Should we talk to the minister and see about removing the ghostly feel? Or should we just move somewhere else? A terraced house would give you more people to talk with . . . being alone is making you even more odd. When I'm not home you might have some company if we lived elsewhere?"

"Have you lost this place in a card game?" I countered. It was usually his gambling habit that forced changes for us.

"No, I'm thinking of you," he whispered.

He was tall and lean and I knew that his policeman's right hook could take the wind out of my lungs if I talked back to him.

Clearing the dishes, I sensed him gawping at me. There was no thanks in him for the work I did to keep his house. No appreciation that I tried to darn his socks and make him good food. But then there was no gratitude in me that he hauled himself into a terrible job every day to do whatever he did. We were like strangers who once humped each other in the vain attempt to bring a screaming child into the world. The lunacy of life was

51

not lost on me. I've thought long and hard about it. Whenever I finally liked the way things were back then, John spoiled things.

"Someone told me there was someone here today," he said.

"No, dear. No one called here."

He smoked a cigar and twiddled with the knob on his new wireless. He meant Mrs Marjorie Fellows, the curtain-twitcher next door in Number 4 who had seen Tim come and go through the front and side entrances.

"Why are you suddenly all cheery and polite?" John asked. "One minute I can't look at you for the temper that's on you and the next you're grinning like the Cheshire Cat?"

John was not the sort to bother with joking or teasing. He truly believed that I was a lunatic. Sometimes he came home early to catch me out or convince me that I needed to see a doctor. Always he tried to make out things were my fault.

The floorboards above him cracked loudly and he looked upwards, sighing. I wondered if Tim had slipped out and gone home to his uninterested father and starving siblings. Or if he was waiting on my soup and cold dinner in the attic.


So, yes, I went back to the Sinful Roses and visited them a few times. Much to Alice's disgust.

I got a sense from Lydia and Alice that they were constant, active members. They recruited candidates and also seemed to have been involved for many years. I've no proof of that – only the memory of a gut-feeling.

There is this annoying oath that women who are

helped must give back to the Roses, and I refused to obey it. I still do. This was and still is the problem. I was almost killed by them because I refused to attend meetings and listen to other women's problems and give them advice. It's unbelievable really. Could you think of anyone less suitable for that role? However, I think too that they were possibly correct to try to remove me. Women are usually loyal creatures. I don't think I'm built like that.

Alice was right to be wary of me from the start and, even though I wasn't scared of too many people in my life, I just knew not to mess with Alice.

Despite this, I never expected the Sinful Roses to have the wherewithal to actually kill anyone. Again, I was naive. I thought it was all hot air. *Pah!* I'll say again that we all need to vigilant. I now believe they are capable of murdering us all.

Alice fascinated me. From her manner, accent and dress, she was English. I don't think she was ever in trouble. I always read the paper from cover to cover, and I have an excellent memory. I didn't recall ever reading about a murdering Alice. There again, I always felt it was not her real name. Hiding our true selves is easier than people think. Is it not? Even John didn't truly know me.

"What do you mean you forgot the time?" John asked, open-mouthed in the kitchen when I'd not made him his supper. "And you do know that your jumper is on inside-out and back-to-front too?"

Being with the Roses changed me forever more. It was like I was lost and was trying to find my place in the world again.

Tim wondered why I had changed my hair and tied

my scarf tightly under my chin and I realised it was
Alice who controlled a lot of my decisions. When with
Tim I pictured her watching us, being impressed by my
naughtiness, eager to join in but I wouldn't let her. It was
a helpful fantasy and I loved thinking of her annoyance
that I was better than her, braver than her and, yes, a
better lover than her.

So, having instructed me, they told me to get on with it.
As simple as that.

But it wasn't that simple.

I took the bus to the house. I'm not sure why I went
there. I didn't have an appointment with them and I had
no errands to do nearby. But when I got off the bus in
Netterby and marched with my blistered heels out the
road, I found myself where I wanted to be.

The house asked me why I was staring over the low
wall at it? I strode up the brushed avenue and clashed the
brass knocker shaped like a lion against the sturdy door.
The echo of it gleaned no results. No one came to my aid.

I retreated to the roadside and leaned against the
pillar a moment. I was conflicted. Conforming and
performing to the Sinful Roses' instructions bothered
me. I hated being dictated to. But I simply couldn't go
through with it alone. I did not want to go forward
without the Roses. If they weren't with me then no-one
would know of my greatness, you see. It would all be a
big, quiet secret. There would be no witness aware of
how I had orchestrated it all. What was the point in
killing if no-one shared in the pleasure? However, Eve
Good did not do others' bidding and it felt like I was
being backed into a corner. I didn't like that.

I watched a large black crow perch on the ridge-tile and saw it soar off to where it nested in the high trees. The curtains were drawn and there was no life about the place bar the hopping wrens and magpies.

What had I hoped to see? What had I thought the trip would achieve? Tim was possibly finished the library books I'd brought him. He was waiting on me to be naked with him and still there I stood. Passers-by noticed me in the spitting rain, gawping at the house.

"It's mostly derelict," said an old man who stopped to chat. "But it's a fine property. Once owned by wealthy people."

"Do you live nearby?" I asked. Attack is the best form of defence.

"Top of the main street. You do know about this place?"

I shook my head.

"You must! It's the scandal of the whole area. Left to that criminal! And her with all sorts of women coming and going all hours of the day and night. I want to know who could want to visit at night?" He began to move on but paused. "You aren't from around here?"

I shook my head again. "I felt drawn to the house. I saw it from the bus."

"Ah …" He pushed the cap back on his grey head and scratched at his nose. "Even the children running around here are afraid of this place. And it a house next to the church an' all, It's a dreadful carry-on."

"And women from all over come here?"

"Yes. Fine-looking women. Like yourself."

Bless him, he was trying to be flirtatious.

"You've such lovely brown hair and the most striking eyes." He stared at me.

I'm sure that I blushed.

He left.

Alice would've wanted to knock sense into me. I imagined her shouting at me *"Go away, you fool!"* but I couldn't leave even when my hat got so heavy with rain that it began to soak through and drip onto my face.

Lydia and Alice knew a great deal about me. They were aware of almost every facet of my boring life. But I knew very little about them.

"It's helpful that you are an only child," Lydia said. "Someone with no family and not too many friends is good. People can let you down, you see. It is important that you are self-reliant and not a talker. You must trust no one with any information about what you intend to do."

Such was their probing, I almost expected for them to know about my Tim in the attic.

A flush came to my cheeks when Lydia mentioned that I had "normal desires".

What desires did she mean? And what desires might they have had? What were normal ones? I had asked them that, hadn't I? Yes, I did, for they laughed and mentioned that some women, like Alice, had unusual passions. What did that mean? My bravery had ended there. I hadn't asked any more.

I watched the rain bounce heavily from the pathway in front of me and thought that I should have trusted them and mentioned my Tim. I worried that a piece of the puzzle had not been presented and that it might have been my undoing. Also I longed to see Alice's face when she heard such a thing.

I should have told them. Tim was just a distraction, a

weakness, but he did have the most glorious ass and an exceptionally long cock.

I'm not embarrassed about the immorality, or the intercourse we had. Tim was my prize and I couldn't let them sneer at what was important to me.

Tim used to work in the garage where John got work done on his vehicles. The affair was all very *Lady Chatterley's Lover* but, even if I do say so myself, it was even more salacious than that.

"I'm Tim Harbour," he'd told me, lowering his beautiful eyes to look at his mucky boots and his two rough hands thrust into poor pockets. "I fix the cars." His dirty finger came out to point at John in the distance. "I mind his."

"You might look after me too?" I moved us both inside the door.

I couldn't resist the innuendo, and it made him grin. I wanted to hold his face and kiss those deep dimples – so I did. I smacked my lips on the two of them, on each cheek right then and there – *kiss* – *kiss*. And then my lips hit him square on the mouth. It was passionate, wrong and perfect!

"I'll not tell a soul," he said after I slipped my tongue into his mouth and we fumbled at each other in the stall that smelt of engine-oil and grease. I believed him but if he told people I didn't care in the slightest. The thought of people knowing had kept me living in a state of bliss. There was something a little sinister in me that enjoyed debauchery.

A couple of nights later, his teeth shone in the gloom when he knocked on the side door. John wasn't home and I expected he wouldn't be, but my problem was –

where could we go so that he wouldn't find us if he did come back?

I decided the attic would be our bedchamber and I thanked God for it.

Tim loved what curves I had left and his hands moved over my naked breasts and it made me die with desire. It was like a disgusting novel; the panting, the perspiring, the thinking I'd die without him. I never understood lust until Tim found the place between my legs. The passion between lovers made sense. There was never enough time to hold him and I never tired of kissing him. It evolved from an animal-like eating, to a lingering, elegant sucking of the best sweet.

"Do you love John?" Tim whispered and found his way inside me. I couldn't think of John then and I didn't answer him. "Do you love me?" He kissed the back of my neck and I suppose in a way I did love him in those moments. But it was silly to love another man when I was a married woman! Why did I need someone younger to make me happy?

"Your mother?" I asked him once. I bit my lip, waiting for the reply. His handsomeness made me hold my breath sometimes.

"Dead. She's dead."

"Ah." The relief flooded me.

It became more and more awkward finding ways and times to get Tim in and out of the house unseen. Therefore, he stayed for far too long. He lost his job and there was no need for him to go home or to leave me. His appetite for food and other things was satisfied. Then he slept, wrote silly love stories or read the library books I brought him. That was his life. All of it. I provided it for him. He was a clever enough young man if things were right, but they weren't and neither was I. He was almost a prisoner, a slave in ways. Was I manipulating him, the way John did to me? Possibly. Did I keep him like a pet? John used to joke about me being his lapdog. I became like an animal he fed and gave love to when he took the notion. Was I doing that to Tim? No. I was always attentive to him. Even when I didn't want to be. Even when I was tired I spent time and effort on being kind to him. Like a dog, he gave me unconditional love and humped at my leg and made me feel attractive.

Oh lord, I liked that. But I didn't force him into being dependent on me. He chose to be with me. There again, I chose to be with John and I still longed for escape. Tim didn't want to escape from me though.

"I'm not your mother," I told Tim when his clothes needed to be washed. "You don't see me as old – like a mother? Do you?"

His look was one I couldn't place. He was fearful of upsetting me. He had never thought about what we were doing. Why would he? He was happy. I let him lie with me. What else was there in his life? Until Tim came along I had nothing good in mine. He was everything exciting in my life.

I was wrong to want people to know about us but I knew I should have told the Sinful Rose. This aching in my guts wouldn't leave and the desire to shock was massive.

After my stint of standing in the rain a small, plain brown envelope with no stamp arrived at my house.

Tearing it open, my breath caught in my chest.

A card inside simply read, in swirling letters:

*Come tomorrow morning 10am.*

*The Sinful Roses*

They came to where I lived? They shouldn't have contacted me. I was almost certain that it was one of their own regulations. They had listed many rules.

1. *Never mention this to anyone. EVER.*

2. *Don't come unannounced or without an appointment.*

3. *Plan the deed meticulously and within three months from now.*

4. *Repaying the debt may take up to three months to fully complete.*

There had been more of course, but instead of listening properly I got lost in the portrait over the mantel and mulling over telling them about my Tim.

What could they want now? It worried me. I figured that they might have heard good things about John? Or that perhaps they'd seen Tim? I had forgotten about standing in the rain.

Something was not right and that piece of card was a sign that things were not well. Not well at all.

John was home early too. Bursting into the house like he was expecting to find me in a passionate embrace on his couch. What was making him suspicious?

"I thought I'd come home early," he said, pulling off his boots and jacket.

He could have checked the attic – but he never did.

"The neighbour said you've had callers. Two visitors. Marjorie saw an elderly woman earlier who dropped something off and a 'trampish-looking chap'? They both worried her so much that she came out on her stick to tell me to buy you a cross dog."

"I think that Marjorie needs poisoning! I told you, I've seen no one all day."

"You didn't see a woman dropping something off? The evenings are darker too. I worry about you being home alone here in this dark cul-de-sac. I just felt that I needed to come home and wasn't I right? Especially if there are prowlers about outside."

He rambled on and on about the need for me to lock doors and how we should be vigilant. He also suggested that I visit Marjorie to check on her.

Murdering the old biddy was all that was on my mind.

# Chapter 8

## Laurie Davenport

As soon as Norah stops reading I start my apologies.

"I cannot believe that woman. Such an awful thing to have to read! I wanted to stop you a few times but curiosity got the better of me."

She laughs loudly and I find myself laughing too.

"Laurie, you can be such a prude," she says, still laughing.

It relieves the tension, but I'm still concerned.

"I'm mortified," I start again. "All that talk about her young lover and murder. As if we'd condone or understand such things? Are you going to be all right?"

"I'll say a few 'Hail Marys' and all will be well. Stop fretting. This is our job right now and she's only trying to shock us. And, it seems to have worked."

"It definitely did!" The room is stuffy and I wonder if we could open a window but I say, "I didn't know women could think such things, never mind write them down."

Norah doesn't answer and I wonder what facial expression she's using. I hate that I cannot tell what she's thinking.

"I'm fine, sir. Honestly, stop worrying. I'm a grown woman. She's not going to shock me."

"Really? I'm aghast that she wouldn't make you

blush, even a little!" I flap my hand in front of my face in a comical fashion. "I thought I might faint."

Norah guffaws.

"Someone needs to tell her that there'll to be no more of that sort of thing," I announce. "But have we learned anything more today – other than that I blush quickly and my scars don't stop it from being noticeable?"

"I didn't notice you were all that uncomfortable when I was reading," Norah says.

I wonder about that. She is bound to have seen me shuffle at my crotch. A blind man could have seen I was aroused by some of the conversation. I'm almost thankful that my eyes cannot give me away now.

But Norah decides to change the subject.

"I can look and we can see if we can piece things together," she says. "She described the house for example. I wondered if she did that on purpose? And it's in Netterby. We can easily find such a house. She also made me extremely nosey about Tim. There cannot be too many garages around there with fellows called Tim having worked in them? Also she gave us names for the women. And the organisation is definitely called the Sinful Roses."

Norah's figure is moving as she's on her feet, softly pacing the floor. I want to take her into a hug and hold her there. Against me. If I put on music, we might dance? I could manage a waltz if we moved a few of the softer, lighter chairs. I didn't enjoy life when I could. Charlotte and I partied, socialised, but we were never happy or content in each other's company.

I suddenly remember. I squint over at where I think Norah is, by the gramophone.

"I've been to Netterby, you know. With Charlotte. About five years back. We went to a party there."

Norah laughs. "The Sinful Roses were throwing the party, no doubt?" she teases.

"Certainly not!" I pretend to be offended. "It was at Ravenscairn House, the home of a very respectable lady – Lady Dornan."

There is a pause, then Norah says, "But might Charlotte have met a Sinful Rose there – or someone who told her about them?"

"It's possible, I suppose," I say, and my heart sinks.

Norah walks over and touches my arm.

"Am I not the best Sherlock Holmes?" she says.

I laugh. "You are."

"And you can be Watson."

"Oh, thank you kindly!"

She begins to pace again. "Eve has not wanted to tell us much of value yet. It's like she's setting the scene, painting us a picture. She's the oddest creature, isn't she?"

"The General will want a report. I'm to telephone him this evening. He'll be glad that she's cooperating. They often tried to get her to tell what she knew and now that she's writing we'll have to keep her at it."

"She recognised the Davenport name. Could it be that she knows your Charlotte?"

"Most unlikely." I find the thought chilling. "A criminal woman like that? Eve has been accused of terrible things. Arson and brutal murders. She did try to kill poor Marjorie Fellows too in the end, didn't she?"

"Marjorie was a key witness. She seems to be the one person who spent the time with Eve and even she has very little information on the other crimes. We're doing well to have this in writing."

More pacing.

"When you visited the north of Ireland where did you usually stay?" she asks.

"Nice hotels in Belfast or sometimes on one of the big estates. My family has friends all over the British Empire." I sound haughty and full of myself. "I felt we were working on our visit, though, and if I showed up at the usual spots I'd be asked about my condition and also about you and our reason for being in Northern Ireland. I wanted to stay somewhere inconspicuous."

"Of course," Norah says and sits with a creak of the couch. "I only wondered if the locals or people you knew over here had any thoughts about our Mrs Eve Good. I'd say the gossip-mill has opinions and information which we would never get from a file."

"Good thinking, Watson," I tease, sitting up to be closer to her.

"Excuse me – *you* are Watson – I'm Sherlock," she says.

"We'll see about that!" I take her hand and like the feel of her skin on mine. "We really are getting somewhere, aren't we?" I ask the air of where I think her face is.

"Yes," Norah says. "I know we've had a terrible time lately but we're learning a lot. It'll all come together."

"I hate giving the likes of Eve a hearing – she doesn't deserve it," I moan.

I suddenly feel very tired.

"Could you help me upstairs, please? I might take a nap." The thought of what I might do to Norah before a nap races across my dirty mind.

"Of course, sir," she says, rising to help me.

"When are you going to use my Christian name? Please?" I insist, holding the material of her sleeve. I lean on her arm and we are in step as we move across the floor from the drawing room into the hall.

"I'll try, Laurie," she relents. "I'll make a call to the General now – let him know of our progress. You rest and I'll do that and come back for you to go to dinner. It's rabbit stew this evening and bread-and-butter pudding."

I yawn in reply. I would like to talk to Freddie myself but Norah knows that I need her to dial in the numbers for me anyhow, so it makes sense for her to relay our investigating to the General.

We reach my bedroom and I become jittery. I sit on the side of the bed with a flop and let her help me with my laces. Might she undress me further if I was brazen enough to suggest it? I've taken to slipping the shoes on and off untied and it is spoiling their neat fit. The laces knot and her shadow tries to untie them and is level with my crotch for an agonising time. If only I were Freddie! He would say something seductive now. I open my mouth to try something and close it again.

"Thank you," I sigh when she's also turned down the bed and mentioned where she left my shoes so that I don't trip on them. "I would be lost without you. I'm extremely grateful for all of your assistance."

"I know that, s– I mean, Laurie. I'll see you in an hour or so."

I make my way to brush my teeth in the washbowl in the corner and realise that it has been almost a week since I thought of taking some sleeping powder or anything else to aid my living.

I carefully make my way back to the welcoming bed

and sink into the pillow. I've changed in a matter of days. I haven't thought of myself much at all. I've been tired and have slept soundly. I've laughed and found pleasure in the company of others and I've enjoyed my food. The list of positives goes on as I lie there in the cool crisp sheets in a clean bed and I am grateful to be alive.

My wife trying to kill me has opened me up to new possibilities. Who knew that would happen?

# Chapter 9

## Norah Walsh

"I'll get that criminal woman transported as soon as I can," the General promises on the telephone.

Fredrick is always full of his own importance. It's wrong that men like Fredrick Ashfield are given any sort of power. It goes right to their dicks.

"If it helps Laurie, then we do it."

I listen to him twitter on about his fondness for Mr Davenport and I must admit that the handsome ass has a sense of loyalty to his dead friend's brother – and yet I wonder if there's something more to his interest in all of this Sinful Roses business. Men in power perhaps know the real reach of the Murdering Wives Club.

I don't like having to explain to Fredrick what a harlot Eve Good is. After all she is a fellow female and I do see some of her traits as admirable. As much as I shouldn't admit it, she fascinates me. The women at home in Meath, huddled around the church doors or the candles for lighting in prayer, would have something to say about her. Since the outbreak of war, Giles' worries about the morality of women and the downfall of society is echoed everywhere. Even with men blowing each other to bits, it is the actions of women that are causing concern on home turf.

If Eve Good were in the midst of holy Irish women, there'd be hell to pay. She'd be well and truly hung out to dry by the god-fearing females who patrol Irish society. They've got opinions about the likes of me too – and I'm nothing of note in comparison to this bitch.

"And why isn't Norah home taking care of her own grieving father then, eh?" these whispering women start. "Working for the British! Traitor to her own, that's what she is."

Daddy, to give him his due, stands up for his only daughter and replies to all gossip, "You know nothing about it. My precious Norah is a patriot, but she's clever and knows how to seize opportunities that present themselves to her. She is her own strong woman."

If any of them had been given a chance to leave Irish shores they'd have grabbed it with both grubby hands. I know that and so do they. I refuse to feel guilty about my choices. Lord Wester was a means to an end: an escape and an education. Being nanny to a lord was cause enough for them to spit at me. If they knew I was his mistress, I would never be able to show my face in Meath again.

Now, in Davenport, I keep to my duty and summarise Eve's letters to Fredrick.

"You could easily read them before you send them on to us," I suggest and then bite my lip. What am I doing? I need him to need me! "But I suppose busy men like you don't have the time for epistles from murderers."

"Continue to telephone regularly and let me know what's happening," Fredrick orders before slamming down the receiver.

I'm just like everyone else under his command now. Again, I should have known this would happen. I am no longer the naive slip of a girl who left Ireland. I know now that I'll have to work hard to achieve anything in this life. Things don't just fall into my lap. Sometimes a woman needs to use everything in her box of tricks to succeed. Eve thinks that she's the only woman to have taken an unsuitable lover. The only one who has thought about terrible things. *Ha!*

I know from her file that she too is an only daughter. Born to devoted parents who spoiled her with kindness and patience. There's no reason why she is such a lunatic. She's ordinary-looking, I suppose. Blonde, petite, with peculiar eyes, that when open spark a fear – even in me.

She married John Good when she was quite young. I cannot recall the exact date of their wedding but I know it made me stop and take note that marrying young, for her, was not a good plan. It seemed to change her and it would have been the same for me. I escaped that bullet but ran into another one.

Lord Wester's idea to take me across the ocean with his family was much more appealing than being shackled to another pig-farmer and a distant cousin of a cousin. And, yes, I had to let a hairy married lord sneak in under my sheets occasionally, but I learned to manipulate that to my advantage in the finish too. Eve Good isn't the only temptress, no matter how much she boasts about it.

The female prison guard and I exchanged glances. She didn't like that blonde bitch either. Yet, Laurie seemed taken with her tales. I suppose they're shocking to the likes of him. Even warfare kept Laurie Davenport from the true realities of murder. From what I can gather, he was an officer spared from the main battles. His responsibilities lay in ordering men about and organising tasks such as building and repairing roads and bridges. It was the laying and clearing of mines that proved to be his downfall. He talks about a mine being an enemy one lodged deep in the mud, but I wonder sometimes if it was one of his own that blew up and maimed him and killed some of his comrades. Perhaps he doesn't remember exactly what happened and wonders? There's more to his war wounds than just the mark of an enemy. He's lost all confidence and belief in himself. Charlotte hasn't helped, but the poor divil pulls at my heartstrings something shocking. There's an innocent vulnerability that I want to fix or perhaps hug out of him.

He likes to touch me, but I can tell from the way he does it that it is because he cannot see me. Like I enjoy bare feet in sand, his fingers in mine ground him in that moment. The touch gives us a connection. It's not because he wants a grope. He's a gentleman and is such good company.

Poor vulnerable Laurie also blushes at the mere mention of sex. How can a man make it almost to his fortieth year and still feel embarrassed by something he should do everything in his power to get? I try not to smirk at his embarrassment. Surely he must have thought of us making love? I've considered it. From when we first met I have daydreamed about him kissing me. I wish that I didn't and I really want to stop the thoughts. Being in Davenport Manor was to be a new direction for me. A chance to prove myself. Yet, Laurie does make my belly flutter with butterflies.

Fredrick won't have told him about us. I'm a dirty little secret that men of power and wealth think they can pass around as a plaything. "Laurie needs a woman like you. But if he knew of my real hope for you being in Davenport Manor, he wouldn't have it," Fredrick said. "You'd be ordered out. Laurie is a good sort, but he's also a right prude. He'd rather be faithful to the whore who's trying to kill him, than fall for a beauty like you. Let's work on him in secret and take this slowly. You're the expert seducer, Norah. I'll leave it to you to make him fall in love with you."

It does hurt that Fredrick can just pass me on to his pal like I'm a worn pair of shoes. I thought he might be even a little bit sorry to hear me agreeing to our spilt. I hate to admit it but sex with Fredrick was fierce fun. If he didn't speak, I quite enjoyed our time together. Being a mistress to the British only bothers me when I think of those at home in Meath. The Irish see the British war with Germany as an emergency to be avoided. The majority have no interest in the invaders' problem. But – they would be interested in what I'm up to, though.

The British and Fredrick worry about the Irish rebels siding with Hitler. This stops Fredrick from trusting me completely. It's possibly not as silly a reaction as I once thought. I may be Irish but I know which side my bread is buttered on. I know who I must be loyal to now.

I had agreed to accompany Laurie to speak to Eve Good before realising where she was imprisoned. Being in Armagh, I was very close to home. Terrifyingly close. Fifty miles to be exact. The island of Ireland is small and my accent was remarked upon. I was very worried that someone might have known someone who would tell of me being in the North with a blind British officer. Every bit of me knew that I needed to get back to Davenport and fast. I had to keep my head down. In the not too distant past, cavorting with an English soldier on Irish soil could get me tarred and feathered and have my red locks shorn off.

The fire worked out for the best and got us back on the boat home quicker than I anticipated. And all these complications are things a canny woman can work with. This danger of being found out in lies and deceit makes it even more exciting. Sad, I know. But a woman in search of adventure uses any means possible to get it.

# Chapter 10

## Norah Walsh

Davenport has its own small flock of hens. There's also a vegetable garden and these days the groundsmen share out the spoils amongst all those who rely on the manor. This means that the house itself only gets a small share of its own produce. Cook knew I wanted one of the newly brought-in eggs fried but she overcooked it and then let it go cold before I ever arrived into the kitchen. Eggs aren't easy to come by but when she left to get more rationed supplies I cooked the last one from the basket.

"She'll let you off this time," Giles says as I pop the top of the cooked egg and watch the yellow ooze onto the fried bread. "I must tell you again that we both are very grateful to you, my dear. You saved Mr Davenport from that fire. He can talk of nothing else. He survived enemy guns to be almost burned in his bed." He shudders.

I want to take credit for the rescue but instead I try to put him at ease. "It was nothing more than a bit of smoke. All was fine. He just cannot see and that makes it harder for him. His imagination is his downfall."

"You're a calm, brave girl," Giles says, patronising me with a pat on the sleeve. "And you had to rush back here before you got to see your own family?"

"I didn't mind that," I say, slurping some sweet tea.

"Did they even know that you were in Ireland?" he asks. "I hope they don't worry about you. Reassure them, won't you, that you're in a good household now, with people to look out for you."

I swallow the food and say, "They know I can take care of myself. It's only my dad left anyhow and he's found himself a new woman to court." Saying that aloud does sting more than I thought it would. It's ten years since my mother passed away, so it's not as if he jumped into another woman's bed in a matter of weeks. But still – he should stay miserable, for my mother will have to stay dead.

"And Mrs Davenport …" Giles says in a whisper. It's as if talking about her might bring her into the kitchen. "It's wrong of me to say this, but I will anyhow. We've never liked her – but we wouldn't want anything to happen to her all the same."

"But she goes missing a lot – she'll turn up," I say, dabbing the corner of my mouth with a hanky. I want to say a great deal but hold my tongue and dig a nail into the palm of my hand.

"The police seem to think it is different this time," Giles says, his eyebrows raised in worry. "Poor, poor Mr Davenport!"

"He's fine. Or he should be. I don't think there's much love lost between them, is there?" My patience is low since the fire and the debacle at the prison and I'm sounding harsh. "I'm more worried that he'll let this set him back. We all have to make light of these events or he'll sink into another bout of fear and not want to come out of the house."

"True. You're right. And you think Mrs Davenport is alive and well and there's nothing to worry about?"

I grimace and say, "Yes. I do. She's just trying to get Laurie's attention. Isn't that her form?"

"Oh, that's just it! You're right!" Giles says, patting me on the arm again. "Yes. That's her. Always causing drama. Never happy with anything. Always looking to be centre stage. We'll not let her win. Norah, I see that you put Mr Davenport's welfare above your own. We think you're marvellous. We really do."

I blush and pull my arm away in fake modesty. "Arrah now, I don't do much. I just know that the war is making us all a little tense. There's no need to go up to meet the rain and worry unnecessarily, that's all."

"We were glad to see you come back here. We were afraid that if you got home to Ireland you might not come back, and Mr Davenport would miss … the company. I'll go check on him now and reassure him that all will fine and dandy."

"Do," I say with a smile.

When I came to Davenport Manor, I expected to be repulsed by a scarred toff. But Laurie has grown on me. He's nothing like Fredrick – which in a way is a blessing. Where Fredrick elbowed his way to the top, Laurie doubts his ability to even live a full life.

Women like Charlotte could never appreciate a man like Laurie Davenport. Yet, society will throw a spoiled brat like her into the arms of a meek man and expect it to work. I know that I could make him happy and I could help him find ways of making me happy.

"You're not the clinging type, Norah, but we're together almost a year and it's wartime," Fredrick Ashfield said three months ago. "No matter how practical a woman you are, I need to move you on, old girl. You're getting too comfortable and will expect things of me. Things that I cannot give you. Even though I've been straight with you from the beginning, I know how you females think. You'll want me to settle down and that's not the life for me. Someone like Laurie Davenport would be a fine match for you instead."

He patted my arse and kissed the top of my head.

Right then and there and him naked in my bed was when I really understood why there were Sinful Roses in the world. Some men just call out to be murdered. They ask for it.

Ashfield is an attractive forty-five-year-old man with a good salary and prospects, and he thinks that he's the best, and only, catch for a girl like me. Yet he couldn't see that I was the one using him. That never entered his little pea-brain. I was a woman, so naturally I was smitten and lying in wait for him to make an honest woman of me. The cheek of it! The anger bubbled inside and I thought of Lord Wester too and his moving me on in case I told his wife or made demands.

Fuck-'em-all! I can see why there's a need for a support group for women who wish to murder the men in their lives. I really can.

# Chapter 11

## Laurie Davenport

Norah links my arm and leads me out into the garden.
I've not been out in the grounds in months. Possibly
years, if you take my time away into account. Before
Norah came, Giles attempted to take a breath of fresh air
with me. It ended in disaster. He tried to push me in that
dreadful wheelchair, and we got stuck and I was
manhandled back into the house by the few elderly
groundsmen that are left. Their own sons no doubt are
dead, and I'm living to burden them further. I was too
mortified to ask Giles to take me out again.

Norah didn't try cajoling me or asking me what I
wanted. She just opened the double doors from the
drawing room out onto the terrace and took me like a
child by the hand and marched me down the steps into
the heart of the garden.

"We were right to get out of the house to read Eve's
epistle," Norah says encouragingly. "It's a nice sunny
day. Let's sit on that bench near the pond and then we
can go inside for some of Giles' tea."

We go and sit.

"You are bossy, you know," I say, glad of the light
breeze and the sound of the birds chirping.

"Is that water deep?" she asks.

"I'd not drown in it. If that's what you mean." I try a chuckle and she joins me. "How are things looking? Have the gardeners been busy?"

"All is tidy. Green. Pretty. I wish you could see it."

I nod for I do wish it wasn't all dappled light and shade and morphing shapes.

I whisper, "I've been wondering if Charlotte took off and is now gone missing because she didn't succeed in killing me. Is she afraid of the Roses?"

"She might have disappeared because she's afraid of them or they might have found her. Who knows? If these Roses even exist at all? I'm not sure I believe Eve Good."

The grass is soft underfoot and a cool breeze fills my lungs as I surreptitiously shuffle my bum over in the seat to be nearer to Norah. Her disbelief in the existence of the Roses has shocked me slightly. She was the very one who wished for us to take off on this adventure. If she thinks it's a wild goose chase, then what are we doing?

I should attack her stance on this, but the day is nice, her being near me is pleasant and I don't want to ruin the moment between us. I wonder how to get closer still to her arm, her side, her body. How might I seduce her? The thought of us naked flits across my mind now at all hours of the day and night. I can almost sense how it will be. Will be? What wishful thinking! A young woman does not need to be burdened with a cripple. However, I'm not disabled in the ways that matter. I feel desire rise in my groin.

"Comfortable?" she asks me and I hear a rustle of pages. "Let's see what this Eve Good has to say for herself now."

Sunshine and warmth should make everything

beautiful. If I was like Freddie I'd have something seductive to say, some flirtation that would bring her into my arms. I've never been good with romance. I try to make words form. I pray that I can make her see me as a whole man. A man with a ... what do my wife's horrid books call it? Wanton desire? A throbbing member?

I cough for she is reading now and I must focus on being read to. But then I recall the reason for me listening and all of the anxious worry returns.

# Chapter 12

## Eve Good

I turned up at the appointed time at their den of sin.

Lydia rubbed her temple and shook the bun in her hair to and fro. "We brought you back here because we're worried that you might not be fit to finish this. Are you able to continue?"

It was then I realised that if I didn't go through with killing John I was in danger. I knew too much. I should have realised this before, but I was without friends, without family and I didn't think ahead like I should have.

I stared at Alice and thought that though she was much the same size as me, she was sturdy and vicious. Lydia was older and greying but I couldn't cope with both of them if they decided to attack me. I considered that if they came at me one at a time, I might swing things in my favour, but I had no weapons and nothing around me looked sharp or heavy enough. It wasn't only fear that made me tremble then. It was the excitement that I was lacking in my life. The thought of danger that worried but also thrilled me.

"Would you harm me?" I asked them.

"To protect ourselves, we would," Alice replied without hesitation. "We need to ensure you're putting things in place."

"I was a little overwhelmed. But I'm putting the steps in motion." It was a lie of course.

"Why were you standing in the rain staring up here on Wednesday? That is prohibited in our list of instructions," Lydia said in a very aggressive manner. "Were you trying to draw attention to us?"

"No. I don't know why I did that. I suppose I felt lost."

"It's all overwhelming," Lydia said. "There's where my worry lies, Eve. I was downtrodden and afraid of my own shadow. I made mistakes despite all of the guidance I received. I fear that you will make mistakes, just like I did. My lack of confidence was what got me imprisoned. You must be ready in your mind and in your heart for this and not slip up."

"How many times have women like you done this?" I asked.

Lydia looked like she might answer, then stopped herself. She patted my arm. "My mistakes have taught me that each Sinful Rose must be fully prepared. We all learn from the mistakes of others. That is why we are here, to guide you and help you through it."

"Lydia, you made very few mistakes!" Alice snapped. "It was your husband's family who caused all of your woes. Eve will not have that worry. Her poor husband hasn't got any family here. Only a sister in Norfolk."

"You know that you must make it all happen soon, Eve," said Lydia. "You remember that, don't you? There may be an extension given, but three months slips by quickly and it is a deadline that it is good to stick to."

I nodded.

"Because of your manner, I think it is a good idea to go through it all again. We will try to support and advise on how best to prepare yourself and what should be said to the authorities. There must never be a mention of this place to anyone when John dies. No matter what the outcome, you must not let us down. We will contact you if you are in trouble – but," she held a finger up at me, "you must never come here again or stand outside or mention us. We will know if you do. You understand that if we hear of you saying anything there will be consequences?"

"Of course." My palms went clammy. I couldn't breathe. I pulled at my collar and tried to stop my heart from pounding. Why was it that I enjoyed being this close to the edge of everything? "But what if I can't go through with it? Can I just forget all about this? I would never tell a soul. I would never speak of this place or anything. I am not stupid. I can be discreet."

Alice started ranting. "*You see! You see! Just like I said! She'll ruin us all! I'll kill you myself if you don't go through with things! Do you hear me?*"

Lydia took no notice of Alice's outburst.

"She'll drag all of us down with her!" Alice said. "Give her the ultimatum. Tell her that she *must* do this within three months because I don't trust her. You have three months from the first day you came here to do what you came here for. Do you hear me, Eve Good? We've never had to use this threat before but for you we will make an exception."

Lydia held her hand up, palm towards Alice. "There's no need for that. All of us normal folk asked such a question. It shows that she is a moral person and that is a good thing. Sit down now please, Alice, and let her alone." She turned to me. "Listen carefully. You must keep things simple. It must look like it is an accident.

83

Plan it for when you don't seem to be in the house or where there are no witnesses. All roads must lead his colleagues to see it as a tragic accident. You are a weak woman in their eyes. Keep it that way."

I was speechless.

Lydia went on like it was a recipe for jam. "John will have told all who will listen that you are weak – this is good. They will never suspect anything but find someone who can vouch for you, befriend them and make yourself invaluable. Reveal no possible motive. All is wonderful in your marriage. Financially you will have the insurance policy and the house and maybe his pension, but you must be heartbroken, worried and upset for the future. Practise this. Over and over. What you will say and how it will seem to them. Think of every angle. Cover it with a story or a line you've practised. Look in the mirror. Does it seem real? Believe it was a travesty, a tragedy. It was all totally out of your control and you are devastated."

Lydia had said all of it before, but I got a deeper understanding then. I couldn't think of it being this simple – but it seemed to be. Her recipe for the perfect murder continued. I'd dreamt of being without John every day for years, fantasised about a life without him. I'd been unable to think of anything else some days but it had always seemed impossible, unobtainable and too great a task. Seeing these women again and knowing they had achieved it helped immensely. If the likes of them could do it, well then, I could too. Sitting there, I realised that killing my husband was achievable. I would finally be free. It was evil but I had to do it now. I was involved and couldn't reverse time.

"We also try to avoid each other in public," Lydia went on. "If we ever bump into one another we must pretend that we have never met. We told you all of this the last day, but we felt with you mooning about outside you hadn't heard anything at all. If we meet in society, or in the future, you don't know anyone and we don't know you."

I decided then that it might be a good time to come clean about Tim. I had been savouring this juicy titbit.

"There's something else that I should tell you," I said. "You mentioned desires, I think, the last time I was here. There may be a slight issue with that ... I have something I need to say …"

Lydia encouraged me with a slight smile. "If this is important, Eve, you must tell us now. If we're not aware of all the facts, the Sinful Roses will not be able to help you later. I disclosed everything and that helped me when I needed it in the darkest of days. Whatever you're embarrassed about, it is probably something we've heard before."

"I have a lover."

Alice's laugh was loud. When she stopped I'm sure I was bright red. I could feel my cheeks were glowing despite the cold.

"Who knows about him?" she asked.

"No one knows about Tim. No one. His name is Tim Harbour, a twenty-year-old mechanic."

"*Twenty?*" Alice squeals. "Younger than you then? What else?"

"'That's all I know. His mother is dead. I've no idea where he lives other than he is with his father and many siblings and they are dirt poor." I stopped and tears

85

started to roll down my cheeks. Thinking of him and how awful it was that I knew this little about him. If I cared, really cared, I'd know everything there was to know about him. Shouldn't I know every detail about someone I loved?

"Would John have any idea at all about this?" Lydia asked.

"No."

"She could pin it all on Tim and walk away," Alice said, lighting another cigarette. "Her lover kills her husband. Not her fault."

"No," Lydia said quietly. "The police will not let Eve get away with having a lover. They'll not like her deceiving John and dig more into the case. This is not good. You were right to tell us this."

"I'd find it hard to tell him to leave," I said, but when I saw their expressions I knew they were sure that I must end it. "How will I say to him that he must go? I can't. He'll wonder at my sudden change of heart. I can't just ask him to leave me. How will I do that?"

"Tell him that you aim to leave John but that you need time and you need him away from the house," said Alice. "Explain that you will contact him later. Tell him that he must not burden you until you can be free or else you will lose everything, and John will have a case to leave you penniless." She seemed well versed in lovers. "Explain that you need him to be strong no matter what he hears and that, if he cares for you at all, he must keep your secret for the relationship to continue."

"Get him out and away from the house, before you do anything though," Lydia said. "That is most important. Getting him away is the first step."

In my imagination I could see John's colleagues finding Tim. The questioning would be terrible.

"Do you not understand you'll need this Tim gone or use him in some way?" Alice asked. "Are you thinking at all about this? Strategically? Have you any plans at all?"

I didn't know how to answer.

"And Tim cannot be murdered too," she said in the next breath. "The likes of you will want to kill more than once. I can feel it in my bones. You're not right in the head."

I couldn't believe that she was even suggesting such a thing.

"One dead man in your life is enough," she said. "It is either Tim or John. You cannot kill them both. You'll need to think of some other way of getting this lover out and gone from the house – but you cannot kill them both. Do you hear me, Eve?"

Alice's eyes sparkled in the greyness of Ravenscairn House.

I decided then and there that she was probably mad.

# Chapter 13

## Laurie Davenport

Ravenscairn. The house where I partied with Charlotte. I feel a little stunned as we walk back to the house.

Giles is by the open door and I smell his hair lacquer as he stands aside to let us enter the house.

"I'm glad to see you taking the air, sir," Giles says. "Excellent."

"We only went to garden and back," I say. "I'm totally useless."

"Men were here, sir. I was about to go for you, but their manner was most distressing. Looking through everything they were. It was upsetting for Cook. I was glad you and your parents did not see the trampling they did over the whole house. They're going to examine the garden and the outhouses later."

"Are they still here?" Norah asks.

"Coming back, I believe," Giles snorts. "Their manner was very uncouth and they took my pistol. I shall want it back no matter what they say. I'll bring you some afternoon tea and sandwiches, sir."

The drawing room is warm even with the cool air from the opened doors. Giles doesn't like the lack of control, and who could blame the poor old bugger? During all our despair Daveport Manor has been our safe haven.

"Those murdering bitches better not come here," I say as Norah sits me down.

I hear her try to open my briefcase which we use to hold her notepads. The lock sticks a little and she mutters.

"There, it is open now," she breathes then. "Giles has a pistol? Did I hear him say that or was I dreaming?"

"You did. I believe he keeps it under his pillow."

"He's full of surprises." She giggles. "I cannot see him using one. Is he a good shot?"

I love to hear her amused and I chuckle along with her. "I've no idea."

Norah slumps into the soft chair by the bookshelves. She never presumes to sit in my favourite chair and I'm grateful to her for that. She is thoughtful all of the time and is nothing like my wife.

"So, let's make a few notes," she says. "The house is called Ravenscairn. And you have actually been there. Unbelievable."

"It really is."

"Two women. Both middleclass. In Ravenscairn – early 1930s? One of the women, Lydia, was in prison before this for murdering her own husband. Alice something-or-other was about Eve's age of twenty-five then, approximately thirty-seven, thirty-eight now then. We know Eve's address was 5 Newburn Crescent, Whinpark, County Down, and she took the bus to Ravenscairn House beside a church. Even if you can't remember where it is exactly, it will be easy to locate."

"Charlotte and I were there in 1930," I say, "It was an old building but it was all newly renovated when we visited for the party. I wonder when exactly Lady Dornan acquired it? I can ask her – she might know who the women are."

"You will need to be careful how you ask her. We don't want to alert the Roses that we are doing well. We need to keep them in the dark and us out of danger."

"Yes, Watson," I tease. I want to remain jolly, but there's a clawing fear grabbing at my gut that I don't admit to. A man should be fit for the fight but I'm not that man any more.

Norah breaks me out of my maudlin thoughts by asking, "Do you know this Lady Dornan well?"

"No, not at all. It was Charlotte who introduced us. But I know they have a house in London too. Her second husband has the title – he attends the House of Lords."

"I feel like asking what happened to Lady Dornan's first husband," Norah says.

"I'm not sure what happened. I never knew him." I gasp. "You mean, you think Lady Dornan is one of these Roses? But she didn't own the house when Eve was visiting it. And no. Lady Dornan wouldn't be party to such things."

Norah grunts slightly. She thinks that I'm naive. But I cannot imagine Lady Dornan allowing such witches into her home. She'd have no reason to be involved in such murderous meanderings.

"Do you think these Roses exist or not?" I question. "In the garden you didn't seem so sure they did."

"It's hard to know," Norah says. "We only have the word of a murderer to go on. It all seems more and more farfetched."

"Could it become known that we're getting letters from Eve? She seemed sure that they had eyes everywhere, which seems impossible."

"Women are more resourceful than men give us credit for," Norah says.

"What might they do to us if they think we are still on their trail? The fire and attack on Eve show what they're capable of."

"From listening to her accounts, they should know more about us than we would like. According to Eve, they investigated her before allowing her into Ravenscairn. They may be following our progress – but I doubt it." Despite her words Norah does sound concerned.

"It's hard to tell what is happening around me," I say. "I cannot see to protect either of us."

"Do you think they may be here, keeping watch?" she asks. "Hopefully, the night guards and patrols will put them off. I don't think the Home Guard are all that pleased with the scant information we've given them."

"They can be in a tizzy if they like but I'm not telling all and sundry that my wife might be a murdering wives club member!" My blood pressure is rising. It's frustration. I am brimming over with lots and lots of frustration.

"There are places to hide in the grounds – but sure Giles and the gardeners and groundsmen would spot people lurking, to say nothing of the night guards?"

"I imagine so," I say. "But it seems these women are well trained. They got to Eve and Charlotte – if that's what happened to her – and ourselves quite easily."

"Maybe."

"The General didn't want to talk about Charlotte's disappearance," I say. "Did he tell you anything at all, Norah? I'm very worried."

"Nothing. He's tight-lipped. No-one wants to upset her father with rumours and gossip. I don't think Fredrick knows anything more."

91

"At least everyone might believe me now. Something is amiss."

"We believed you."

I don't like to cast doubt on Norah's word, but I never felt believed until Eve Good said that she considered murdering her husband. It seemed far too unbelievable. Normal, ordinary women don't admit to planning to murder their husbands. Yet Eve Good is living proof that they do consider it. If the fire was deliberate, then dealing with her has become a very dangerous pursuit. For now, it stands to reason therefore that these Sinful Roses do exist and want to stop all investigations.

"Eve is our only way into this murky world then?" I say. "But, surely, there must be more women who know about this?"

Norah breathes in sharply. "A Murdering Wives Club," she says in a slow, low tone. "A support group for women wishing to kill their husbands. If people do know about it, Eve Good is the only one brave or stupid enough to talk about it."

"Perhaps it is all in her fanciful imagination?" I say. "For I cannot see why a woman would need to kill her husband. Surely she doesn't want to take such risks?"

We fall silent for while.

"It's hard for a man to understand why women might need to be part of something powerful," she says then. "None of us like to be vulnerable and alone. This group must help women who feel trapped or scared. But here's another thing that occurs to me. The way Eve describes John Good, he sounds like a brute, but that is what Eve wants us to think. From my reading of the files, John Good was a good policeman from a nice family. His sister said that Eve was always a bitch and they warned John against marrying her, but Eve manipulated him. It seems that she wished them to live beyond their means in more affluent areas. He had a good record with his job and was well liked by his peers. So what if she's deceiving us? Painting a false picture of the man to justify her actions? It may be that there was no reason for Eve to want him gone other than for the freedom, the insurance money and his pension."

I ponder this. "That's quite possible," I say at last. "And Charlotte would have had the same reasons." I let the truth sink in. "She would have had the estate and no burdensome cripple of a husband. There's none of the Davenports left and she could have inherited the lot. She hoped I'd die in Italy."

"You didn't oblige. And so she needed help and guidance. She contacted the Roses. Or perhaps they advised her to encourage you to enlist?"

"Her father made me feel like a downright coward and Charlotte insisted I sit the tests and interviews to become an officer." My mouth goes dry. "She wanted the war to kill me – for her."

"Maybe. But this Lydia and Alice took Eve through each step on the way to murdering John. Who are these women? Eve knew about the Roses before. Her cousin Tilly from Inishowen told her. That means the women or at least Lydia is known in the south of Ireland too. Perhaps the Roses in Ravenscairn came up from the south? We will have to question this cousin. Search out this Lydia."

"Why would Charlotte want to be involved in such things?" I ask myself more than Norah. "I would have granted her a divorce and settled some money on her. Surely she knew that?"

"I could do with that tea now," she says, rising. "Don't trouble yourself with the whys – that will all be revealed no doubt as time goes on. No point in fretting."

"If someone you loved tried to kill you, would you not fret?" I ask her angrily, getting to my feet. "If you came home wounded, hurt beyond repair and wanted your wife to simply love you and she turned her back on you and tried to murder you in cold blood, would you not worry? If she then went missing when you started asking questions, would you not panic? And if you were almost burned in a stranger's house for talking to a killer, would you not have questions?"

There's a silence. I've been angry with her when I shouldn't have been.

"I'm sorry," I say, wiping my eyes with the back of my hand. "This is not your fault. I just wish I knew what I did to deserve this punishment."

Her perfume is close, her hands reach mine and she sinks into my embrace. I lean a chin on soft curls and her curves lean into my chest and groin. I kiss the top of her head and smell her hair. She sighs and moves her head. Fingers encircle the back of my neck and draw my head downwards. Full lips meet mine. I take Norah's face in trembling hands and kiss her properly, taking in an urgent tongue to meet my own. Moaning, we kiss until I hear the door open. It's too late to move, but we jolt apart.

Giles booms out, "*Tea!*" The tray rattles. "*Tea for two!*" he says and he doesn't sound surprised or cross.

"Thank you, Giles," says Norah, sounding breathless.

A desperate uncertainty washes over me. How on earth did that happen? Will that blissful union ever occur again? I truly hope that it does.

# Chapter 14

## Norah Walsh

Finally, we kissed. Sitting with him in the garden and watching him touch off his scars made me pity him but also see the good man underneath. Charlotte Davenport does not realise what she's abandoned here in this lovely place.

I can still taste him, feel his hands around my face and it makes me tingle. But I sip my tea and watch the little birds hop about the lawn. Laurie is sitting staring into the distance and I want to face his chair towards this window and point out the sundial I have just found in the distant corner of one of the large flower beds. The gardeners must have cut around the old ornament and I make the promise to Laurie in my heart that I will kiss him again near it someday soon.

Fredrick wants this to become a liaison. Does Laurie? Do I?

"Norah?" Laurie asks for my whereabouts in the room. The light is very bright today and he must be having difficulty with it. "I cannot find your pretty silhouette."

"I'm here," I say but I don't move. I shouldn't have kissed him. This was not planned. Much as I am aware of Fredrick's hopes, I wanted this to be a different situation for me. My time in Davenport so far makes me feel worthwhile – it's where I'm finally doing a real job, finding a good purpose, using my brains and wit, rather than my looks.

Laurie's been a good colleague. There have been no expectations, no lurid remarks and no groping of my arse. I've felt safe here. I curl my fingers around the cup and really look at the wonderful man in the antique chair.

From where I'm standing, I raise my voice and say, "If Charlotte contacted the Sinful Roses and became one of them, she is a fool."

The doorbell rings.

"That might be the post," I say.

Giles comes in with the silver tray.

"Second post is here and there is correspondence for Mr Davenport from the General."

"More from Eve?" Laurie asks.

"I'd say so," I reply and take the envelopes off the tray. "Thank you, Giles."

He stays a few seconds, looking between us for signs of what we are thinking and doing now. He sways in the doorframe, holding on to the doorknob and raises an eyebrow, as if questioning me. About what? About Laurie and me? What can I tell him? I have absolutely no idea what is happening between us. What I do know I cannot tell Giles. I'm a bitch. Right this minute my conscience tells me that I'm worse than Eve Good, worse than any of these criminals. Poor Laurie!

Giles shrugs and leaves, realising he's not going to get any information or satisfaction.

I tear open one of the envelopes and scan the pages.

"Yes, there's more here from Eve," I tell the side of Laurie's face. It is the unmarked side and he is very handsome. I should tell him that I barely notice his scars now, but I don't want to mention the unmentionable. There are many scars and secrets between us.

Instead, I settle myself into the warm fabric of the chair next to him and start to read.

# Chapter 15

## Eve Good

My heart leapt at the thought of life without my husband, but I couldn't bring myself to plan his murder. I busied myself instead with visiting and befriending Marjorie in Number 4. I was excellent at it. I became a cheery and helpful Christian. There was no sign of Tim, and although I went to the top of the house to try to smell him, there was little comfort in it.

I moved the mattress back to the far bedroom and sprinkled some dust on any surface that I thought needed it up in the attic. It didn't look very convincing when I stared at it.

An accident should have been easy to come up with. But John wasn't clumsy and I was a good bit smaller than him. My mind froze when I thought of time marching on. I hadn't a clue of what I was going to do. How would I kill my husband? And better still how would I make it look like an accident? Bugger Lydia and her crew! They had been of little help. All they did was make me nervous.

Marjorie was enjoying my visits and she found excuses for me to stay longer each time. At least she made me feel useful.

"John's a great man," Marjorie said, twirling pearls between her fingers.

"He is. I'm blessed to have him."

"I can see your house from here," Marjorie told me, touching her grey curls, "but the bushes and trees are growing too large and are starting to block my view of the side door especially. I'll need a gardener soon enough. Who do you use?"

"John does it," I said, thinking of how he perched high on the ladder to branch a tree. Perhaps he might fall from there if I suggested it needed doing?

Marjorie had set the seed of an idea. It mulled around and I made a pie for her dinner and rinsed out some of her smalls to set on the clothesline.

"They'll not dry out there," Marjorie told me.

But I wanted to look at the trees and think.

"I also worry about people stealing them," she added as I headed for the back door. "There are far too many layabouts sneaking about this cul-de-sac."

Afterwards I placed the extra pastry into a bowl and tied my scarf tightly around my head. I strode with confidence through our gate and looked intently at the trees. They stood like high statues in the crisp sun and their leaves were scattered everywhere. Out of the corner of my eye, I saw the glint of John's car. It was pulled in at the side of the house.

My back door was unlocked. I went in and placed the bowl on the kitchen table.

"*John?*" I called out. "*John? It's only after three!*"

I had washed the hallway tiles before I left and they were dry. I hung my coat on the hook near the kitchen, checked my face in the little mirror and went up the hall. It was then that I saw John's head.

His thinning hair showed that his scalp was blueish

and he was lying at a strange angle on the stairs. Some of him was on the last few steps and his head and shoulders were on the hard tiles which were streaked with blood.

"*John!*"

He didn't reply. I could not see his eyes from where I was. I should have walked around him and seen if they were open. But I couldn't move.

"*Dear God! John, answer me, please!*"

He had fallen. Hit his head.

Dear Lord, let him be dead. "*John? Answer me!*"

I didn't want him to answer and I murmured prayers. "*Please don't answer me, John. Yes, I was bad woman.*" I hoped that he had stopped breathing.

I didn't touch him. I should have tried to rouse him, but he might have stirred and come back and then what would I have done? No, it was better the way he was. What made him fall? Who made him fall …?

I ran back up the hall and out the side door. I raced as quickly as I could up to the main road. The phone box was a long way down that road. It was empty. I dialled for an ambulance and then found myself circling each number for John's work with my finger and found my panting eased while I waited on someone to answer.

"*Hullo! Help me, please.* It's John, my husband John. He's fallen – he's at the foot of the stairs. I was at a neighbour's. He's at home. I don't know what … Please send someone quickly. Yes. Sergeant John Good, Number 5, Newburn Crescent, Newburn. My darling John! Please hurry. Please send help. I can't move him. *Please come now!*"

I was impressed with myself when I slammed down

the receiver. I didn't let them ask me questions. I sounded very upset. Didn't I sound distraught? I was distressed and in shock. I didn't know what the hell had happened to John. I wasn't even sure if he was really dead or if it was just wishful thinking.

Did wishing it make it happen? Was it a lucky coincidence or something else? No one other than the women in Ravenscairn knew about my plans. Could they have done it? Would they? My mind was muddled.

I looked up at the trees moving at the side of our house and realised that I had nothing to get away with. I didn't do anything. I didn't toss John down the stairs. It was an accident. I merely came home to find him in this state. I had nothing to fear. It was a tragic accident plain and simple.

Inside, I peered through the bannisters at his slumped body. I couldn't see his face well, nor did I want to, but I could tell that his body was lifeless. He was dead. There was no question about that. Sergeant John Good was gone and I knew nothing at all about it. The mirror near the side door showed me that I was smiling. I practised crying and waited to hear his colleagues coming to save him.

They all came rushing in.

"Dear Lord, I'm afraid that you might be too late," I sob. "My darling John! Poor darling John!"

There were many men in the house. They gave me some whiskey and one of them brought a woman in, possibly a police secretary, to sit with me in the parlour.

"John's a good man," she said.

I wondered if he had bedded her. She seemed very concerned about him.

I shivered despite the heat of the whiskey.

"Mrs Good?"

A man I recognised as Constable Irvine stepped into the room.

"I'm sorry. I'm afraid the doctor says that he's definitely gone," he said.

But before he was finished I sobbed and aimed to keep crying.

Irvine went on in a measured calm way that sent a fear through me. "We can tell that his heel caught in the carpet and he lost his footing. There was nothing to be done for him. We are very sorry for your loss."

I groaned a bit. Uncertain suddenly of how grief-stricken a loving wife should be. Tears formed in fear and I was glad of them. I wiped my cheeks and chanced a look at the uniformed man with the large greying moustache and the probing eyes.

"They asked me to speak with you as we've met before. We're taking him away. We've done all we can here, I'm afraid, and now it is a case of us helping you as much as we can."

"I have no one other than John. No one."

"Yes," Irvine said with sorrow.

I was a good actress because I even began to feel sorry for myself.

"How can I manage without him?" I sobbed.

Nobody said anything. I sniffed.

"He did worry about you," the woman said. "John was a good man. I'm sorry for your loss."

That made me glare at her.

"Apparently John told his colleagues that he wanted you to see a doctor," Irving said, coming closer. "That's why he was home early – he said he had made an appointment for you. So, you must try to focus on staying well."

I stayed silent. I thought it was an odd statement as I always had refused to see any of John's mind-men. Irvine reminded me of a bad smell in a small space.

"We'll all miss him," he continued, glancing around the room.

"Yes," said the woman.

"Would you like to see him?" Irvine asked in that toneless way.

I disliked his moustache too.

"No. Thank you."

"We cannot leave you alone," said the woman. "Is there anywhere we could take you?"

"I'll go to stay with Marjorie on the corner. I look after her now and again."

"She's been out to the road to see what's happening. A kind old soul."

"Caring for her will keep me busy."

"But don't let her annoy you with talk of intruders."

"Intruders?" I asked and I didn't have to pretend to be startled – I was.

"She's saying that perhaps John didn't fall –"

I gasped and he stopped.

"Don't worry," Irvine said. "None of us like to think it can all end with no explanation. Even a woman her age doesn't like to think of ... the end." He rubbed down his moustache with his thumb and forefinger. "We can help you with the arrangements. Anything you need, We look after our own."

"Thank you."

"What about his family?"

"Like me, he was mostly alone. He has a sister somewhere in England. I'll try to contact her."

"John mentioned that you were worried about the future?"

"Me? Was I?" I was starting to come out of myself a bit more.

"You're a fine woman, Mrs Good. Once our men are done in the hall I'll take you over to Marjorie's."

"Aren't they finished yet? That carpet should have been changed long ago ... I've got caught on those threads many times."

"Don't distress yourself now, Mrs Good. You're not at fault here. This is just one of life's horrible tragedies."

I moaned a little and he patted my hand awkwardly. I was uncomfortable with him near me. "Will I ever be able to get my heart to stop pounding like this?" I asked him. "Will this all be a horrid dream in the morning? I'll never get over this. Never. My darling John is gone for good. Gone for good." I hid my face in a cushion and my shoulders shook.

The cushion hid my grin. I was a monster, an evil woman.

But the wonder of it was – I did not kill John Good.

# Chapter 16

## Laurie Davenport

"Irvine. Is he in your files?" I snap at Norah the moment she's finished reading.

"Yes," Norah sighs. "I did research who was involved in Eve's case at the start of all of this and I tried to contact him. But I'm afraid that he's not available to question. He enlisted and has been reported missing in action. Many of the men who were involved in this initial investigation are no longer with us. We are thwarted at every turn."

"Tim Harbour. Any joy locating him?"

"Not yet. I'd say the lad would be long gone by now. This all happened many years ago. He might have emigrated or be lost in the war too. We cannot find him."

"Tilly? Her cousin?" I try next.

"She knows very little more. I finally got her to a telephone yesterday while you had your nap and I got her to speak to me. But the poor woman had a breakdown following Eve's trial. I had to tread very carefully. All she knew about the murder of her husband Frank is in the files. Gruesome stuff which I won't read to you unless I have to. Tilly did tell us how women contact the Sinful Roses though. Their reputation spreads by word of mouth, of course – but actual contact is made through a newspaper advertisement."

"*A what?*" I ask, pulling myself to stand and pace about. "They advertise? In what paper?"

"Apparently it is in select women's magazines and national papers. It is a simple mention of Ravenscairn House being open to appointments. I haven't noticed them myself. She says the ads alert women to the opening of a 'Ravenscairn location' that then is open for a few months. These locations can be anywhere. It seems the only fixed location is Lydia's home, Ravenscairn House. Of course, as Eve knew the actual house she didn't have to wait for an advertisement – she wrote to the house directly. Women have to write to the address given, stating their name, address and that they wish to be a Sinful Rose. It is understood that they will be investigated discreetly and so the women must wait on a reply which gives them an appointment."

"And it is sitting there in papers and magazines?" I ask, bewildered by such a blatant business. "My good God!"

"We'll have to see if one is advertised close by," Norah says from where she is sitting on the creaking couch. "If we find such a place, we might go take a look at it. I should drive us, you know. We could ask Giles to take out your car?"

It hasn't occurred to me that Norah can drive. I forget that she's a capable woman.

"I'm not sure that I would let even *you* drive my Crossley. Charlotte was keen to get behind the wheel but I was having none of that. Women are not good drivers."

"Hiring cars is expensive. When there's one sitting at the manor it seems silly that I'm not allowed to drive it," Norah says, sounding determined.

I can hear that she doesn't like me mentioning Charlotte and I go to sit on the couch too.

"I need talk to you about a few other things." I search for her hand.

She doesn't give it to me, and I smooth mine over the soft seat instead.

"There's no need to bring up that kiss," she replies. "We have work to do. Is it about work?"

Everything in me that was hopeful curls into a ball and silently crushes itself. She regrets the kiss. She doesn't want it to happen again. Norah doesn't want me. My temples ache, my heart sinks and I think instantly of morphine.

"Let's discuss the case instead," she says confidently.

"I think one of us should telephone Lady Dornan," I say, heartbroken that Norah is cross about our glorious kiss. "We should arrange a visit to London to meet with her if she hasn't moved permanently to County Down to be away from this blessed war."

"I'm glad that you finally think that she may be Charlotte's contact. I've thought for quite some time that she's a person of interest. I've asked the General to look into her past."

"Have you now? You and Freddie have long conversations when I'm not about? How cosy – you and Freddie!" I say childishly.

"You think I do nothing all day?" she snaps. "I know you do! You men seem to think that women are incapable of thinking and achieving. I work hard while you snooze upstairs or sit about in here feeling sorry for yourself!"

The truth of that hits close to the bone but I refuse to agree with her. How dare she think I'm wallowing in self-pity! She has no idea of all that I've endured – or all that I worry about. Not a clue!

My temper rises to meet hers. "I do hear you constantly on the telephone. Is that what you call work?"

I can feel the resentment rising within me that she wants to forget our kiss. It makes me angry that she wants to reject me and something that was so nice. It was she who kissed me! She gave me hope. And now she's angry and nasty. It's cruel of her.

"I've put a great deal of thought into this case for you, you know," she says. "Even though I think it's all a load of rubbish, I'm here because of you."

"I don't believe a word of it! It's more likely that you're trying to please Freddie. You're probably sweet-talking him for more perfume! Yes, that's what I think you're doing!" How I came up with something so jealous-sounding and silly I'm not sure but it doesn't stop me folding my arms and scowling. I'm angry with her.

Norah is furious too. "Despite listening to that Eve woman's words for hours, you think that we women are all worried about things like nylons and lipstick!" she says, rising from the couch with a dramatic flounce. "There are women fighting and working hard in this war and men choose to turn a blind eye to it."

I hear her sit down again. There is a pause.

"I'm sorry. I'm sorry to use that phrase. It came out. But women are doing everything a man does to fight and survive for the good of mankind. Why do you still think we're not capable of evil deeds too? We are capable of doing whatever we put our minds to."

"I hear you," I say quietly, thinking that I'd rather be kissing her than having this conversation. "I know that you're a very capable young woman but I must say that you sound like one of those fervent agitators."

"And so what if I do?" Norah asks.

"Let's talk about this later," I say, searching again for her hand. I want to hold it. But I find her knee. I squeeze it and she moves away. Oh dear. I have alienated Norah. "Shall you or I telephone Lady Dornan?"

"You do it!" she snaps.

"Can you dial the number for me later?"

"We'll have to teach you the way to do it for yourself. And let you practise."

I scratch into my hairline and say, "Good idea."

"Do you believe Eve?" Norah asks, sounding mellower. "Do you believe her that John fell?"

"Do you?" I ask for I'm not certain what she wishes me to say and I don't want to annoy her further. "I'm almost afraid to give my opinion."

"What a silly thing to say! I'm not that much of a cow."

I think on that for a time and then say, "I don't believe her. She wanted him out of her life and she killed others. I'm curious to know how she's going to explain all her other crimes away."

"She makes out that the women almost forced her into an impossible string of events. As if all of her wrongdoings are their fault. It beggars belief!"

"It all does."

"Eve wants us to think that she went on a whim and got embroiled in a mess," Norah says. "What nonsense! I'm almost feeling sorry for the Sinful Roses. It sounds like they are there for the good of oppressed women and this Eve has ruined things for them."

"Oppressed women?" I ask gingerly, hoping I don't

get attacked for querying her logic. "You think that these Roses have a moral compass?"

"It sounds like they were set up with the intention of freeing women from the tyranny of their husbands. They do nothing wrong themselves other than discuss crimes. We could have a hard job proving that these women are actual criminals."

I sit open-mouthed.

"Their ethos is to support vulnerable women and this Eve has ridden roughshod over everything and spoiled things," she says. "They knew she was a loose cannon. This Alice woman was right. I'm angry for the Sinful Roses. I know, I know, I know that's wrong. But there are many malicious men out there who are brutes to their lovely wives. I can understand why there is a need for such support. I can see why women engage with the process."

"Sweet Lord!"

"There will always be those who break the rules but Eve was, and is, a total liability. They needed to stamp Eve out. I can see why. She's a vile bitch!"

"Let me get my ducks in a row here. You're saying that you believe that the Roses are upstanding women? With a worthy cause? Do you think that they're righteous people? These are criminals who tried to kill us and have kidnapped or murdered my wife!"

Norah replies slowly, "We don't know that's the case yet. Your wife is known for running off for no reason other than she likes the drama and worry it causes. These other women might only have threatened Eve. I don't trust or believe Eve Good. She could have easily harmed herself when she was cornered and now she aims to blame the Roses so that she is considered interesting."

"That's plausible, I suppose. Well done – you've thought of a new angle to this."

As soon as I say it, I realise I'm trying to flatter her. Norah might strike out at being patronised. I hold my breath and indeed she does.

"It's my job, Laurie, and I'm as clever as any man," she says coldly.

"Oh, dear," I mutter.

Norah has got a bee in her bonnet and I have failed to remove it. What is a man to do with a woman who thinks that a Murdering Wives Club is a good, understandable idea? I am at a loss.

There's an opening of the door and the clink of teacups. Giles' tea is welcome.

"Is everything all right, sir?" he asks and Norah marches heavily out of the room.

"Women are hard to fathom," I say.

Giles and I talk about the weather, Cook, and the grounds, before he returns to mentioning Norah.

"She is on the phone to the General now and sounds quite animated – can you hear her, sir?" he whispers. "She's a fiery one."

I can indeed hear her talking on the phone in the hall and realise the door has been left ajar.

"Yes, I can hear it. But you think she's a good woman, Giles? You like her? Yes? You think she's a good egg?"

Giles pours the tea and I wait. "We all like her, sir. But it's not our opinion that's important. Do *you* think she is a good woman and do *you* like her?"

I sit back in the chair and touch my scar. When I am with Norah, I am a man again. A whole man with a handsome face who is still blind but empowered. I have a purpose and a passion for livng. Is this Norah's doing? Or my own? I credit Norah with my transformation and I am grateful to her for it. The fact she has a mind and opinions of her own are to be expected, and someday I might understand them. I want to. Charlotte was never one for debate or philosophy. I doubt she cared much about anyone, other than herself. Politics or women's rights in the world was something that never arose. Maybe it mattered to her too but I never knew? Did I make her terribly unhappy? Is there something wrong with *me*? I know I promised myself to be less compliant when I returned home from Italy, but I want to please Norah. I just don't know how to do that. I might ask Freddie what perfume she likes.

"Any word of Mrs Davenport?" Giles asks, interrupting my thoughts. "There are salad sandwiches on the plate there, sir."

The guilt stabs me like a knife for being disloyal to our marriage. I'm having immoral thoughts about wooing Norah. More than thoughts, they are full-blown fantasies.

"No word of my wife. No."

"If you don't mind me saying so, sir, she was never the woman for you. She's flighty. You need a solid woman. Someone who is kind and good-natured."

We both can hear Norah losing her patience with the Freddie. She is loud and shrill all the way from the hall.

Giles chuckles.

"The work we are doing is frustrating Norah," I tell him. "She talked about herself maybe driving the Crossley."

Giles is silent.

"I know," I say. "Times have changed, haven't they?

112

When did we ever think that I'd consider anyone else driving my car? But it makes sense. Could we look out the keys and giving her a trial run?"

"I suppose so, sir. If you insist. And those men were about again and bothered Cook this morning. She's looking to talk to you about their prowling around in the muck and dragging it back inside. She's talking about hiring someone to clean. She's not got the time. I warned her not to bother you, and that I'd see to cleaning it myself."

"Could we hire someone part-time?" I suggest. "I cannot see the dust and dirt but we need to keep standards up."

"I was going to suggest Norah might –" Giles stops and Norah's voice is louder still.

She is stating her case for women's rights rather strongly to the General. She is wasting her time for Freddie is a man's man if ever there was one.

"Perhaps that's not her role in the household though?" Giles says, obviously hearing Norah's speech about the detective work she's capable of. "Let me see if we can find someone else."

"That's settled then," I say. "Let's not annoy Norah with too much today. She just seems to be in a bad mood. It will pass."

"I certainly hope so, sir."

Giles leaves and I cock an ear to eavesdrop on Norah but the call must be over for there is no high-pitched woman's voice in the hall.

The proposed questioning of Lady Dornan is bothering me. She's a lady of some standing with property and connections. I shall have to tread very carefully. Suddenly I hope that Norah hasn't telephoned in the current mood she's in. Such questioning will take tact and decorum. Lady Dornan is a woman of steel. And will I be fit for the task? I have annoyed the unflappable Norah.

Retracing my steps through the day, I cannot for the life of me see what has happened to make Norah this angry so quickly. Perhaps our kiss has concerned her? Perhaps she's feeling it was a bad idea? She kissed me. This is all her doing, yet somehow I know that it is I who will have to mend things. Whatever shall I do?

I'm about to put on some music to help me think when Norah comes in. She walks towards me.

I aim to speak first. "Before you say another thing, I want you to know that our kiss meant the world to me. I hoped that you might have dinner with me here this evening?"

Norah sniffs. Is she upset? I cannot see, it is most frustrating.

"I cannot this evening. I'm sorry. Another time perhaps?"

"That's fine – and I've asked Giles to look out the car for us to use. Actually it will be for you to drive from now on."

"I hope you don't think that I kissed you to get privileges?" she says.

"Of course not." My gut clenches. I've done the wrong thing yet again. She is still cross with me. Dear Lord in heaven, a man has a terrible time of it in this world. "I just wanted to mention both things to you before something else distracted me."

"I don't think we should ever kiss again," Norah says. "It was my fault that it happened. It shouldn't have – I'm sorry."

The disappointment hits me like a slap.

"We won't talk about it again," she states. "Agreed?"

I gulp and nod. "Agreed."

"I rang that Lady Dornan and you're not going to believe this," she says. "She's coming to see us tomorrow."

# Chapter 17

## Norah Walsh

I told Laurie about the Sinful Roses advertisement. It came out in a moment of weakness. What a complete arse I am! In trying to reverse our relationship, I've taken to arguing with him. It's a Fredrick tactic. When not wanting to commit or make promises, he would cause us to fight. I shouldn't have kissed Laurie and I most definitely shouldn't have mentioned the Sinful Roses advertisement. My only saving grace is, Laurie will never be able to find it in a newspaper by himself.

As soon as I had the words out I wanted to take them back. I hate hiding things from him and I do enjoy the game of being detectives. In trying to be too clever I slipped up. It's a sad state of affairs that I am here under a veil of lies. This was to be easier than it's turning out to be. I wasn't supposed to care about the man. I was going to use all of this Sinful Roses business to my advantage. My female heart is failing me. Or maybe it's somewhere lower down that's taking over my brain!

It pains me to look out on Davenport Manor's gardens. It all looks very beautiful in the morning light. The dew makes everything sparkle as the slight early morning fog lifts. Strong branches silently swing on the mighty oaks. I feel pity for Laurie as I watch the scene.

116

He should see this beauty. The lawn stretches out to meet the evergreen shrubbery and I can see on through the tunnel they make to the rented farmland scattered with sheep. If those at home could see me now, what would they think?

The long window panes are in need of a clean and a spider has made its home in the top corner, webbing its prey in broad daylight. And standing here in the dappled sunshine of a foreign land, I feel at home for the first time. Possibly ever. It's like I've been here before, in a past life. Stood on this very spot, looked out on this same view, and had the same loving feelings towards the house and its owner. I shake myself and wait on the feeling to pass, but it doesn't.

The house is in good repair, considering it has been neglected for years. It's not being used for the army in the usual ways big homes are being commandeered, and I'm glad of that.

"It's not big enough," Fredrick said when I wondered aloud why they hadn't spoiled the peace of the corridors and grounds with their big boots and nasty guns. "And Charlotte's father, Laurie's father-in-law, is an influential bugger. Another problem. Whatever the spoilt little whore wants, the little whore gets, and I think that's why Laurie was put in the worst possible danger on his posting to the Royal Engineers in Italy."

I shake my curls and run a finger over my throat and toss out hair from my collar. A gardener doffs his cap. "You think that you're Lady of the Manor," the voices in my head sneers. "Getting notions." My conscience always tries to talk sense to me, but I rarely listen. I've always wanted more out of life. Always saw myself as something more. I understand why women seek out the likes of the Sinful Roses or ask to be involved in the war effort. Anything is better than the drudgery of normal life. I relate to Eve's boredom.

Fredrick said on the phone already this morning that she'll be moved soon from Armagh to his headquarters at Thistleforth House. That is perhaps ten miles away and so she will be available to tell tales to Laurie. Thankfully, she's still refusing to speak with a woman in the room and I'm glad of that. I hate looking at her. Possibly because I can see that we're not that much different from one another. Eve Good wants to be like me. She has ambitions beyond her station too. And look where they got her. No-one to care at all.

The guards I met in the women's goal had little sympathy for her. It's for the best that we're all back in England. I'm not as exposed, Laurie is at home and once Eve is brought here she'll be on unfamiliar territory for a while. She'll need to settle in. The Roses might also take time to find her. It will give me some time.

"Get Laurie's confidence built up soon," Fredrick says when I telephone. "That Charlotte will turn up and want to move back in. By all accounts this disappearance is to extract ransom from her own father. I doubt it has anything to do with Roses or the likes of them. Keep an eye on Laurie, for he'd pay up his last shilling for the cow."

"We cannot have that," I agree – too quickly. "I wouldn't want Charlotte Davenport back. I'll do everything in my power to stop her."

Fredrick pauses and I can hear him drag on a cigarette.

"Laurie is much better without her," I add quickly.

"Does Laurie want her back though?" he questions cruelly. "The sap probably does. He cannot see what's good for him. He cannot see you, my dear. Make him see you."

"I hate when you mock like that," I say. "You know that he won't want her back and you know that I've more to me than being just a wife or lover!"

"Do you now?" Fredrick says with a sniff. "You women are full of yourselves these days. You can talk all you like. It's actions that count. Like these so-called Sinful Roses – women can talk all they like about killing – but they don't do it very well. For instance, is there anything of note from what this Eve Good is saying? Any other scandalous women to report to your superior?"

Instead of answering him, I go on to ask how they will move her to his base at Thistleforth House where she'll be imprisoned. I ask about how secure it is.

He refuses to be deflected. "I know that you're hinting at being here full-time, Norah Walsh," he says. "It's not going to happen. We both know how much you want to be one of the Special Op Executives here and, no, Norah, you cannot become one of them. Stop asking me. It will never be possible for a southern Irishwoman to become an SOE. You are getting access to Eve Good. That's as much responsibility as I can give you. Anyhow, I'm not going to discuss any more of this on the line right now."

Fredrick waggles the women who go to war at me regularly. It is like a carrot on a string. I don't know as much about this band of secretly trained women as I would like. But I do know that they are a vital band of females and even the likes of Fredrick Ashfield respects them. If only he felt I was good enough to join their ranks! Once I get this case solved, I will make him see sense.

It's my turn to ignore what he has said. "Is Thistleforth House ready for Eve Good, though?" I ask again. "She won't escape, will she?" The thought of a lunatic, murdering woman on the loose is enough to tip the public into total panic. But Fredrick wouldn't allow that to happen. Thistleforth is his baby, so he isn't going to let a pesky woman sully his reputation. I let the image of me helping Eve abscond race across my mind, and I smile. It would serve him right if I did!

"A blind ex-solider playing detective is enough for you to worry about," Fredrick says. "Keep him in line, won't you, Norah? And hurry up with the seduction. He's in need of a good time."

Fredrick is being a cad and he doesn't care. It disgusts me. Laurie Davenport is to be a means to an end. But now he's more than that. Fredrick ruins things with his lurid suggestions and orders. I'm a piece of meat he's chewed and spat out for Laurie to taste now. *Yuck!*

Laurie's kiss was a good surprise. On many levels it changed me. An electric current switched on and it lit up all that I was and where I was headed. It made me question my own motives, and Laurie's gentle nature lulled me into the trap of loving that kiss and wanting more of the same. There's a safe, gentle passion between us that is tearing me asunder. I cannot fall for a blind man almost fifteen years older than me. Not now! Not when the world is at my feet and I can achieve things. These feelings are coming at the worst possible time. I've many things I can and should do. Falling for a man is not one of those things!

I don't normally want more kisses from any man. I've learned to put up with more, but I've never had butterflies or my heart aching for love of that kind. Never. And now I'm going soft on a man just when I might actually find a little power of my very own. It has got to stop. Must end.

I open the envelope on the tray from Eve Good and scan the first few pages. I'm eager to start for the day, but am even more thrilled at seeing Laurie's smile as he comes into the room. No amount of talking to myself is helping me see sense. His lips turn upwards again when I move nearer to where he is standing. How handsome he looks, and he cannot see what I see. And I doubt that Laurie Davenport realises that he could seduce me in a heart-beat and this makes me feel for him all the more.

# Chapter 18

### Eve Good

Lydia warned me not to go to Ravenscairn again. *"Whatever happens you must wait."* I could hear her as plain as day. Did she mean that to be the case, even if I didn't kill John? Was I still to wait then? Would they believe that I didn't do it? Of course they wouldn't believe me! And, regardless, I was supposed to help others now? But how was I supposed to do that when I did nothing myself?

This was ludicrous – and I aimed to tell them! I had to let them know that it was all an accident. A tragic accident that I had nothing to do with.

I wondered then if maybe the women knew that it was not an accident? That maybe a Sinful Rose did it? I thought too that Tim might have had something to do with John's fall.

Tim knew the house well and he was a sturdy lad. He might have caught John unawares and have given him a neat shove to his death. It could easily have been an accident with no malice. Perhaps John found Tim in the house and they had a scuffle? My mind tortured me.

No one even hinted that I might have pushed John. There weren't any odd glances or comments. Everyone was full of pity and sympathy and I lapped it up. I maintained the facade well. Of that I am proud. I must be mad to be proud of that.

* * *

I decided to take Marjorie to the Christmas Carol Service in Netterby. Of course, she didn't want to go. Snow had started falling. I badgered her into the hired car and ignored her moans. I abandoned her in a church pew with the excuse of checking that the driver was definitely waiting in the village until we'd finished singing Christmas carols.

In the winter darkness Ravenscairn was a silhouette in the snow. Elegant as ever, it was frozen in time. The bare trees were still and silent of crows. There was not even a flicker of light about the windows and the curtains were drawn.

There were no footprints to the front or the rear and, although it was only a month since John died, surely I should have heard something from the women by now? Ravenscairn House looked empty.

When I returned to Marjorie she hissed, "There's a lady wearing a coat like yours," and she pointed in the direction of the choir stalls.

There, singing her heart out, was Alice. And, yes, oddly enough, she was wearing a red coat similar to mine in cut. It took maybe ten minutes for her gaze to meet mine and then she nodded knowingly.

On the way out she shook the minister's hand for a long spell, like she knew him.

I shuffled Marjorie forward.

"Please don't pull me, dear."

"The car," I mumbled and elbowed my way forward without my elderly charge.

I sidled past the minister's back when he leaned in to kiss a babe in arms and I caught up with a striding Alice.

"Do not talk to me," she mumbled out of the side of her mouth.

People were walking in our direction but were on the other side of the street.

"If you must, come to Ravenscairn on Christmas Eve."

"Christmas Eve?" I asked, unsure of the hushed instructions.

"Happy Christmas," she said for the benefit of no one. "Now fuck off."

I took Marjorie home.

When I reached my house, near the side door there was a hidden shadowy figure. In fear I tried to reverse but the figure moved towards me.

"Tim?"

He was cold in every sense. His coat would suit an elderly man and covered him to well below his knees. A scarf was tight up over his mouth and his face was almost hidden.

"I've been here a few times but the doors are always locked. Since when did you need a locked door?"

He was harsh. Extremely hard.

"I did see you at John's funeral but I couldn't speak to you then and there," I said. "And I had no way of contacting you. I couldn't chance being seen. Come inside – you must be frozen. It's good to see you."

There was snow on his boots and coat and it fell on my hall tiles. I moved right to go towards the kitchen, but he headed for the bottom of the stairs.

"What happened to John? He just fell?" he asked, looking up the stairs and pulling the scarf from his face. "Here?" He examined the scene and then bent down by the door to see it all more clearly.

"I was waiting to come and get you."

He sat on the second step. John lay about there.

"You ignored me," he said. "You didn't come to get me when he was gone. You don't care about me at all. I know you, Eve. Don't lie to me, like you lie to everyone else. I'm not stupid. I know what's what."

"How could I speak to you at John's funeral? What would it have looked like?"

"Like you were speaking to someone. Or were you worried that people might think that you killed your husband?"

Suddenly, there was a rap on the front door. A loud one. Someone had used the brass knocker and only strangers do that. If I ever had visitors they would come to the side door or tap on the back door and come on in.

Tim fled into the parlour.

With my coat on, I went to open the door but when I stepped into the hall I could see Constable Irvine's distorted face in the bulbous glass, peering in. He waved in a cheery way.

"Hello," I said, opening the front door. "I was just going out."

"I just stopped in with Marjorie and she said you were only back from church. Going out again?"

"I felt that I needed a stroll."

"In the snow?"

I moved us towards the kitchen. I hoped Tim would make his way to the attic or out of the house. But something told me he was still in the parlour – hiding.

"What can I do for you?" I asked.

"I was passing and thought I'd check how you were coping."

He looked at my red coat as I took it off and took good stock of my new dress.

"Thank you for calling, I'm not used to visitors."

"That's odd. I was sure I could hear you talking to someone." He smiled under that awful moustache.

I had practised questions and answers but I had long since forgotten them. Thinking I was scot-free. The right words weren't coming.

Irvine spoke slowly. Each word was considered and rehearsed. His tone was smooth and velvety and made the hairs on the back of my neck stand up.

"I must tell you that it has been reported to us that you were acting very strangely weeks before John's accident? Were you? Weren't you supposed to attend a psychiatrist?"

"I don't know why John told you that – that he had made an appointment for me. He said nothing to me about any such thing. I was more content and I was making a life for myself. For us. John didn't like me to seem normal. He liked me to be a bit 'cuckoo'. It made him look like a saint. John was no saint, no matter what you all think."

I had let my mouth and temper get the better of me.

Constable Irvine took out a notepad and wrote something down, grimacing. "None of us are saints, Mrs Good. But, right now, I think you are acting very strangely indeed."

The Constable finally went up the hallway on the dot of eight. The clock started chiming in the parlour. He cheekily pushed back the open door and pointed at the mantel. "What a fine clock! I've stayed far too long." His gaze swept the room.

My heart beat again in the correct rhythm because Tim was not there.

The snow was falling again but there were more than Irvine's footsteps visible. He looked at the path and was bound to notice the other set of men's shoes leading away from the front door. He said nothing about it and neither did I.

The pressure on me was immense. A mountain of worry sat on each shoulder.

The Ravenscairn meetings seemed a long time away. I would have liked guidance and answers right at that moment. I thought being without John would have made me happy but it was making me even more insecure, less sure of my fate, less content and a great deal more lonely. I was also back in the position of wanting to poison Marjorie. She was getting more demanding. I had no need of her then. The Roses had been wrong about so much. I didn't need Marjorie to vouch for me and she was just a burden. I hadn't needed to seem more normal or have someone to speak on my behalf if things turned sour. I saw her as a sullen, spoilt brat who thought they were owed unconditional devotion.

There was no reason to hasten things unless she really irritated me, but I found myself thinking of what might be possible. There were no stairs to throw her down. She stuck to the one level. Her home was on a slightly raised hill up from mine but the path wasn't treacherous.

Her fire cracked in the hearth and sparks flew onto her rug. Flames. Yes, they could spread easily through this house and she might die from the smoke. They say that it is the fumes that get to the lungs first.

\* \* \*

Ravenscairn was beautifully bedraggled on Christmas Eve. A Miss Havisham of houses. She was abandoned to the elements but stuck still in time like a broken clock.

"Lydia, I didn't kill him. I know nothing of how he died. I don't need ... I feel I don't deserve to be a Sinful Rose woman. John simply had an accident. I don't know what to do now." I'd practised these lines and out they poured.

Lydia laughed as she poured whiskies. "You're good at lying, I'll give you that. But you've no need to pretend here. We know what's what. You must stop that nonsense. You will be of great benefit to others. Once you set foot in this room, once you swore that oath to us, there was a cycle of events put into motion. Regardless of what you may think, we're not stupid women. I stood up for you, Eve. Don't let me down now. There's no need for you to pretend here. We don't think you are a bad person. We understand that sometimes men bring us to the brink and we can either push them over it or jump ourselves. You pushed back. You were brave."

*"But I'm not brave at all. That's what I'm trying to tell you.* I'm in shock about all of this. It's been weeks, but still I don't know how it happened. Please tell me what happened to my John? I think you know!"

Lydia was the first to break the painful silence that fell.

"Are you saying you wish to leave the group, Eve? Are you saying you don't need us any more? This is a serious matter. We aimed to help you and you come here shouting that you owe us nothing. We asked for nothing but loyalty."

"Threatening me isn't helping," I said breathlessly.

Alice cocked her head to one side. "Eve, we've done nothing. We've merely supported you in your endeavours. If you are not happy to be a Sinful Rose then that's your decision. However, we will not take kindly to it. If we cannot trust you to tell us the truth, can we trust you at all?"

"I know nothing though, Lydia," I say. "I know nothing of note. Apart from this house, and where it sits. I know nothing that could damage anyone."

"I told you, Lydia," Alice said and pointed at me. "If you think that we will fall for your lies, Eve, you've lost your mind. You are bound to us now, regardless of what you say. I can promise you something here and now …" she leant forward in the chair, "if you let Lydia down by speaking of us or if you refuse to keep your promises to us, then I personally will stop you breathing for good. Do you hear me, Mrs Eve Good?" She lit a cigarette. "Lydia didn't realise that there are mad bitches in the world. She took it that sane women might need to murder but failed to realise that the insane ones, like you, would too."

"I'm not mad."

"You most certainly are if you think that I'm going to put up with you. I'd kill you here and now only you'd make a mess of this nice room and we'd have to dispose of your corpse. I know from experience that that is not so easy to do."

She saw that I was afraid of her.

"Regardless of your pretending, Eve, you are one of us now," Lydia said.

"I'll have to help others to kill their husbands?"

"And that would be against your conscience?" Alice scoffed. "Lydia, we are now in bed with a mad bitch who is a loose cannon. And I told you all this would happen."

"It's not that bad," Lydia said. "Eve isn't saying she won't help us in the future. She is just saying that she isn't sure she has the stomach for any more death and we all ... well, most of us know how that feels."

"She's got the stomach for it all right!" Alice spat. Froth formed at the corners of her lovely mouth. "This one is cruel in the worst sense of the word. And now she's trying to get out of her agreement. But, Eve darling, we all know that the police aren't fully finished with you. We all know that you are a liar. Don't count your chickens. You might need us more than you realise."

"I'm not trying to get out of anything. I realise I might need help. Honestly, I'm only saying that I don't know what to do any more. I am lost."

"For the love of God, I don't need this!" Alice snapped. "You knew and know full well what we do here. Be very careful about shrugging us off."

"You've done *nothing* for me. Nothing! What is so great about the Sinful Roses? I came to a strange house, listened to rules and regulations and got scared half to death and that's about it. You women have done *nothing* for me, other than confuse and threaten me!"

"*Ha!*" Alice called out. "You see, Lydia. I bloody well knew it. Just you remember, Eve, that *nothing* is all we did. Talking about it is *all* we did." She nodded at Lydia. "Don't let her blackmail us. She can say what she likes but she will incriminate herself if she mentions us. She is the one with the problem here."

"My husband *fell* … that's if you had nothing to do with it."

Alice made a lurch for me but Lydia grabbed her arm.

"*I'll kill her!*" Alice said, her forehead creased. "You are some piece of work, Eve Good! I'll kill you with my bare hands! You wanted advice on the way to dispatch your so-called brute of a husband to the hereafter. You got that. You should be here asking for help in getting rid of the police from your door. But no. The bold Eve Good thinks she's scot-free. You come here, use us, and then think you're going to win in the end. *You bad bitch!*"

"Eve, I think you're being very hasty," Lydia grunted. "I was arrested many months after my husband was shot. You may need us yet. It is very early days and you are all alone in this world. It could make more sense to keep us on side."

"I've not got the stomach for killing like you have. That's all I am trying to say. I haven't killed my husband and I'll be of no use to any other woman. I might be more of a liability than anything else."

"*Pah!*" said Alice.

"Regardless of how your husband died," said Lydia, "you are one of us now and you agreed to the rules. You sat there in that chair and listened and nodded and made an oath."

"I did. But the whole thing is blurry to me. I didn't really understand what I was doing. I don't recall it word for word. And, because John fell and wasn't pushed I'm concerned that I will be of no use. I hate to say it again but you did very little for me. Unless one of you pushed John down the stairs for me? Tell me! Did you?"

"I should've insisted you had nothing to do with us

at the start of all of this like I wanted to." Alice used a hanky and wiped the spittle away from her chin. "You're spoiling everything and don't deserve Lydia's patience."

"You're killers," I pointed out. "I'm not."

Lydia's glass was empty. "Are you willing to acknowledge the oath you made?" she said.

*"I can't be of use!"* I shrieked. *"Aren't you listening?"*

"There's no choice in the matter," Alice said.

"What I'm trying to say," Lydia said, "if you both would let me, is that there are many ways that the Sinful Roses can help you, Eve. And there are many ways that you can help us as well. Let's wait and see what happens. Don't be hasty and cut yourself off from those who could protect you."

"No matter what you think of me, I can't kill or help others to do it. I'm simply not like that."

Lydia rolled her eyes at Alice. "Eve, you came here wanting to kill your husband. Don't get all moral on us now. What's done is done. We'll have to think on what you're saying. This is all very unfair. It was I who insisted that you needed us and now here we are in this mess."

"I'm sorry, Lydia." I caught Alice's glare and added, "Well, if I can't stop all of this I may have to just make the best of it."

'"*Make the best of it!*'" Alice copied my tone. "You're some bitch!"

# Chapter 19

## Laurie Davenport

I've never really been fit for the nastiness in this world. For my entire life, I've hidden away from reality. Going off to war was supposed to make a man of me. The naivety of it! Do I believe Eve Good walked blindly into the Sinful Roses? Possibly. For I walked into a marriage and off to war without an iota of sense. Norah, however, thinks women are much more scheming and plot their lives out more. I envy them. I wonder what plans Norah has? If only I had the gumption to ask her.

"These wives in the report?" I ask Norah. "The ones suspected of murder who started all of this – where are they now?"

"At home, I presume."

"And can we question them?"

"All of the files say they are above reproach. One was proved to be having an affair and talked about her husband's death but talking about murder and committing it are two different things and there was nothing the police found to incriminate either of them. One husband had a shooting accident, the other would you believe fell from a third-storey balcony. Both have expensive lawyers and neither will talk any more about the 'accidents'."

"I'm glad we're almost finished with that Eve

woman," I admit. "She is warping my morals."

"She led us to Lady Dornan. Speaking of Her Ladyship, where is she? Look at the time! It's well after two and she said she'd be here at half past one."

Norah puffs the cushions. She does it regularly and it's a comforting sound. I can picture her by the couch, her red hair loose around her shoulders, her face concentrating on shaking my mother's cushions. They will possibly be the ones with the gold tassels. My mother would have liked Norah. She might have raised an objection to an Irish Catholic stealing my heart, but I like to think that she'd have approved eventually. Father would never have approved and this makes Norah all the more appealing.

"Before Lady Dornan arrives, I should tell you that I've found out something rather interesting about her. However, I want to see if she comes clean about it first. I'm warning you it's going to shock you. But let's see if she's honest about her past first. I'll go see if Giles has anything nice for lunch after they leave."

Norah puts on one of my records and leaves the room. What on earth is in Lady Dornan's past?

"Pardon me, Pretty Baby" by Rudy Valée continues to fill the parlour and takes me back to when Charlotte and I danced cheek to cheek on this very floor. Where could Charlotte be? We snuggled in each other's arms and moved easily over the wooden floor and Persian rug. I thought I was in love. But I didn't know what those feelings were at all. Interest, intrigue maybe. Lust – definitely. I was bored waiting to be a husband. Tired of trying to find the perfect woman.

Going off to war gave everything a different sheen. If the casualties of war were anything to go by, the rest of my life was perhaps a few years at most, and I wanted to have sex. Unlike Freddie and Ian, I wanted a wife. I craved stability and security. The irony.

Norah, even when we argue, lights up the darkness in my head. I can understand the romance novelists and their depictions of love. I rub my chin and admit to myself that I want to hear and feel Norah close to me more and more. I ache if I think she's not happy with me or if she's absent for a few hours. When she's in the manor, I'm content but there's a deep longing to smell her perfumed skin or touch her in some way. I never had those sensations with Charlotte. When I am alone, I imagine Norah in my arms all the time. How we might fit together in my bed? How her back might feel when she's naked? Could she ever think of me with this kind of affection? Could I or should I ask Norah to dance? Can I still dance?

There's a knock to the door and Giles enters, declaring, *"Lady Dornan and ... Mrs Davenport, sir!"*

I leap to my feet and stumble towards the door. *"Charlotte? Charlotte? Charlotte is here?"*

Giles must have stopped the music for there's nothing but the tread of feet and the swish of material past me into the room.

"I believe there's been a search party out for me, Laurie?" Charlotte says.

It really is Charlotte. She is back. I barely remember to breathe.

"What on earth is going on?" I manage to say.

"I'm here too, Laurie!" Lady Dornan's voice rings out like a church bell.

She is known for her loud demeanour. I'd forgotten that.

135

"Charlotte turned up at my door recently and I thought we should make the journey together. You *did* want to see me? You look like you're not glad to see either of us!"

"I'll bring some tea, sir," Giles says.

I can tell he's surprised but calm. I try to be the same way. My shock simmers down and I sit. I aim to listen. Some of my best recent insights have happened when I've been silent.

"May we sit down at all?" Charlotte asks. She flops into the chair she knows is my favourite one.

I can picture her lounging back, legs elegantly crossed. And she's smoking. I can smell the long cigarette and imagine the holder balanced in her slender fingers. That blonde hair is possibly under a fashionable, expensive hat and her petite frame clothed in a designer jacket and skirt. She's possibly wearing my mother's pearls. I should ask for them to be returned.

Lady Dornan sits noisily and I try to recall her face. She was never pleasant-looking, more distinguished. I remembered she had a sharp nose and was shockingly thin. Yes. We joked she should be called Lady Lollipop.

"I've been abroad," Charlotte says. "I was unaware that my departure caused so much worry. That was until I spoke with Lady Dornan."

"Where were you?" I ask, not fully caring. "Where abroad? We are at war!"

"All over the place. Does it matter?"

"I believe you have questions about my house in Netterby?" Lady Dornan says.

The tension in the room is suddenly palpable.

"Eh, yes," I say. Where on earth is Norah? I could do

with her back-up and the information she has. Also women are scaring me these days and I am literally in the dark about what to do or say next.

"Laurie, you seem shocked," Charlotte says. "This isn't the warm welcome home I was expecting."

She's mocking me. "What do you want?" I ask curtly.

"Yes, let's cut to the chase. I'm here because I want a divorce," she says with a dramatic pause. "I understand the prenuptial agreement will see me left with very little, but I think we both know we should never have married and, to be frank, I'm in need of my freedom."

"We can discuss that later," I reply. It's typical of Charlotte to air our dirty linen in public. "Are the police aware that you are in one piece?"

Charlotte no doubts shrugs, for there's the standard careless grunt from her.

"I shall tell them that you're safe and well and not one bit concerned about the chaos you've caused," I say and then direct my conversation to where I think Lady Dornan is sitting. "It's also the authorities who are interested in the comings and goings to your house in County Down."

"I beg your pardon? Comings and goings? Whatever do you mean? To my house?"

"Yes, Ravenscairn. Is the house still called that?"

"I've changed the name. It's now called The Old Rectory."

"I'm working with General Ashfield," I say, wondering how much I should share. I am ill-prepared. Norah had planned to do the questioning and I agreed for I'm tired of not seeing people's reactions to my questions. "Your house came up in some enquiries that I'm making."

"How odd!"

"How odd that you didn't tell us Charlotte was alive and well and coming with you!" I snap. "It might have prepared us. We might have had less worry."

"I wasn't sure that Charlotte would agree to come," she says. "I knew that since you've come home from the war she's been troubled by your behaviour. But, here we are. I think it is fair to say, Charlotte, that you felt you should come and say your piece and I suppose me being here means that you're safe to do so."

"What?" I sit forward. "Safe? Why is she not safe in Davenport Manor? This was her home."

Charlotte coughs and says, "You can see his temper building for yourself. This is what I've been dealing with, Lydia."

My heart jumps and I barely hold back a gasp. *Lydia!* Lady Lydia Dornan! Surely she is not the woman of Eve's stories? Is Lady Lydia of Ravenscairn and the Sinful Roses sitting in my drawing room with my murder-hungry wife?

"Are you quite all right?" Charlotte asks. "You're pale as snow."

"As if you care! Have you made out to Lady Dornan here that I'm a cad? I've never given you even a cross word, Charlotte. I'm now a blind cripple. I cannot harm a fly." I instantly regret saying that. Pointing out my frailties is not exactly a good move when I am alone with two dangerous women. "Where is Giles with that tea?" I ask loudly.

"The war has scarred you terribly," Lady Dornan says. "It is changing men irrevocably. And there's no sign of it ending. This rationing is terrible. I'm surprised that you can get your hands on tea."

138

"Laurie would never do without," Charlotte chips in. "His friends, like that snob General Ashfield, see him well cared for."

"And your vehicle, Charlotte? It was just abandoned. And not a word! You don't care much for anyone else, do you?"

"It wasn't my automobile and it has been returned to the owner. No harm done and you don't need me. You never have. This divorce will be a relief to us both."

I was about to tell her that when I returned home I needed her desperately, but thankfully Giles arrives with the tray. The tinkling of the cups is very pleasing.

Giles pours the tea and hands the cups around, then says, "I'll be just outside, sir, and I've had the men guarding the house return that item I needed for protection."

"Men guarding the manor?" Charlotte scoffs.

Giles leaves. I never wanted him to stay more in all of my life.

"What do you need them for?" Charlotte asks. "Where are they? I didn't see any."

"Well, you wouldn't if they're good at their job," I tell the room and sip my tea. I neglect to mention that they don't come to the manor until dusk. "It is to do with my new job. Top secret and all that."

"And this job led you to investigating Ravenscairn?" Lady Dornan asks.

"It was part of my investigation, yes," I say. "You shouldn't have come all of this way. I only wished to know about the house before you purchased it. Who did you buy it from, for instance?"

"If you must know I inherited it from a rich American relative."

"I see. And was that relative renting it out to someone before that?"

"I have no idea. My solicitor dealt with the transfer of property."

"Do you spend any time there now?" I ask.

"It is shut up now. My husband is taken up with matters here in London."

"That's right. Your second husband. And what does he do?"

"What are all these questions about? He sits in the House of Lords and runs a company that supplies materials to the army."

"And your first husband?"

Charlotte interrupts. "Lady Dornan has kindly let me stay with her in London. The bombing is fierce so we might stay here for a couple of nights."

"That's not possible," I say quickly.

"Laurie, don't be difficult," Charlotte says. "This is wartime and you must make exceptions. I'm your wife."

"I think this is the opportune time for you to take the last of your belongings and go for good. Lady Dornan has her big car with her, no doubt, and you can drive away into the sunset knowing I will gladly grant your divorce."

"Laurie!" she gasps. "You are really a cold fish. Have you no heart left?"

"Perhaps it's for the best, Charlotte," Lady Dornan says, setting down her china cup with a clink. "It's time for you to start anew. I can see that you are a deeply troubled man, Laurie – and, Charlotte, you have your whole life ahead of you."

If I fling the cup I might just hit the shadow of one of them. I grip the handle and take a soothing sip instead.

"I may be in touch with more questions," I tell them, praying inwardly that they both leave and let me be. "Good day to you both. I shan't get up."

Giles opens the door with a flourish. He must have been eavesdropping.

I could hug him when he booms, "The maid has packed all of Mrs Davenport's things and she's left them in the hall! I can help take them outside. Let me get your coats."

I can tell that Charlotte lingers, watching me, as Lady Dornan walks to the door.

"Goodbye, Charlotte," I say to the shadowy figure.

"This is not over," she whispers. "Do you hear me, Laurie? This is not over by a long shot."

"It most certainly is."

The figure moves away and I close my eyes. Little changes in what I see but everything has altered in how I feel. I'm relieved to be rid of my wife. Overjoyed to be free of that unbearable tension and the resentment she carries around. And more than delighted to be alive and safe.

Norah's scent tiptoes into the room and she comes directly to my chair. She hunkers down and places a hand on my knee. "I'm here," she murmurs. "Giles and I heard everything. We were right outside."

I want to tell Norah that I'm a brave man who wasn't in the least afraid of two women in my own house, but I cannot lie to her.

"They're both in the Murdering Wives Club," I tell Norah. "I might be blind but even I can tell that they are Sinful Roses."

# Chapter 20

## Laurie Davenport

Norah has poured us whiskeys. It's the first time in days that I think of my morphine stash. My head and joints ache.

"Why didn't I think of her being the Lydia from the Sinful Roses?" I say. "She owns the bloody house!"

"I suppose you didn't know her first name – she's normally referred to as Lady Dornan. And Eve said Lydia was a criminal. Lady Dornan didn't fit who we were looking for until I spoke with Fredrick and he sent over some papers just now. And now that I see her, Lady Dornan fits the description Eve gave us. In the photographs we have of her she looks different. I had almost discounted her until I came across some scandalous tales from the past. This is going to make you scream out loud – Lady Dornan was once known as Lydia Babbington. And wait for it, Laurie. You're going to have a fit when I tell you this. Lydia Babbington murdered her first husband and did fifteen years for his murder. She was given a reprieve some years ago. Her present husband, Lord Dornan, has a liking for dangerous women, it seems. He visited her and other women prisoners. But took a shine to one in particular and proposed and married Lydia a year after her release."

"Good gracious!" I take a large gulp of whiskey.

"I know. Apparently Lord Dornan fell in love with her when she was incarcerated. It was only a short time after her time in prison that she married a lord and became a lady!"

"I cannot believe it!"

"It was a scandal for a time. Now rarely spoken about. Lady Dornan did a good job reinventing herself."

"I'll say! Did you see the two of them? What did Charlotte look like, do you think? Well? Tired?"

"She's a very beautiful woman. I can see why you married her."

"I'm glad that you can for I'm at a loss. She's a stranger to me now. What was I thinking marrying her? It was the romance of war. I was such a mammy's boy and she was rebellious, flirtatious and, I suppose, salacious."

"Don't feel bad about it. As I said before, most men do their thinking with an organ much lower than their brain."

I laugh. Norah's right, of course. She is in much better humour. How has she got me laughing about all of this? She's a marvel.

"Charlotte isn't coming back," I say with a satisfaction that fades. "She'll not be back," I say again, letting it sink in. The finality of it thumps pain between my eyes.

"The General will be glad too," Norah says.

Is Norah happy at Charlotte being gone for good? I suppose she might be. I hope that she's delighted.

"Are you going to be all right, Laurie?" Norah asks after I have finished most of my whiskey. "You're very quiet and pale. I'm sorry I was snappy this last while. I think Eve Good is a bad influence on me."

"I barely noticed," I lie.

"We still don't have a lot of proof that these women have done much wrong," she says with a long sigh. "The General is at pains to point out that the most we have on them is that they are part of a subversive organisation. But then they can say they meet to discuss jam recipes and occasionally one of the members' husbands meet with a sticky accident. There's very little proof of any wrongdoing."

I hold my glass aloft, hoping Norah might refill it for me. I easily could try to do it myself and I am going to have to make an attempt to look after myself if my wife is divorcing me.

Norah is dutifully at the whiskey decanter.

"Perhaps it is all over for us now?" I say. "With Charlotte alive and yet gone for good there's no need for me to be involved in this mess, is there?"

"And what about the crimes and the men who might lose their lives in the future?" Norah asks.

"I suppose. But a blind man like me is not exactly going to change all of that, now is he? I mean we must be realistic about this, Norah. This is pointless. I am pointless."

"There it is again. This sorry-for-yourself nonsense. Giles told me that he was delighted to see the old you coming back. All fight and vigour you were. Where is that Laurie Davenport? I want him to come back home."

Perhaps it is the whiskey talking for she sounds emotional.

"We've hit a dead end though, haven't we?" I say. "I know Lydia might be Lady Dornan but what of it? I didn't ask her much for I was afraid to let something

144

slip. I was worried I'd alert them to what we know. And, to be totally honest, I was petrified of them both. I was scared of two women in my own home."

"That's understandable. I thought I'd antagonise them further if I came in. Mrs Davenport would resent me being here. Although I'm sure she's aware of my existence. Lady Dornan knows you have an assistant because I took her calls but I doubt they know we're a strong team hot on their heels."

"I don't have your enthusiasm about being close to making this stick. Sherlock Holmes wasn't a blind fool."

"I thought I was Sherlock and you were Watson?"

I snort.

"Anyhow, Watson, I've a plan I want to tell you about," she said. "If these Sinful Roses are real then I've thought of a way to infiltrate them right at the heart of their organisation. The only thing is, it will take time to worm my way into the club."

"That's not a good idea!"

"It most definitely is. We can look out for an advertisement for a Ravenscairn close by and write to them and wait."

"They'll look into the applications. They'll know that you're not married! It will not work at all. No way is this a plan of attack. They won't let you in – even if they don't know you are my assistant."

"Very few people know about our connection," Norah says. "And I can always get married. People are marrying quickly these days because of the war. Finding a husband is the easiest part to all of this."

My heart sinks. Norah wants to marry someone.

She takes a deep breath. "General Ashfield has no

wife and with your help I'm sure that I can persuade him to be bait in this case. He won't be an easy man to kill, I grant you, but that's a good thing. It will make my plight all the greater. This group seem to often help women with military or police husbands and I'm sure I can persuade the Roses that I want to murder a general! Especially Ashfield. He's a snob. I'll have to say that I married him for his money and status. He's not ugly but I couldn't marry him for love. And of course my Irish family will not approve and therefore they won't attend the wedding. He's the perfect bad husband for me."

I cannot reply. I'm dumbstruck. She cannot be serious.

"This is the best way to get the information I need. Sorry, I should say that this is how *we* get the information *we* need. If I'm a Sinful Rose I'll be trusted and learn what we need to know from the inside. I can be a spy in their camp."

"Please stop, Norah. This is making me weak with worry. There's no way that the General would agree to this and there's no way that I'll let you do it."

"Let me?" Norah sounds cross. "It's not up to you to let me do anything! I'm a grown woman and I've a mind of my own. The General was saying similar things yesterday when I suggested it on the phone. He thinks that I'm a frail female. The cheek!"

"He doesn't think this is a good plan either then? Well, I'm glad of that."

"He's afraid of commitment. Even if it's a false marriage, he's afraid of even the pretence. I've told him that we can forge the papers. It doesn't have to be real!"

I stop myself from pointing out that I'm roaringly

jealous of such an idea. I throw the remaining whiskey into my mouth. How do I dissuade her without making her more determined? Women!

"Eve is coming to the end of her tale," Norah says. "She may add small pieces of information but we are not gaining ground quickly enough. I can become one of them. What better way is there?"

"And how can I remain involved?" I ask her.

She taps a nail on the glass. She is thinking.

"Are we not a team?" I ask. "Going into this will mean you'll be in grave danger. You'll have three months to do the deed or they might murder you. Think on that for a moment. This isn't something you can march into lightly. Look at Eve Good and where she ended up. You could die, Norah!"

"They've not killed Charlotte," Norah says. "I've been thinking a lot about all of this. Eve said that Lydia mentioned that were other ways to help the Roses. I think although Charlotte failed to kill you – they like her. They didn't give Eve another choice because, well, they could see she is unstable and would never follow their rules. They needed rid of her, but Charlotte might have convinced them that she needs more time or can provide something else that they need. Money maybe? Or loyalty? Although Lydia or Lady Dornan came here with Charlotte to keep a close eye on her, wouldn't you say?"

"Perhaps." Norah is making sense and I pause for a moment before asking, "I might still be in danger then?"

"Perhaps," Norah replies. "But wouldn't I know all of the answers if I was involved with them? I could snoop and find out what Charlotte is up to."

"But you might be given total strangers to deal with!

They might not even know Charlotte. You might learn nothing at all and put yourself in even more danger!"

"Eve wanted out from the moment she went into Ravenscairn," Norah says. "I believe that much is true. She realised she didn't need them like normal women do. She is self-obsessed – she didn't want to know about the others at all. Because she is Eve and only Eve matters. But I'll be different. I'll be going into Ravenscairn to learn all that I can and because I want to be there. I'll make them trust me."

"This is ludicrous. I forbid it," I say.

Norah goes on regardless, walking over all my protests. "I will find out all the answers if I become a Rose. I'm eager to see this advertisement. I wonder when and where it will appear."

Norah is far too good at being a detective. My headache is worsening. I'm not cut out for this business.

"Eve will tell us soon who tried to kill her," I say. "I'm convinced that she will tell us about her being found on the road to Belfast. She was shot twice, wasn't she, and left for dead? She might implicate Lady Dornan. We should show her a photograph."

"Yes," Norah says. "She wouldn't say who shot her but her cousin and Marjorie Fellows came forward and Eve was found guilty of murder, attempted murder and arson. The police didn't care too much about who tried to kill Eve. Especially if she wouldn't talk to them. But, if she admits to who it was now, we might be able to get the Roses on an actual crime. We might be able to prove they were involved in the attempted murders of Eve and ourselves."

"You know, I thought once I returned home that I would be free from worry. But this is a whole lot worse.

148

Men with guns across battlefields are a lot easier to deal with! I think we are still in enough danger without you adding to it, Norah. Please listen to me. I don't think it is a responsible idea to put your head in the lion's mouth. I know the more I refuse to let you, the more you will want to do this. And I don't want to drive you into it. If I am adamant I don't want you to do it, you will want it more. And if I encourage you to do it and something happens, I'll never forgive myself. And really I cannot bear to think of you in any more danger on my account."

"I want to help, Laurie. I came here to find out what was happening to you and others. And I think I'm quite good at it. I can do this and we'll put these criminals behind bars where they belong."

"It sounds like you're longing for adventure and you want to be a hero," I say.

"And would that be a silly want?" Norah asks. "Don't men go off to war for adventure and to be heroic?"

I open and close my mouth. She has got me there.

# Chapter 21

## Norah Walsh

"Laurie did well," Giles says as we walk back towards the kitchen together. "He did well to see them both off. That took courage. I'm very proud of him. Thanks to you, he's got a new strength of character, Norah."

It is kind of Giles to give me credit when I had stayed out of the drama.

"It was such a relief to see them drive around the far corner of the avenue and out that end gate. Gone," he says triumphantly.

"Laurie did very well," I say as if he's a boy at school. "There's a lot happening with his work for the General too and he's coping with it all. I'm very proud of his progress."

"And aren't you a strong woman?" Giles says, swinging the kitchen door open expertly with his back. "Dealing with dangerous wives."

I smirk. If only Giles knew about all that I cope with.

"She's a very beautiful woman," I say to him as I help by putting cups and saucers onto the shining silver tray. "I mean Charlotte. She's a good-looking woman."

Giles grunts and places the large, brass kettle onto the hot plate.

"Laurie has regretted marrying her for some time, hasn't he?" I ask even though I already know the answer.

"She wants a divorce. Should he give it to her so easily? She'd be entitled to things. It might break up this estate?"

"Never. The Davenports have good lawyers and this place is locked up tight from the likes of that Charlotte."

I let my shoulders relax. "That's good news. As we'd say at home, it's all tied up tighter than a duck's arse then?"

Giles laughs and agrees but then starts ranting about gold diggers and wanton women with no morals.

All I can do is sit on the stool by the warmth of the stove and wait on the kettle. I do agree with him that in that way men are vulnerable. But, though sometimes a woman manages to damage their pocket and reputation, but it seldom hurts them for long.

As Giles opens the tea canister the aroma of it fills the air.

"Laurie will be back to his old self sooner than we think," I say to Giles as well as myself. "We need to keep this momentum going. Keep him moving on with his life. I'll drive us both over to Thistleforth and visit Fredrick. It'll get him out of lingering in that parlour and thinking too much about things outside his control. It might be late when we get back. But Cook is off today anyhow and we might find something to eat over there."

"Whatever you think is best," Giles says, filling the teapot with a long high pour from the heavy kettle. He's showing off his strength and abilities to make tea. "I think you were right to let him deal with the women alone. It gave him confidence. He so badly needs to feel manly again. It's hard for a woman like you to understand, but Mr Davenport has lost more than his eyesight. It's his whole manhood that is at stake. Charlotte has condemned him to a fate worse than death."

"That's a bit over the top, Giles," I say with a snort, but I know in ways he's right.

I wonder whether the Sinful Roses might see Laurie's fate as sealed and Charlotte might be let go from their clutches. They might be persuaded that Laurie is dead in all the ways that matter. Eve Good is a different kettle of fish for the Sinful Roses to deal with. She's not just a murdering wife. She's killed more than a husband. She went on a rampage when her husband plummeted to his death.

"Did he fall or was he pushed?" I mutter to myself.

"Pardon?" Giles asks.

"Oh … nothing."

"Then he came home broken and maimed and she was off cavorting and making a spectacle of herself. When she was here, we lived in fear. Cook will be pleased to know he saw her off. That was not an easy thing for a man of principle to do. He made oaths to love, honour and protect her. *Huh!* He's finally going to get some peace. Over the top it may be but I'm glad, Miss Walsh."

Giles is passionate about his employer and it is nice to see. Laurie has indeed stared death in the face and become blind because of it. He lost his entire family and he neither deserved or caused this tragedy. He also does not deserve someone like me in his life. But I am falling in love – and much as I try to stop it I can't.

I nod at Giles and smile. "My worry is that once this work is done, he'll not need me any more …" I stop myself for I cannot think of the future. I don't want to think about having to leave Laurie or Davenport Manor, but I'll have to. Regardless of what happens with Eve Good, an end will come and Laurie and I will part ways. That makes me very sad.

Giles has lifted the tray aloft but he stops and places it back onto the table with a clink. His hand takes mine and he leans down to peer into my eyes. "Fredrick is not a nice man, but he knows his duty and does it. He cares for Mr Davenport and sent you here for a reason. We both know what that reason is. He wants you to love Mr Davenport and bring him back to a full life. I can also see that you're a good woman. Allowing Mr Davenport to depend on you and, yes, care for you, is not a bad thing." He holds a finger aloft to silence me. "But you should have faced that Charlotte today. You mustn't feel one bit guilty about taking her position in Mr Davenport's home ... or heart. Don't let her ruin the one good thing that has happened to Mr Davenport in years. And, before you wonder, Miss Walsh, that one good thing is most definitely you."

"I don't know about that," I say.

Giles lets go of my hand and lifts the tray with new purpose. "Bring in Cook's oaten biscuits, would you? They're beside the egg basket in a tin with a horse and hounds on the front."

Nibbling on an oaten biscuit, I sit beside Laurie at our favourite spot beside the glass double-doors leading out onto the terrace.

He doesn't speak for a long time.

I break the silence. "Once we've finished this, let's drive over to Thistleforth and get more of Eve's account from Fredrick – and find out all we can about these wretched Sinful Roses, eh?"

# Chapter 22

## Laurie Davenport

I cannot drive, read, or admire the woman I'm falling for. My wife wants a divorce and I'm trying to prove that she's out to kill me. What in the world is happening to me? I'm like a sitting duck waiting to be shot. To get me moving and motivated, Norah and I have come to Thistleforth House and she has asked to see the General. It's reported back almost immediately that Freddie is too busy to meet with us and we linger in the corridor like strays.

"Don't look so dejected. It's me he doesn't want to see," Norah says, touching my arm. Her face moves towards my ear and I shiver when she whispers, "He knows there are things here at Thistleforth that I want to be involved in and he's avoiding me."

I want to ask what things? But an image of a naked Norah in Freddie's bed flashes before me. Were they lovers? Are they still? I reach out for her wrist and hold it. I pull her closer and touch my lips lightly off her cheek. "Forget him," I whisper against the softness of her. She smells heavenly. "We're a team now. You and me, Watson."

"Yes," she murmurs.

I wish we weren't in a cold corridor with footsteps passing. I could quite easily slip an arm around her waist and fold her against this passion stirring between my legs. Thankfully, she doesn't move away from me and leans against my chest with her forehead against my chin. We breathe in unison and I move my mouth downwards and find skin with my lips. I kiss it.

She sighs and says, "We shouldn't … I've ambitions, Laurie. I want to be more than a ..."

"*Shhh*," I urge. I don't want to hear about Norah's desires as something tells me that they don't include me.

A kiss finds her forehead again and I feel the tickle of curls against my face. I nuzzle into her hair and find the smooth side of a tightening neck.

"You're so beautiful," I whisper and hold either side of her slim waist with my hands. "Let's go home?" I urge, breathless at being this intimate in a cold corridor.

"This isn't right," she says quietly without moving. "Nice and all as it feels, this is wrong. We shouldn't, Laurie."

I suck gently near her earlobe and she shudders. My crotch hardens but she moves my hands from her sides and steps backwards.

Her fingers touch off my hand and she grabs it to squeeze it reassuringly as she says, "We should stop now. You're still married, Mr Davenport, and I'm a good Catholic girl."

I suddenly become self-conscious and wonder who might be within earshot. There are doors opening and closing and the noise of chattering comes from further along the corridor. Why can I not find this seductive bravery when I'm at home in the manor? When I have her alone, why can't I move and be like this?

"Let's get what we came here for," she says and I hear her footsteps clip off and away from me.

I want to thump something hard. I curl my fist into a tight ball and grimace. Why did fate bring Norah into my life now? Why am I being tempted with images of a glorious future and steamy lovemaking? Norah is right – we're not meant to be tempted this way. I just wish someone would tell my tormented libido.

I stand waiting on her to return. It feels like five minutes. Then the cool air around me is replaced with a warm glow and her aroma.

"Did you get Eve's letter?" I ask, not wanting to know if she got to see Freddie. He would kiss her for sure. He wouldn't stand there like a lunatic with his mouth hanging open and his underwear embarrassingly and uncomfortably tight.

"Yes," she answers. She takes my arm and we set off.

"Her letters should really be sent directly to Davenport," I say, wanting to keep distance between Norah and Freddie. Something outside of Davenport will take her away from me and it burns me in my guts to think of it.

Sitting into the car, I resent not being able to drive. I miss it terribly. Norah is quiet and I hate not being able to see her. The engine roars and it's not me making it sound so good. Anger bubbles and thoughts of not seeing what's right in front of me surface.

"What is between you and Freddie?" I ask Norah and then hold up a hand to stop her answering. "No. Don't tell me. I don't want to know. Let's not spoil things. We should stick to the job at hand. As soon as we get home let's see what else this Eve Good can tell us and just move on."

Norah mutters agreement. "That is for the best, Laurie. We have a job to do. We shouldn't get distracted."

I want to gush that I don't want us to succeed for then she will leave me. I also don't want to know any more about her and Freddie. I'd rather stay in the dark and cling to Norah. Yes, that is what I want – Norah in the dark with me and not much talking at all.

The rain comes on just as we park at the front door. It patters on the windshield and roof. I was just about to ask Norah to walk with me in the garden but now that's not possible. She let me kiss her face only a while earlier but it seems like a dream now as I stumble my way up the front steps.

"I'll take your arm," she offers from behind me. "Wait a moment!"

I don't do as she wishes and fumble to find the doorknob by myself. I stride across the hall, counting my way to my usual spot in the sunshine. Who needs her? I certainly don't need to beg any woman to be with me. I don't need Norah!

All is going fine until I miscalculate my journey and my arm clips off the fern in my mother's Belleek china pot, sitting on the hall table. It crashes to the floor and scatters earth everywhere. The smell of soil mingles with my curses and I kick a large piece of pot ahead of me. It clatters off the skirting board and shatters some more. Temper tantrums are usual in children and it takes all of my resolve not to stamp my feet or lie down in the dirt strewn across the floor and kick up my heels. I shout out in anger instead, a long, anguished groan.

I creak my tightened neck and jaw-line towards the front door and call, "*Norah, it seems that I do need you! Can you help me, please?*"

"It's all right, Laurie, it's only a plant," she says from

the end of the hall. "Can you make your way into the parlour? I'll help Giles clear this up and be with you in a minute."

What I want to say disappears with her footsteps towards the kitchen. I should just take Norah up the stairs and make passionate love to her. That's what any normal man would do.

But here, in the dark, I am not the man Norah needs.

# Chapter 23

## Norah Walsh

Seeing Laurie lose his patience with a potted plant is new. I like it. There's a glimpse of the man that he is. Finally, I'm getting to see a fire or passion in him. It's a pity the accident comes from him trying to be independent but I think it also happened because of his jealousy or frustration with me. I like that he's jealous. Should I encourage this or not? It seems to be reviving Laurie but also it's unfair if I'm not planning on following through with my flirtations. It's unfair to give him mixed signals. It's not good for me either. I'm torn in two. On one hand there's the chance at happiness … perhaps . . . and on the other there is the chance to be a woman of substance. What do I want? Or which do I want more?

His kisses are so delicate, so thoughtful, so delicious. I get lost when he touches me like that. The sensations are too intense to forget or ignore. Then, in the middle of the romance, my sense comes back to me and I push him away. The distress to myself is bad enough but, as I lift the shards of china, I realise that I'm also playing with a broken man's emotions. It's disgusting. I need to make up my mind and stick to a course of action.

"I'll try to glue it," Giles says. "It's a family piece."

"Oh dear," I say, smiling. "That kick he gave it didn't

help. He was walking by himself."

"Ah," Giles says knowingly. "Go do whatever it is you were doing together. Go on. I'll finish here." There's a kind wink from him.

I hate that I have vital information that I'm keeping to myself. These are good men and it's unfair not to reveal all that I know, to Laurie especially. It's very unfair indeed!

Taking the envelope with Eve's letters into the parlour, I wait on Laurie to smile at me. Usually he does and when it happens my belly-butterflies swirl and all is fine with the world. However, just now there are no smiles from Laurie to greet me. A silent, sullen expression is facing out towards the rainswept gardens. I cannot blame him.

"Will I read this to you?" I ask him when he doesn't acknowledge me. "We cannot give up now," I try as I drag a chair closer to him. "Let's see what Eve Good has to say for herself today."

# Chapter 24

## Eve Good

I was leaving Marjorie's one day when I found a man on his knees looking in the flowerbed under some of her rosebushes. He was portly with thick spectacles and receding dark hair. It was Cedric her nephew. Terribly boring and moist-handshaking Cedric Fellows. He was starting to visit more regularly. Marjorie was pleased and I was suspicious.

I wrote to Tilly, telling her about everything. I asked her too if she had recovered from the bout of influenza which prevented her from coming to John's funeral. Tilly had always been able to read between the lines – she knew how I felt about things. A distant cousin she might be, but there was lots of my blood in her veins all the same. If she became a Sinful Rose then maybe things might not be quite so bad. We could be in this mess together. I thought it would be easier with the likes of Tilly in my corner. I would have an ally, a comrade. I muttered a little prayer that she might be led to consider it, then licked the envelope closed and placed a stamp in the corner.

Also, Lydia and the others help women in peril, women on the brink of ruin and disaster. It is laudable in many ways. When one looks at it, they provide a great

161

service and they receive no monetary reward. What do we gain from helping others, other than danger? Maybe that was part of the attraction too?

John was dead weeks by then. If I had pushed him, I'd be empowered and full of pride, elated with a sense of achievement. Without the Sinful Roses there was very little else in my life. Much as it pained me to think this or admit to it, there it was – the truth of the draw to such a place and such people. Alone and vulnerable I was at their mercy and, in looking at it all, I was lifted by their interest in me and my existence meant something. Waiting on the meetings gave purpose to my weeks, excitement to my thoughts, urges to my lethargy.

The women, Alice and Lydia, made me feel dangerous and vicious. Alice called me terrible names and accused me of dreadful things. Although it was unprovoked and undeserved, I did like to think she thought I was dangerous. I found myself smirking in the street, knowing she saw a badness in me.

The next day, Lydia, Alice and I were in the Ravenscairn parlour.

"Why did you let me join if I'm so bad?" I asked Lydia.

"There were many reasons. Your bruises, the meek nature you had – back then, the lack of nice things, the lack of children which I understand can break a woman, the longing looks you made when I mentioned freedom and independence. And …" She stopped.

I forced the issue. "And what else made you go against Alice's protests?"

"If you must know, it was your address," she admitted.

I could tell that she didn't want to discuss it with me.

162

She had that tight-lipped look she did so well.

"What do you mean?" I asked.

There was no reply.

"I've a right to know why and how you picked me," I demanded.

"You live beside a Mrs Marjorie Fellows," Lydia said.

The gasp from me was loud.

"And before you ask, no, Marjorie doesn't know me. I don't know Mrs Fellows. But I know her nephew. Knew him."

"Cedric?"

"Yes."

"He visits his aunt. You can't leave it there and not say any more. How is Cedric significant?"

"Cedric came to visit me in prison. He's a special friend of mine."

My mouth fell open.

Lydia went on. "He also did a lot to secure my release. I was grateful to him. He knows nothing of us here. Don't lose the run of yourself. He's merely a good man who read about me in the paper he works for. Nothing more than that. I felt it was a sign to help you. You lived near Cedric's aunt – and needed help. Your husband was a policeman too and I felt …"

"Guilty."

"It was a sign and you seemed lost."

*"She's a liability, Lydia!"* Alice shouted. "Give the order and I'll get rid of Eve Good. Let me do the deed."

"I'm to be called Eve Kanaster from now on. My maiden name."

Alice laughed. Her mouth was wide in glee. "Ain't you *Good* any more?" she drawled. "It's not often I feel sorry for any man, but I'm starting to feel very sorry for poor John Good. That poor bloody bastard. He had no clue what he was dealing with. Poor sod."

It was starting to dawn on me that the Sinful Roses were nothing but a liability to me. Their anger was plain to see and they refused to listen to my claims of innocence.

I left Ravenscairn certain that I was going to have to tread the rest of the journey alone. Alice's threats rang in my ears and I found myself packing a suitcase.

Tilly, my cousin, had written and invited me to Inishowen. She gave instructions for me to ignore her husband Frank and to bring warm clothes.

I was still packing when Cedric knocked on the door. He was looking for *rent*! It turned out that the weasel was my landlord and I never knew. Unbelievable. John had rented the house! *Rented* it! And from the likes of Cedric who lorded it over me. He also hire-purchased the car. *Pah!* Hire-purchase was a word I barely knew – how had John stooped so low? I felt sick to the pit of my stomach but I didn't waste any time getting ready to leave.

Shaking with anger and, though I hate to admit it, fear too, I kept packing that small suitcase I kept on top of the wardrobe.

The greens of the world flashed by as I took the bus to Tilly's.

Glensmal was a nice detached house with a view of Lough Foyle. With access to the shore and its pathways, it took the full force of the weather but its two storeys were strong and true.

Tilly looked through me at her front door.

164

"Have I changed that much?" I asked her squinting blue eyes. "Surely you know me?"

"It's like you're a different person. My goodness! Your weight? Your hair? The scarf? I barely recognised you."

"I simply had to get away. I know you probably asked out of politeness but I needed to escape to someone or somewhere."

"Not another word. Sit you down and I'll make us a cuppa." Tilly took my case in her thin hands and lugged it into the narrow porch.

The thick walls were painted a canary yellow and had a deep warmth to them. Ever the good housewife, her kitchen was spotless and the floor clean enough to eat off.

She moved elegantly. Tilly was a beauty.

"I'm glad you went to Ravenscairn." Tilly was always one to see the glass half-full instead of half-empty. "But now you have John's insurance money, the house, everything all for yourself."

She was pleased, but I was far from content.

"No annoyance, no ill treatment any more," she went on. "Time to come here. Money to buy yourself nice things like this coat." She rubbed my sleeve.

She really couldn't understand my predicament at all.

"John is gone – enjoy it," she whispered. "Stop feeling guilty. He deserved it. From the tales you've told me, he was dreadful to you. You endured many years of being afraid. You're free now. Make the most of things."

"You could join me, Tilly." I pulled on her arm. "They say that I must advise others. I could help you be free too. These women mean what they say and I must help them. It was your idea for me to meet Lydia."

"But they don't want you to actually do anything? Do

they? You all just talk about it? Thrash out the pros and cons – like we are doing now. Shocking behaviour. But the likes of you will love all of that! The scandal, the naughtiness of it."

I suppose I did like it. I've always wanted her away from the beast Frank Hockley from the day and hour he proposed to her. She seemed to be enjoying all this talk of killing and it might be the glimmer of hope.

"John fell to spite me," I told her.

Tilly laughed. "I'm glad for you, Eve. Freedom must feel nice."

"You see it as a game. You think that it is not real but it is, Silly Tilly. Being alone is very nice but you have to work hard to achieve being an independent woman with means." My gut clenches. I don't like being a liar, it doesn't suit me at all. Tilly knows me better than anyone else and her opinion of me matters and this throws me off kilter a little.

"Eve, there's no one better than you to deal with the likes of the Sinful Roses."

"But I'm not able. You're wrong, Tilly. Very wrong. I need you with me."

"You've never needed anyone."

"You could be one too, Tilly. It would be easy and we could be together and you could live out all those fantasies you used to dream about! Say you will, please! Say you'll be one? Go on. You could be just like me."

I took her hand.

She asked, "What do you mean?"

"Let's kill that beast of a husband of yours. Let's bash Frank Hockley's skull in."

# Chapter 25

## Norah Walsh

Laurie and I discuss the madness of Eve for a time once I'm finished reading. She's definitely deranged and the more we're reading the more Laurie's thinking she's untrustworthy. I don't dissuade him of this notion, for Eve Good is most definitely a deranged lunatic!

I don't want to contact Fredrick but Laurie asks me to.

I decide while dialling and waiting for him to answer that I'm right about the men's relationship. Fredrick doesn't like seeing Laurie's disfigurement. It has taken me a little while to figure out why, but now I think it's because he hates to witness a good man's struggle. Laurie's blindness and life now fills Fredrick with guilt and fear. Telephone conversations are easier. He can control the situation. He also doesn't like seeing me face to face any more. There is something very sad about men's need to be on top of their emotions and every situation.

"You were busy earlier when we called to Thistleforth?" I say to Fredrick. "Laurie was disappointed at not seeing you."

"Tell me what's happening and stop coming here, Norah. Until Eve Good arrives there is no reason for you to be in Thistleforth. I'll deliver all relevant things to the manor."

When I read Eve Good's words to Laurie, I can never quite believe my ears. Summarising to Fredrick over the telephone doesn't help much.

"She should be writing a novel," Fredrick says as I munch on cheese on toast. "She was living in Northern Ireland but it could be an international club of murdering wives? Lady Dornan's lawyer and husband have been asking about my interest in their house in Ravenscairn. It's as if she's a lady of impeccable reputation regardless of her past! They seem to forget that she's a convicted murderess. And Charlotte is living with her now! Playing the poor, thrown-out wife of a returning damaged soldier. What a bitch!"

He laughs a lot at that. I stay quiet though I itch to object to his attitudes to women.

Women have stepped forward over these war years and have shown their mettle. With able-bodied men all off fighting, the female sex have taken on their work and are making the most of the situation at home and in the work place. Alone. Men like Fredrick don't or won't notice this. They possibly have turned a deaf ear to the rumours of the Sinful Roses organisation for decades.

They must have. For even I've heard about the Sinful Roses.

What I know is what most women know. The Sinful Roses is not a totally *secret* organisation but they are an organisation with many secrets. Most women I know gossip about the Sinful Roses and fact mingles with fiction no doubt. We all enjoy the badness that surrounds the tales about them. Of course all of the whispers are just out of earshot of any male relation or friend. There has always been an unspoken respect for the Sinful

Roses code of womanhood. It isn't that we ever actually know a member or wish to be part of it all. But there's a romance to their bravery and the need for their guidance is the stuff of gossip.

No-one knows who the pitiful women who need the Sinful Roses are. But it's accepted that some poor souls are at their wits' end with no choices and the men were in need of 'it'. We never really consider what 'it' is. Whatever befalls the bastards will be warranted because the Sinful Roses reign over the whole process. They manage and judge each individual case. There's a moral logic to the whole process that is accepted. It's understood that to speak of them is a dangerous pursuit. If people refer others to them, it is because the situation is dire and there are no other solutions.

It is also known that they are ungodly, unholy women. Well, how could they not be? If you sup with the devil then you must reap the consequences.

Until I met Eve Good I always thought they were almost infallible. A Sinful Rose could do no wrong. But now God love 'em, it's clear that they have had a large problem for many years. The likes of Eve Good was not expected to exist. Even by those who must be considered the most awful of women, Eve Good is a very dangerous exception. She's upsetting the way of things.

"It stands to reason that these Roses want Eve gone," Fredrick says.

"Yes," I agree. "She's setting back the cause of women's rights by decades. All the good work done by women in the factories and in the army goes to nothing with the nonsense she's spouting about wives murdering their husbands."

169

"Good men coming home from war, like Laurie Davenport, don't need the Sinful Roses taking potshots at them. Get it sorted, Norah. Get it sorted," Fredrick orders and hangs up.

Dragging Laurie around after me is a hindrance really. I sway between pity, to being persuaded he needs me, to pleasure in his company, to wanting him to care for me. Guilt has made me lose my patience with him. Being mean to Laurie and trying to keep him at arm's length is like kicking a gorgeous puppy. He's not a stupid man and he'll sense that I'm hiding things from him, not telling him all that I know about the Roses. Even I cannot keep a lid on all that is happening in the wings of this drama. There's only so long a powder keg of explosives will sit quietly in the corner. It'll be necessary to light a fuse under all of this no doubt – but not yet.

Fredrick doesn't think it's all that dangerous. Until recently, I didn't either. I thought I could simply contact the Ravenscairn House from the advertisement in the paper and ask to become one of them. Of course, I wouldn't want to murder anyone, but if they let me in then I'd be able to build a case and prove to Fredrick that I'm made for more than being someone's harlot!

I hadn't expected Laurie to be such a likeable divil. I hadn't expected to care about what happened to him or so deeply. Nor had I anticipated the many disgusting deeds of Eve Good. It's becoming more and more obvious that she deserves the death penalty. Who will give her this punishment first is the question?

So long as she doesn't drag my head into the noose with her. And that is looking more and more likely.

# Chapter 26

## Norah Walsh

I have opened a can of worms. Another envelope from Thistleforth has arrived.

My head is splitting with a headache and the whole entire mess is worrying me. Eve Good's story is almost at an end and Laurie will then want to start asking her direct questions. He'll now be able to talk with her if she is just up the road. But Laurie cannot question Eve. Not now!

There's a lot left to do and I cannot see how I'm going to see it all through. When I said I'd be a good nursemaid for a crippled ex-solider, it all sounded very adventurous and of course Norah Walsh fell for the bait.

Looking back, I was easily fooled. But there'll be no treating me like a whore any more. Fredrick Ashfield wanted rid of me, and he saw Laurie needed someone. Hole in one for that bastard. Two birds with one stone and if I found anything out about the Roses, well, it would be extra ammunition for his growing reputation.

But I can tell that he wants the whole caper tied up in a nice neat bow. I'm not fulfilling any of the duties assigned to me. I've not seduced Laurie, I've not fully left Fredrick's life, and I'm telling him very little about the Sinful Roses. There's only so long I can walk this tightrope, between all of these things. I know I'll have to give them all something and soon. The panic is rising. The vultures are circling and I'm starting to look tasty to them all.

Cook's quiet personality does a lot to ease my whirring mind these days. Watching or helping her work has stopped the voices in my head. *Traitor to her own kind.*

Giles potters about and always tries to assess what I'm thinking. He's a good sort. A bachelor who seems uninterested in women. Nothing seems to make him deviate from his course of duty and service. It's the English way, isn't it?

It seems that the Roses are the same. They've never left their course of wanting shot of Eve Good. I cannot blame them. She is a large liability. A singing canary they want to take down a mine full of gas.

I've not told a soul that I've found the advertisement for Ravenscairn and the Sinful Roses in *The Times*, a few days ago now.

It read:

**5th July 1944. Friends of the Sinful Roses be advised that a Ravenscairn House is open for the next three months. Send personal details to c/o Sinful Roses PO Box 77 at 208 Kensington High St, Kensington, London. Appointments will be given if investigations establish need.**

I replied to the advertisement with shaking hands. I wrote down the Davenport telephone number and thought a long time about the words, finally writing, *Please call the number above for urgent information about Mrs Eve Good.* No signature.

Eerily, despite me not giving them an address, a short

note has just come in the post: *The Sinful Roses will contact you in due course.*

That's me told!

A brandy from the decanter on the sideboard in the dining room does nothing but burn my throat. I'm shaking like a leaf. Communication with them is going to be difficult. Giles and Laurie have ears like hawks for telephone calls and Giles mentioned Cook's eavesdropping tendencies too.

Letters are intercepted by Giles for the silver tray and although Laurie cannot see them, I know Giles reports almost all correspondence. I cannot lie well to Laurie at all. I am sure he must know when I'm hiding things from him. He cannot see my uncertainty but he must sense it?

Letters to Thistleforth are noted down too. How on earth will they contact me? I hope they are discreet. We will be planning clandestine meetings perhaps in the cover of darkness at the far gate of the manor's grounds or over the telephone in the dead of night. I cannot be caught out and be considered a Sinful Rose!

I find it easier to be hostile with Laurie to get time away from him and also to throw him slightly off guard. But that hot and cold behaviour is not what he needs right now. Aggressive women are the very thing he should be hiding from, and if I continue the way that I'm going, I'll be asked to leave before I've sorted this mess out. If he orders me out, I'll be rightly in the soup then. No access to Eve Good or Laurie Davenport and with the annoyed Sinful Roses baying for my blood as well.

It is time to tread carefully – very carefully indeed.

# Chapter 27

## Laurie Davenport

"I am going to find a way into the Sinful Roses even if means marrying Fredrick Ashfield," Norah said again this morning.

She is adamant about marrying Freddie. The whole idea gives me a pain in my guts.

Giles knows about it and he and I are discussing things. I need an advisor to help and have ordered him to sit into my favourite chair. I sense that he finds it hard to drink tea with me. It's possibly the first time we've been on the one level in any way.

"I'm not sure what to say, sir," he breathes out in a long sigh. "This is extremely worrying. I fear that Miss Walsh will get in too deep if she takes on a full organisation of such women."

"Could there be many of them?" I ask. "There cannot be lots of women wanting to murder their husbands?" I shake my head. "Not that many surely?"

"You'd think not, sir," Giles says, "but there's quite a movement of women libertarians. This is the extreme side of it, I grant you, but once people move out of their role in life, this kind of thing is bound to happen. I was saying to Cook, once people don't know their purpose in life, it is a very dangerous thing."

"But the likes of Lady Dornan?" I say with a tutting sound. "She's an ex-convict! And yet she is considered acceptable company by people who should know better."

"Didn't you know that, sir? She's infamous. Oh yes, sir. She was a notorious criminal years before she married Lord Dornan. I was telling Norah in the kitchen earlier that even before they came visiting here the other day I knew that Lady Dornan was a bad person for young Mrs Davenport to be involved with. You were possibly too young to remember the scandal at the time she was convicted. But yes, the loud Lydia Babbington was imprisoned for murdering her policeman husband. May he rest in peace."

"*A policeman!*" I gasp. "Norah did mention it but I didn't ask too many details. I think my understanding of people is gone. Completely gone."

"Lady Dornan changed her name and has hid her past well. How would a young fellow like you suspect a thing? Especially when there's no talk about it any more. But it's definitely her. I followed the case myself. It was in the newspapers for months. Cook and I knew her immediately when she appeared in the society pages but, of course, money makes a lot go away. And married to a lord, well …"

"But murder? And a policeman? And she's walking free?"

"She had influential friends. Did fifteen years in the women's prison and then got let out of there into a care home. Not long after, she inherited property from some American heiress and married a lord. In a matter of years she was loose on the world again. If she was a lowly servant of course that would be a totally different matter.

But she had people to vouch for her character and to smooth the waters of justice. All these kinds of things are brushed under the carpet and he was meant to have been a less than lawful man. The rumours about him helped Lady Dornan's case for clemency. And she's considered to be an old woman now. You young fellows wouldn't have cared about her reputation."

"It was Charlotte who suggested us travelling to Belfast and I never dreamt of women like that existing, never mind that I would socialise with them. How naive was I?"

"Why would you think of such things, sir?" he says. "Your own mother was a walking saint. We all adored her. There was never any reason for you to know about the badness in the world. You're a kind chap with no need to know of such evil."

"Thank you, Giles." I stop to ponder and add, "That means Lydia Dornan is most definitely a Sinful Rose, who helps others to murder? And Charlotte is caught up with them and I may still be in danger?"

"And there was another woman at these meetings with this Eve woman?" Giles asks. "An Alice. And more possible murders elsewhere?"

"Yes."

"But Mrs Davenport wants a divorce. That might be an end to your part in all of this?"

"I had hoped that, but when she was leaving she whispered, 'This is not finished.' It made me shudder."

I cannot see Giles but the shadow of him moves and a hand grasps mine. "You're a wonderful young man, Mr Davenport. This will all work itself out. But I don't like the thought of you visiting that criminal woman, Eve Good,

176

either. What does the General think of all of this?"

"Freddie talks to Norah. I haven't spoken to him much. I didn't want to bother him because I'm grateful to him for believing in me and letting me do this. Hearing Eve Good's story is fascinating. I wouldn't admit it to her, but she's an unusual woman and her viciousness is nearing its peak. Yet I'm more enthralled than ever. You should hear her accounts!"

"I can imagine!"

"She just writes about the most horrendous things in such a matter-of-fact manner. I cannot breathe sometimes and yet I cannot stop listening either. It's macabre."

"I think I understand what you mean. Myself and Cook love tales of trials and courtroom antics. Lady Dornan is still in my mind. She gave the papers plenty to print. What a character she was! She never admitted that she was guilty and she needed sedation in the witness box and was dragged in kicking and screaming and left that way on many occasions. I think it was her husband's family who raised the alarm that something wasn't right and she would holler obscenities at them. The articles were great reads at the time. Her name was in every paper, but she manipulated everyone. Myself and Cook were disappointed when Eve Good was a silent defendant. We were kept in the dark about her motivations and it was very frustrating."

"She's not silent now, I can tell you. And she's making me sympathise with her. How strange is that? And I know that she did it all to herself. Still, I find myself feeling sorry for her when I'm brushing my teeth or sitting in that chair. It's madness what she can manipulate in me. One of her victims was Cedric

Fellows. He owned the *Belfast Times* newspaper. Do you remember the accounts of his murder?"

"Not especially."

"I fear we're coming to his murder soon. These killing women are manipulative, like you said. That is the word. Manipulative!"

Giles pours us more tea. I'm thoroughly enjoying his company and wonder should I tell him that.

"Perhaps Norah is right about getting into the club?" Giles says. "It makes sense to let a woman find out what is happening. And she will be a strong woman who they cannot sway to their way of thinking."

I recall something. "Norah is a sympathiser though. She sees their cause as a just one. According to her, it's like women's emancipation from under the tyranny of brutish husbands. I worry about her getting involved for many reasons."

"I'm sure."

"I know that she sees Eve as a criminal too and wishes to find whoever tried to kill us. And I suppose she wants to incriminate Charlotte."

"Yes. She'll want to do that most of all. You do know that she has a soft spot for you, sir?"

"Me?" I say, quite pleased by that remark. "I doubt that."

"Weren't you having a moment together when I barged in the other day? She's an attractive woman. Young and unmarried and according to Cook she has no man in her life. Her family are far away and she's in need of a gentleman to keep her right."

"Indeed." I nod seriously. "Mind you, she'd not agree that she needs looking after."

"Well, none of them do," Giles says with the authority

of a bachelor. "I think you would make a fine couple. What do you feel for her?"

"I would say Freddie would have something to say about that," I muse. "He's her employer and she wants to marry him for this pretence business. Perhaps there's a history there? Perhaps she has feelings for him? And I doubt she will want to be involved with the likes of me. An Englishman and her a good Catholic Irish girl!"

"That's not what I asked," Giles says. "How do you feel about Norah?"

"I know so little about her. I think I've learned that before I fall in love again I should know everything about someone. I won't make the same mistake again."

Giles grunts. He's not convinced and neither am I.

"I should talk to Freddie about these plans of hers," I decide. "Might you ring his number for me, Giles? I must ask him what he makes of this plan of hers and if he's willing for us to continue with this work. He might put a stop to the whole thing and I don't want that. This has been good for me. Much and all as it is scaring me senseless at times."

"We all need a purpose in life."

I nibble at a biscuit and ponder on Giles' life purpose. It never occurred to me before that servants had little choice in their life's work. It all depends on the whims and needs of an employer. In ways, we are similar. My future depends on my own tenacity or abilities, but also on Freddie's opinion. I suddenly can see why Norah wants to continue with this plan of hers. She wants to take control. I almost applaud her.

"I should give Norah my blessing to do this?" I say to Giles. "Shouldn't I?"

"I doubt you have much say in the matter, sir. It strikes me that Miss Walsh will do what she wants to. That's the way the world is changing. I'm not sure it is a good thing but there we have it. I must get on for it will be almost dinner time and Cook will have my hide. You see, she's in charge even though I'm supposed to be." He laughs.

"I needed and enjoyed our chat," I say to Giles. "Of course, all of this is top secret."

"Mum's the word, sir. Your secrets are safe with me. Will I put that call through for you now?"

"Thank you, Giles."


Freddie answers on the second ring himself. "What?" he says in that barking manner of his. "Who is this?"

"It's Laurie. I'm calling about Norah."

"It took you long enough. I know she wants to marry me but I've told her no. I told her that you were the man for her and I would never take her from you. So – there's no need to challenge me to a duel."

"I think you should marry her, Freddie," I say. "We need her to infiltrate the Sinful Roses. I think our use of Eve Good is coming to a conclusion."

"And you wish *me* to marry your Norah?" he asks, amused. "And wait for her to kill me?"

"She'd never do that."

"And what makes you so sure? Your wife tried to bump you off, remember?" Freddie scoffs and it hurts me more than I'd care to admit. "Norah will have to do the deed or the Sinful Roses will have something to say about it. Do you want to put her in danger? Put me in danger too, no doubt? Really? Do you want that?"

"What else is there to do, Freddie? If you can think of something else then say it."

Freddie's heavy breathing is audible and then he says, "Damn it! Tell Norah that we're now engaged and I'm far from pleased about it! On your head be it, Laurie Davenport old chap. And after forcing my hand on this, there's no way that you're going to be my best man!"

# Chapter 28

## Norah Walsh

Eve's letters have arrived and I'm caught between reading them to Laurie and burning them in the grate. If I lie and say Eve has not sent any more letters, he'll insist on speaking to Freddie about it. Yet, reading about her crimes digs us both in deeper.

Once I am called to meet the Sinful Roses, they will want to know what she has told us. They will want to protect those named by her. How will I face them? How will I protect us both from their anger? If I don't read on, we still know very little. I could just explain to the Sinful Roses that we know nothing. Somehow I doubt there will be much explaining allowed.

Laurie is not keen on me joining their ranks and I can understand why. I wonder what the hell I was thinking, replying to that advertisement. I suppose once Eve Good started involving us in the whole thing, our fate was sealed. I had to do something and it's done now.

As I brush my hair and put on some lipstick in the large, gilded hall mirror, I decide that speaking directly to the Roses and accessing how they feel about us might be one good way of ensuring our safety. Waiting to hear from them again is hard. I can see why Eve Good described waiting and meeting them in detail. It sticks in the mind like glue – wondering, anticipating, worrying.

And I really want to drive into London and sit and watch the address from *The Times*. Laurie will miss me if I go and that's a dangerous idea. I'll sit tight here in the safety of Davenport Manor.

But how can I brazen this out? Convincing the Roses that Laurie and myself will just leave them be is not possible. They're not that naive and we're walking headlong over a cliff. Jesus Christ Almighty, what have I done!

I pick up the post from the silver tray on the hallstand by the telephone. Giles has not delivered it to Laurie yet. There's a brown envelope from Eve. She has been very busy indeed.

Laurie is in his chair by the window and I sigh as I enter the room. When I see him my heart usually does a flutter but now it is one of worry as well as lust. He's still vulnerable. Unable to see and still trying to come to terms with all that has happened. This is all so unfair to him.

"Are you ready to listen to Eve's letter?" I ask.

There is his smile. Despite the scars, he's still a lovely man. It breaks my heart that I'm keeping secrets from him.

*It's for the best*, my conscience tells me as I unfold the pages and start to read.

# Chapter 29

## Eve Good

Staying with Tilly brought me no comfort. Frank's breathing and the sound of him eating grated on my nerves. Once you've considered killing someone, their presence sends you into a spin – their every annoying habit is magnified. Why couldn't he just be gone?

But it was not looking promising. It seemed more and more like Tilly wouldn't do the necessary. She wouldn't even discuss it. I understood that there were many trials and tribulations. It wasn't easy stomaching the "murder" word and I did understand Tilly's reluctance. I was not built for it and neither was she. But, once ideas sneaked in, I found it hard to let them out again.

"Can you try not to antagonise Frank, please?" Tilly asked me while we folded sheets. "He retaliates then by asking you to leave."

"I think my time here must come to an end. I'll do Frank in myself if he doesn't stop picking at his teeth and scratching himself. *It's unendurable!* You have to endure a lot. I couldn't put up with all you have to deal with."

"Arrah now, I don't think he's all that bad," Tilly said. "He provides for me and has been a good father. He's good-humoured when you're not here. These Sinful Roses sound scary. I'm not sure I could deal with the likes of them or the guilt. I'm much better off staying the way I am. Please don't make me get involved. I'm content the way I am."

I sighed, tired with the same old day, the same old conversation and the same old lack of gumption. Tilly used to be full of life, full of fever for the unknown – she enjoyed putting salt in the sugar bowl and scalding frogs. The two of used to get up to a lot of mischief. We were always great at making babies cry. We used to try and outdo each other at that game.

I stared at her. I knew she was a different woman.

When we do venture out conversations range from the price of flour to the lack of fuel or the price of it for a vehicle she never sat in. How boring. Tilly never moved more than a few miles and, if she did, it was mostly on foot. Round and round in circles of housework she went. I thought that there must be more of the world out there for her, for me and for us.

"Ending things though?" she whispered at me. "Is it necessary? Really?"

"I can go where I like, do what I want and be who I like," I told her. "That's worth anything."

"But what about us going to hell? It's a sin!"

"Since when did you care about such things? Since Frank got his hands on you. That's since when. Lord above, Tilly, I'm tired."

"You might have sold your soul, but I can't do it. I can't even think about it."

In my head I was screaming at her that I'd harm him over and over again. But, like with John, I had not thought it through very well.

I didn't realise that until Frank was bleeding profusely

from his abdomen and Tilly was shrieking and scaring the geese outside. The smell of manure lifted off Frank's clothes. They seeped with blood and he stared at me. Then he reached out for Tilly who was screeching by the range.

*"You've slashed him! You've slashed him!"* Tilly's hands were in her hair and Frank slumped to his knees.

Weakened, he muttered, *"Bitch."*

I was on top of his torso, thrashing down on his neck with the knife and hitting bone. It might have been his face. I couldn't see through the anger. Frank was a strong man and the knife was not as sharp as it could be. The tossing he did dislodged me off him and the kitchen floor was slippery. I knocked against the table and sent the dishes crashing. His moans were animal. Those hardened claws grabbed at my dress and my swoops with the knife were frenzied and crazed.

There was blood in my face. His own features were cut open and there was blood spurting from his neck. Down he went like a ton of bricks, grasping at his many wounds. There were more than a few places where it flowed and the noises in his throat were guttural and long. Searching for air, for life, he slid in the fluids from him and he flailed about a bit.

Tilly's howling was uncontrolled.

I caught my breath and fixed my hair back. On my hunkers I could see Frank was not dying. Bloodied and injured he was still dangerous and wouldn't bloody die! Despite all the bleeding and moaning, he was still here. Frank Hockley was a stubborn ox. He didn't move though and lay heaped on the floor. He hoped I was finished with him and would give up.

186

Tilly had stopped shrieking.

It was then that I heard a click from behind me. Glancing around, I saw Tilly was armed. Frank's culling rifle was cocked and shaking.

"Good idea, Tilly, finish him off!" I stood back out of the way and took a look out of the windows. No nosey neighbours had come to hinder our progress. "The shot might alert someone though. Maybe we should wait for him to bleed out?"

The sobbing from her was pitiful and Frank's snorting was off-putting. I looked again out of the low windows. The geese had settled.

"You can't love him now anyhow. Not in this state. He has half a face and those noises are worse than when he's eating."

It was the *whoosh* of a small piece of metal past my ear that wakened me fully. The pump of the rifle refilling and the unnatural shout from Tilly when she fired again. It made me leap.

There was a burning smell of powder. In a huddle of fear I ducked low, but I had no shelter. The table housed the injured animal that still might have life in it and the floor had no protection against a bullet. Tilly was thrown and rubbing at her shoulder, gasping between sobs.

"*Don't shoot this way*," I ordered, not taking my eyes off her.

Tilly was determined now, her eye aiming the mean-looking weapon again. Her shoes clipped on the tiles and as she stood above me the metal cylinder came level with my ear. She was panting.

"*Don't do this, Tilly. Don't. Give me the rifle*," I begged, reaching out.

The barrel wasn't hot like I feared and I slowly wrapped my fingers around it. "You're no killer, Tilly. You love me like a sister."

Holding my breath, I listened to her sob and felt the grip she had on the weapon go slack and I took it off her with one pull. The butt thumped the floor and she retreated to fall onto her knees by the meat near the table. She cried over him, whimpering sweet somethings into the mess of him and swallowed hard to make herself stop crying.

She leant up towards me and pleaded, "Please don't harm us any more. Please, Eve. He's a good man. For me, please. Please? No more."

"You landed me in this mess and then you won't help me out of it. Tried to kill me! I'm beyond cross."

What a pathetic creature she had become. She made a praying gesture with her hands, mouthing "please" at me. A good person would have nodded and reassured her, but that person wasn't in me.

Silly Tilly had let me down. She didn't want to be in my company any more, she didn't wish to be a Rose even though it was she who landed me in the nest of snakes to begin with. I couldn't hide my anger. I took to nibbling the side of my nails.

When I looked again, Tilly was kissing Frank's bloody hand and praying.

"*Which will it be, Glensmal?*" I said aloud to the house.

Tilly muffled her crying in her hands. She was probably right. I'm a little unhinged when I'm annoyed.

Frank Hockley's body tipped over the wheelbarrow and slumped back onto the back step. Tilly had a basin and

188

was staring at the blood, like it was poison. I was sure he wasn't breathing but Tilly wasn't pleased we didn't call the doctor and police.

The ground behind the henhouse was hard under the spade. I had no idea that digging was so difficult. Watching men labour in the past, it all looked rather pleasant and quick. The spade was not liking my foot and the ground was far too tough – even breaking the surface at times took all my effort and concentration.

"Could we burn him?" I muttered and realised Tilly was not with me.

Returning to the house, I saw she was on her knees mopping the floor. I silently took the rifle back out with me in case she intended to use it again. She could have gone for help or run for the shore and its path, but I trusted that she was in a state of shock.

I went back and resumed digging. I managed nothing but a low trench and tossed Frank over into it. It wasn't much of a grave. His belly would protrude and covering him in wouldn't make him hidden, that was for sure. There was no sign of neighbours or Tilly. The sheepdog came for a sniff at his old master. I poked and pulled earth from around his corpse with the spade in an attempt to lower the level of the soil . . . and saw his arm twitch.

The thud of the spade from a height made a satisfying noise on his skull. A few more for good luck and I half-heartedly covered in the trench and its cargo.

Sweating, panting and semi-pleased with my work, I went back to the house. I found Tilly sitting wide-eyed at the kitchen table, her arms and face clean and the floor wet but free of blood.

"Good work." I placed the kettle on to boil.

There wasn't a word from her. It was as if she was the one who died but still remained breathing and sitting in the kitchen. Her tea was untouched and even the dog stealing a march in over her cleaned floors didn't spark a reaction. The silence was deafening and I just knew that she wouldn't leave with me, and that the bond we'd shared was gone out like the tide. There was an eerie lostness to her I'd never seen in anyone before. Like she'd been broken and couldn't be fixed.

"Tilly." I placed my hand on her arm. It was warm to the touch but she didn't acknowledge me. "You need to eat. What could we have? He's gone now and we can say he's run off and you'll be left with all of this. We could rent out the farmland if it's all too much. I understand that you won't leave here. I see that now."

There was no answer.

After I made scrambled eggs and bacon with more piping hot tea she spoke at last.

"Will you kill me?" she whispered. "Will you?"

"Of course not. I don't kill women. Well, except my mother and that was not violent. It was a quiet slipping away. And what I hope to do to Marjorie."

I sat and watched her drink the tea as I devoured the eggs and bacon. There was no Frank barging in the door and I could see Tilly glance at the clock.

"He should only be home now." Her eyes glistened. "He came home to tell me he was worried and that I should get you on the bus." Her voice cracked. "My Frank."

"He's strong, I'll give him that." The bacon was salty and I poured myself more tea. "I'd say he's probably not even dead."

Finally her swollen eyes meet mine. "*What?*"

190

"It's hard to tell, but he's covered over now anyway."

The way she asked, *"Did you bury him alive?"* made even me shudder.

I shook my shoulders. "I didn't manage to dig deep enough. I'll have to go out again and finish the job. I shut in those geese – they were all interested in scraping where I was digging." The rain lashed the window and I wondered aloud, "Will that soften the ground or make it harder to cover him, I wonder?"

"Where will I say Frank is?" Tilly asked.

There was a coldness to her that was new, and I could still see her with the rifle and moved the knife on the table further away from her.

The night drew on with me hauling and sweating despite the mizzling rain. I had said nothing to Tilly as I went out to start the arduous task of burying the remains of her dead husband a bit deeper.

"Never again will I kill a man without a plan. So much for support groups. Now I truly am an expert in all forms of killing," I told Tilly's back while I peeled off my clothes by the range and tiptoed upstairs to wash.

"I need you to leave," Tilly said, still unmoved from the table when I came back downstairs. "Get the bus away in the morning."

"But they'll want answers."

"And bring me the rifle in."

My breath held in my chest.

"Did you hear me? In the morning, I want you to leave after you bring me the rifle in. Away with you and don't come back."

I nodded. All of my troubles melted away as I sunk my teeth into the butter icing on the sponge cake I'd cut.

My arms were tired. The cake crumbled away and I let it. When I'd swallowed it all down, I told her, "I'll miss you, Tilly. You're all I've got left. I can't just leave you like this. There will be questions to answer and we know you're not a good liar."

"You must go."

She was losing her mind. Poor weak Tilly. There was nothing more to be done. Some women are just not meant to be freed. Like a caged animal or a tamed bird, there was no way they can ever be wild and free again. It had never occurred to me that this would have left her like this. She was not strong like me, not willing to work for her independence. Not needing it, like I did.

I packed my case with many damp and dirty clothes, and I couldn't help but smile. I'd miss Tilly, but her wanting the rifle would be the best solution for all of us.

A woman who seemingly murdered her husband would have great remorse, wouldn't she? Indeed she would, poor, poor, silly Tilly. I snuggled into the bed for the last time for a few short hours. I pondered on whether Tilly was at the kitchen table and whether she might find the rifle herself in the dark and not miss me if I fell asleep.

But there was no sound of movement at all. I decided in the gloom that Tilly loved me and she'd never harm me.

In the glum air of the house in the morning, with both reluctance and a guilty hopefulness, I propped the weapon against the turf basket. With purpose and poise, I approached the statue sitting on the chair looking forlornly out the far window. I kissed the top of her hair and whispered, "I love you, Tilly. You are free now."

My shoes pinched me as I lugged my case to the

village square. From the vantage point on the corner I watched the lough between the buildings and wondered where my evil temper came from. Like the sea it swells and sweeps back retreating into some dark corners within me, to burst forth again.

Suddenly something frightened the birds in the trees by the post office and they flapped squawking into the early morning. The bus swung into the square and I watched the crows circle high above me and hoped that maybe they were startled by a rifle shot further along the shore.

Back in Newburn Crescent, Cedric Fellows was in Marjorie's kitchen at Number 4, making toast and two cheese sandwiches. I watched him through the back window, licking his fingers. He spied me and I found myself waving back. He swung open the door and I walked down the steps and in the back door.

"Hullo." His apron was clean and his shirtsleeves were rolled up over the pushed-back sleeves of his thick jumper. There was a smell of toasted bread and the steam rose off a teapot, with the tea cosy sitting waiting to be popped over it.

"I was just thinking outside there now that as you're here I needn't bother coming on in," I said, not wishing to see him. I was even losing my guilt about not visiting Marjorie regularly. There were other things on my mind. I also was thinking that Marjorie's role in my life might change. "I don't want to be here, if you are."

Cedric was taken aback by my remark and stood rubbing the butter off his fingers with a cloth, uncertain of what to say next.

"But I am in now," I added, looking around me. There

was a warmth I didn't remember as usual in the room and I saw that he had lit the large range cooker against the far wall. "It's cosy in here."

"Aunt Margie would rather die of cold than spend money on keeping warm."

Cedric's glasses slipped on his nose and he pushed them back up, all the while looking at me like I was a vision of some kind. I thought for a while he looked almost lustful.

"Are you sure you won't stay for tea?" he said. "I'd better get this in to her ladyship while the tea is still hot, as I'd say that it has been a few days since she has eaten. She seems quite weak. I thought she might like a cheese sandwich."

They looked very unappealing, but I said nothing.

"Aunt Margie has missed you. If I knew you were busy I might have called on Saturday or Sunday. Maybe we could make a rota of sorts?"

I must have given him a murderous look as he took a step backwards, palms facing out, and muttered, "Of course there's no obligation for you to do anything at all. It is merely that you … I mean … there's no need to include you in any rota. I just meant … Aunt Margie is fond of you. And Father and I also thought that you might benefit from some payment for your time. We felt you've been left rather … how might I put this … that you might need assistance for giving Aunt Margie assistance. Oh dear me, I can be clumsy with the spoken word. Around women especially, I tend to say the wrong thing. Could you perhaps try to take the best of what I said and work with that?"

"You wish to pay me to visit your aunt?"

"Concisely put. I know your pride might stop you …"

"I'm a widow – I can't have too much pride, Mr Fellows."

"I didn't want to insult you ..."

"Insult me? Of course you didn't." But he had. I had started to boil. "Thank you for your kindness, Mr Fellows."

He put the tea cosy on the teapot, swirled the pot expertly and set it on the tray that I liked. Then he placed the sandwiches on one plate after cutting them into triangles minus the crusts.

He chuckled and poked at his spectacles. "Call me Cedric, please." There were damp patches on his knees, and his jumper had a hole at the back under the arm that I spotted when he turned with the tray to go down the hallway. "She'll be glad to see you. I'd say she's not been up out of the chair much in the last couple of days. There's quite a strong smell ..." He turned and whispered, "Perhaps you might help her to have a little wash?"

I closed my eyes to hide my despair and shook my head, muttering, "The poor soul. The poor, poor soul."

"She'll not allow me to help her like that," he said, moving on down the hall.

"Nor me," I said. "I've tried to suggest it but she refuses and I dare not annoy her further."

"I understand. Especially since she thinks highly of you and we all tread on thin ice with her moods."

I opened the door and the whiff was pungent. Urine and something else I didn't want to investigate or have to wash away. Money would not make me deal with bodily fluids – or solids either.

"You do know," Cedric whispered, "that she's had the solicitor here and had me witness an amendment to her will?"

"Will?"

Marjorie snored slightly as Cedric set down the tray on the low table.

"Yes, in your favour," he whispered. "She's a generous soul, is Aunt Margie. She said she knows what it's like not to have a man about the house. And she says that you were like a daughter to her in recent weeks. I did tell her it was a hasty decision, but Margie has always been known for being hasty. And if you're good to her, like I am, then why shouldn't she be good to you? She was adamant."

His tone was sincere but I wondered if Cedric was all that happy behind that smile of his.

"I don't know what to say." I wanted to know what or how much she had left me but I didn't dare ask.

Then he changed the subject.

"You might know someone to cut those bushes?" he said. "She wants to be able to see your front door and the side of the house through her window better. She likes to keep an eye on things and your help would be invaluable to me."

I looked at the dusty, dingy room and the old things cluttering it. I wondered if a woman like Marjorie had anything to leave to anyone. But I guessed that the house alone was worth a fair few bob. My blood simmered down a good bit and I tried not to grin. There was a solution to some of my problems slumbering in the chair beside me.

I sat down with a new-found hope.

"I know looking at her and this room, you'd never think that Aunt Margie has a bob to her name." Cedric smiled again as he sat down. "But there you go. Appearances can be deceiving."

"They sure can."

"Cheese triangle?" He held out the plate.

"No, thank you. I've just eaten. Do you visit other women, Mr Fellows?"

"Pardon?" His cheeks flushed a little.

"Do you care for other aunts or other women? Call on them? Make them cheese sandwiches?"

"I'm busy with work and Father and ... coming here ... I'm not sure what you mean?"

He handed me a cup and saucer with a gold trim.

"Has Marjorie any other family?" I asked.

"My father is the only remaining sibling she has. The rest have passed away. Quite sad really."

"Your father is still alive?"

"Oh yes. I live with him. My mother is gone now and Father insists I live with him and that I call in here on Marjorie."

"Do you call on any other women?"

He had no idea why I was asking him such questions and I should've stopped. But I couldn't.

"Do you visit prisons for instance?" I said loudly and Marjorie opened one eye.

Cedric's finger went to his lips and his eyes widened. Marjorie murmured but resumed her snoring. "*Shh*, don't waken her. She's peaceful."

I couldn't see why he was afraid of admitting to visiting women prisoners. I sensed Cedric was a strange man. He looked at me with lust far too often but something told me that he wasn't the marrying kind. It was all very odd.

I sipped at my tea, thinking it tasted a little bitter. There was no sugar on the tray. I set my cup and saucer down.

"I must go." I felt like I should leave. I cannot explain it, but everything made me fearful suddenly. My female intuition poked at me to rise off the seat.

"I find women like you fascinating," he said. "Sandwich? Please take one. I hate waste."

"No, thank you."

"That one has beetroot chutney in it too. Delicious chutney, I make it myself. I helped Mother to do it all my life and now it's my turn to take the reins." He smoothed down his apron. "I loved Mummy. She was a very clever woman. Like you are. Modest and quiet and no one knew just how talented she was. Her mind worked away all the time. She was never dull and always thought through problems. I can see that you are the same. Fascinating."

I wasn't sure how to answer him. I simply stared.

"Poor Aunt Margie isn't the brightest button. She demands respect rather than earns it. You, however, don't need anyone's respect. I find that interesting."

Alice flashed before me. I wished she respected me, but I didn't tell Cedric that.

"Am I insulting you?" he asked, munching on a cheese sandwich and then slurping his tea.

"Not at all. I like to think that I'm clever and interesting."

"Most women get insulted at the slightest thing. Mummy did for instance. Clever lady, but she worried about her reputation. Do you worry about such things?"

"I do. I've been called quite a few nasty things since John died. I'm not used to it."

"Like what?"

"*Murderer* for one."

I'm not sure why, but Cedric was making me say things that I normally wouldn't. He didn't even flinch at such a word. He chewed at the bread, swallowed it and sipped nosily from the cup, wiped the side of his mouth with his hanky and then smiled.

"Are you certain I cannot tempt you to a sandwich? Marjorie will need fresh ones when she wakens."

"Thank you, I'm quite full." My stomach growled and made a liar of me.

I wanted to leave and stay all at the same time. I stood there teetering between staying and going. I sat on the chair's edge, watching him intently.

"I'm interested in what you've said there, Cedric. What else fascinates you about women?"

"Everything about them really. Considering you all have weak physiques, women must use other methods to survive. Like in the Bible, Eve tempted Adam. Women have lots of ways of corrupting the world around them, or moulding it to suit their needs. Like my mother – she convinced my father that the new carriage was for his status but it was simply because she liked to be driven about in style. You should learn to drive. That is a fine car."

"I don't need fine things. I never had them with John. He spent our money foolishly. On things like that car. I'm frugal now and I don't want to drive."

"You sound insulted. You see, I do this all the time!" He smiled.

It irked me. He irked me.

"With a name like Eve Good, how could you be a bad person?"

"I intend to be called Eve Kanaster from now on."

"Name change ... why?"

"A fresh start." The noise of him chewing and swallowing was disgusting.

"You asked me about prison." He took a look at his aunt. She was out for the count. "How did you know about me visiting the women's prison?"

"Marjorie mentioned it."

"She wouldn't know about that," he said, eyeing me suspiciously. "I told no one about my visits there."

"As you say, you find women fascinating. Some of the most intriguing women are in prison, I'd imagine."

"Were you ever in one?" he asked.

"No. Never."

"They are stark places. Women who go in there are never the same afterwards. I got curious when I set the type for the articles about the trials of those women. I wanted to know what criminal women were really like. I'm drawn to them."

"*I see!*" My tone was high-pitched with disgust.

"It's for their minds, nothing more. For instance, I visited a fascinating woman called Lydia Babbington in prison. You must have read about her? She was notorious. Aunt Margie even followed her plight. Mrs Babbington shot her husband, a policeman! It was a scandal ... many years ago now. Do you know who I mean?"

"Yes, I do."

"Aunt Margie even thought she saw her here on the street recently. It brought me back to when I read about her first and to when we all heard the tales of her antics in the courtroom. Fascinating woman. Absolutely mesmerising when you're in her company. I miss chatting with her."

"What was Lydia Babbington like?"

"Normal. Adamant she was innocent. She kept telling

me she was not guilty of anything at all. The whole experience was difficult for her. She seemed pained at Edward's death. She was genuinely sorry that her husband had been killed. She made no secret of the fact that it was an arranged rather than a love match, but she was shocked to be in the dock and then in prison. It almost broke her. She was passionate about her innocence. She always carried herself with a high dignity, though. She's still a truly remarkable woman, I'm sure."

"What do you think convinced the jury of her guilt then?"

"There were many problems. The dogs being one."

"Dogs?"

"No one heard them bark. There were two cross dogs in the yard and, if a stranger had been there, they've have alerted the neighbours and everyone else. They never barked that evening. No one heard them. Lydia was alone in the house and it was known she didn't have it easy with her husband. One of the reasons I may never marry. Unhappy wives are a dangerous thing."

"Do you think she was guilty then? Do you think she shot him?"

"She most definitely killed him."

"Did she admit it?"

"No. But I always felt she was driven to the worst kind of crime by the worst kind of man."

"Did you tell her that?"

"I never lied to her but I was not forward with her. I respected her too much."

"You respected her?"

"I felt Lydia was pushed to the edge of the moral abyss. She was driven to do the evil deed. It was against

201

her nature. Whatever happened in the house that night, she snapped. She convinced herself she did not have anything to do with it. I found myself visiting her over and over again, to know more about her. Like I say, she was fascinating. What drives a woman like her to do what she did?"

I got to my feet. "I must go."

"I need to talk with you about your rent," Cedric said. "Don't get up. Finish your tea."

"I'm leaving now."

"I wish you wouldn't go, Eve Kanaster," Cedric said to my back. "We have a lot to discuss about your future. Sit back down. Things were just getting interesting."

But I didn't want to hear any more from that vile man. Discussing the rent indeed! Where was a widow to pull money from? What did he expect me to do that would be interesting? The shiver I got told me I'd not like his suggestion on how I might pay my rent. The whole scenario was all leaving a bad taste in my mouth. Also, when he looked at me it felt like he knew I was a Sinful Rose and I didn't want that at all. There was no way I was going to stay one minute longer listening to him sort out my life or finances. The cheek!

I suppose it was then that I was sure I would kill him. I just didn't know how or when I would do it.


Number 5, Newburn Crescent stood as I had left it. John's car sat pulled in at the side of the house. No one had set foot in his car since he drove it home on that fateful day. The police had wanted to see his things and went through his pockets. No doubt they searched his car too, but it all looked untouched. I slid inside onto the leather seat. The pedals were not near my feet and the seat was well back from the steering wheel. I rubbed the chrome finish and peered at the dials. How might I move such a machine? The crank of a key, the pull on the lever and the push of particular pedals. But which ones and in what order?

There was a slight scent of John lingering in there. His hat was on the passenger seat. Placed there in haste, still at the edge. I lifted it and sniffed it. John's hair and scalp always had a pleasant smell. My fingers rubbed the rim and inside the maker's label was yellowed.

Stuck in the material on the inner rim was a piece of cardboard. A square of white was placed there for safekeeping, I plucked it out and turned it over.

*Mrs Alice Longmire, 53 Marshall Meadows,*
*Netterby, Co Down*

The ink swirls were pristine. I couldn't believe it! How was Alice's calling card in my John's hat? Why might he have kept it there? When did he meet her? The thoughts clattered in on top of one another.

I put the card into my pocket and scanned the car. Like a demon, I rooted around for some sign of how he knew Alice-bleeding-Longmire. Ranting, cursing and clambering about inside the small space, I hurt my hand ramming it hither and thither with fury. Alice knew my John before he died. Where did they meet? Why did they meet? Alice never said that she knew him. How dare she shock me in such a manner. How bloody dare she!

John liked to keep his cars well. As with everything else he could not afford, he kept it like a new pin. Everything in its place, including me.

There it was, as plain as day – her name. Alice-fucking-Longmire, that killing woman I brought into our lives. She spied on me, talked with John – probably seduced him. For what? For sport? Then killed him? Lydia mentioned her unusual passions. What might John have thought of her?

She'd be just his type. He always liked the exotic, beautiful and confident women in films. What man would say no to taking her card? What man would refuse to do anything with her? How did I not know about this? How did I not know? I knew about his other women, of course I did. I'm far from stupid.

They must have met in the time between me going to Ravenscairn and John lying here at the bottom of the stairs. When else would it be? I was busy then. Distracted by Tim and my plan-making. Things might have slipped through the usual tight net I held on John's comings and goings and on his moods. It was remiss of me. She burrowed her way in. I was seething!

I ignored the post on the mat, stepped over it and headed for the whiskey decanter in the parlour.

I lit the fire and watched the flames leap up the chimney and I thought Ravenscairn would burn well, with all of its wooden furniture, large drapes and rugs. Alice and Lydia could easily be trapped inside and their bodies would burn with it. Their screams would be covered by the crackling flames.

After I finished my whiskey, I searched through all of our things with a finetooth comb and found nothing further which could push me in the direction of knowing why Alice Longmire gave him her card.

When I was passing by the front door in a flurry of searching further for answers, the lock turned on the front door and in walked Cedric Fellows.

"Ah! You're in," he said. "I felt you left before I got a chance to explain. I've been trying to find ways to help you, Eve." His shoes moved on the letters on the mat. He pointed at them. "You've got many official letters about the rent that is owed. I know that you're good to my Aunt Margie and we wish to help you, but the debt is getting a little out of hand. In the past I never said anything to you about my arrangement with your husband, as he asked me not to. And I felt it prudent to follow his wishes, especially following his circumstances of his death. But you've been ignoring all correspondence and not trying in the slightest to even pay a little of the rent that is owed. I cannot allow this to continue – but perhaps we might come to some sort of arrangement?"

"*Stop!*" I covered my ears. "*Stop!*" Curses came to my mind and my mouth dried.

I lashed out at him, hitting him square across the jaw. His glasses skimmed clean across the tiles. He touched his face and I held both of my hands to my mouth.

He leant down to get his spectacles, groaning. Something in me moved me to kick the glasses forward and through his legs. They landed on the step outside. Without a word he went to retrieve them. His body inside and his bald head out, level with the door frame.

One swift slam thudded the heavy door off what I thought should be his ear. I couldn't see very well at the angle I was at but I bashed the door again regardless of its mark. Another thump. Then another. I possibly hit his shoulder and I swung again with the door and there was an almighty crunch. It must have been his skull. His body slumped forwards and I heard and saw his face hit the hard step with a wallop. His body crumpled outside. He moaned.

My heel made his ear bleed. A rock from the flowerbed made blood gush from his face and forehead. Over and over the dirty stone sank into the skin and blood flew. It all made a nasty mess of the doorstep and the door itself.

I stopped to breathe.

"Oh dear me. A man does not accidentally jam his own bald head in a door. Dear me, I'll never learn."

I shook his shoulders and poked at what is left of his face. Nothing much happened. His chest wasn't moving up and down but I've known that to happen and then them still to be moving or their lungs to come back. Mother especially didn't stop breathing despite all the medication. But then I didn't wish to harm her, it was more to help. She wished to be on her way to be with Father.

I found some sheets and laid them on the hall floor. Cumbersome job that it was, I dragged him inside and heaved him unceremoniously onto them and closed the front door with my foot. I hauled him in the sheets towards the cubbyhole under the stairs which was clear of clutter. I had sold everything of any value so I propped the nasty fellow against the broom. Once I got him settled I located a long skewer from the kitchen and pulling back his shirt stabbed where I thought his heart should be. It was harder than I thought to get it into him. Why is killing not easy?

"A good hard blow to just above the ear," Lydia had said. "But that's no accident. Only use it in emergencies. Only hit there if totally necessary and then make it look like a fall. I learned some skills in prison."

Her words must've stuck in my brain for a reason and I know my capabilities are better than this. My talents are not being used to their finest. I am flying off the handle far too readily.

Closing the small door on the cubby I noticed red streaks on my clean hall tiles. He was lying on my broom and the mop was wedged behind him, so – on my hands and knees – I wiped and washed all away with a basin, wire brush and soapy water.

"Such a quiet cul-de-sac," I mused and went out into the garden and strolled past the bushes and into the street. There was not a being there to know what had happened. I glanced up at Marjorie's window where she usually sat. Dread filled me. She might have seen my front door. She'd have watched Cedric come over here.

"Cedric never came over – no, I've not seen him, Marjorie," I practised in the little mirror that hung in the hall. "I wonder where he might be? Of course he'll visit soon. He left his coat herewith you? How strange? The weather is much better, isn't it? Are you sure you wouldn't like more tea? It's a lot safer around here since Cedric started calling. No prowlers. Yes, indeed. We're very lucky to be neighbours. Perhaps, though, I should move in. Especially if Cedric is missing. What do you think? Of course I'll look after you, Marjorie. It's the least I can do. We women should stick together. Men are fickle creatures and perhaps he has found a lady friend."

And when I looked again Constable Irvine was at the door of Number 4.

# Chapter 30

## Eve Good

Since John's fall, all the men in my life have scared me. Irvine, Tim and now Cedric were all – in one way or another – intimidating. Why must a woman alone be tortured at every turn? I should have been enjoying the pleasure of freedom but I was drowning in worry. What was Irvine doing in the cul-de-sac again? My heart thumped in my chest.

The wind was getting up and the rain lashed the panes on the front door. The draughts banged a door on the second floor and it made me jump. Irvine was next door and I had a corpse under my stairs.

I checked the attic carefully and all of the rooms, locking the ones I could before tiptoeing my way back down. I always tried to step on the last few stairs extra hard. I sensed John's body still there to be trodden upon.

The knock on the front door startled me and there was Irvine's face and waving fingers in the pane at the side of the door.

I opened the door.

"Constable."

"Mrs Good. I thought you might've been with Mrs Fellows next door but there's no answer there. May I come in? I've something to tell you."

I moved aside and let him in to drip on the floor. I stood waiting on an explanation on the tiles where John's head spilled open. Irvine looked like he wanted to sit down or move further into the house. But I couldn't face inviting him! How could I have a policeman in my house considering what I was hiding?

"We've had a word with a fellow called Tim Harbour. He came forward with information."

Irvine removed his wet cap.

The pause was one where a good woman would bring the man into the parlour or into the kitchen even, but I remained on the tiles that killed my husband.

"He told us that he knew you and had some things he wanted to get off his chest."

"*Huh!*"

"He says that you and he were ... intimate, Mrs Good." He coughed.

"I beg your pardon?"

"Yes. The little runt says that it was you who threw yourself into his arms. And there's more ..." Irvine said. "Perhaps you should sit down."

"I'm fine, thank you."

"He also said ... now let me get this correct ..." He took a notebook from his pocket. "He says, and I quote ... please excuse the language now, Mrs Good, these are his words not mine: '*I gave her a good poking many a time in their house in Newburn. She used to let me stay in secret in her attic.*'"

I could feel the colour drain from my cheeks. "He said that?"

Irvine glanced at the notebook and twitched his moustache to the side. "He said ... '*I used to stay for days at a time in that big house of theirs. She'd bring me food and her husband never knew. He was hardly ever there but even when he was we'd still be at it like rabbits in his attic. That Good man drank and snored like a train. She liked to … she liked to have me when he was downstairs. It seemed to make her more frisky.'"*

I began to cry and held in the curses. "I can't speak. I …"

"I have to ask you, Mrs Good," Irvine was cautious. "I have to ask you this, I'm afraid. Is he telling us the truth?"

I closed my eyes and muttered through my teeth, "I can't believe you'd even consider these vile … oh, my dear Lord! What a nasty boy he is!"

"Has he been in this house?" he asked. "Did you let him in here like he says?"

*"No! Never!* Still less up to our attic! I've no words. Why would he say such a thing? Such things about me?"

"He's a boy with no morals or breeding, Mrs Good. A real piece of work. I'm sorry I've had to trouble you with this." Irvine's eyes were full of pity.

I could barely breathe. I wiped the tears from my cheeks.

"He told us that he felt that it was you who had something to do with John's accident. Did he mention this to you then?"

I slumped to sit on the stairs. Ironically, it was onto the exact step where John's crotch lay all those weeks ago now.

"Harbour said and I quote … *'I think she pushed that John Good to his death. She's got the nerve to do it and try to get away with it. She told me that she would get rid of him and we could be together. She said I had to leave the house and not contact her for six months. That we'd be together then. But then I heard about his accident. I'm telling you that she got rid of him all right. But she doesn't want a bit of me now that she's not got a husband downstairs. I'm of no use to her any more. She got rid*

210

*of us both and I'm not going back to her as she'd knock me down the stairs too.'"*

My heart leapt. I was as weak as water, innocent as Christ himself was when wrongly accused. "I can't breathe!" I pulled at the collar of my blouse. "I simply can't cope with this."

"It's a lot to take in, Mrs Good. I'm very sorry," Irvine said.

"What else is there? Is there more in that blessed notebook?"

"Just that you were never happy with John and, of course, more about how you were having a torrid love affair with this Tim lad. More indiscreet details."

"Ridiculous. Awful lies."

He hunkered down and looked directly at me. "He says that John was bad to you and that you have money now and freedom."

"The lying –"

"Try not to concern yourself about this now. I just wanted to ask you for your side of things. If you see or hear anything else you must tell us. Mrs Good, do you hear me? We are here to help you." Irvine looked up the stairs. "Can I take a look around the rest of the house?"

I rolled my eyes and held my breast. If he was to look under the stairs!

Irvine placed his hand on the bannister, his left foot on the first step. "Let me peek into this attic and check around the rest of the house. It'll put my mind at ease."

"There's been no one up there for years. The doors are mostly locked."

Irvine didn't listen and on up he went. He was back fairly quickly.

"The key was in the lock of attic," Irvine said, smoothing out the bloody moustache. He didn't talk about what else he found, or what he didn't find.

"I'm a widow alone and this is not fair. I can't take much more of this. Why are men trying to ruin what little bit of confidence and contentment I have left?"

"Don't worry, Mrs Good. All will turn out for the best. Wait until you see. It will all be fine. And, when I spoke to your neighbour Cedric Fellows the other day he said you were a woman of remarkable character. A good Christian woman who takes his aunt to church. He likes his big words, doesn't he? A woman of 'fortitude', I think he said. He said that he finds you fascinating. Men are still interested in you, Mrs Good. Doesn't that make you feel better?"

"I don't care what men think of me," I replied slowly.

He left with a curt nod of his head and I breathed a sigh of relief. My secret was safe but it wouldn't be for long.

Whether or not Cedric was rotting, the fear of him decomposing greeted me in the hallway the following day. I had to do something. What a disaster it was! I had to get rid of the problem immediately. I also needed to be gone from Newburn Crescent. It wouldn't be long until word came from Inishowen about Tilly and Frank too. Constable Irvine would be back before I knew it!

The card sat on the hall table looking at me.

*Mrs Alice Longmire, 53 Marshall Meadows,*
*Netterby, Co Down*

There was an eagle barely visible, embossed on the card. I ran my fingers over it. I could afford to travel to Netterby. Alice would have to take me in and she'd know what to do.

\* \* \*

On the Old Netterby Road stood a terrace of houses, majestic two-storeys with nice bay windows on the ground floor. The gardens were small but perfectly formed. Each one was manicured and starting to blossom with daffodils and an odd early tulip. Splashed with colour and gardening know-how, they all looked nice and orderly, especially Number 53.

A smattering of grass and a well-swept path led to a door that seemed to be newly painted in a bright red. The residences were nice but it was not a neighbourhood I would have imagined a lady like Alice living in. But then again, where else would a murdering woman live?

I went around to the back. Alice was in the kitchen. She was looking through bags of shopping, pulling out a blouse and holding it up to the light.

Then she saw me.

She let me in the back door, into the small kitchen

"You have some nerve coming here."

I held out the card to her. "I found this. You gave this to my husband. Explain yourself."

"Oh, I met him a few times. I needed to get some information about you and to assess him and your situation – from the horse's mouth. Enough to convince me you were not a genuine victim – you were bad news."

That sounded convincing – sounded like what Alice would do.

"I'm in need of help," I said. "Things are falling apart for me."

"The cheek of you is unbelievable. Have you been arrested?"

"No."

She shrugged, indifferent to my suffering. "Get rid of that expression, Eve Good. I'm not going to let you hurt me."

"I need somewhere to stay. My landlord is dead and anyhow he was making me move. John owned nothing and I am destitute. Can I stay here?"

She laughed. The room closed in on me like it does when I'm angry.

"I need a place to hide," I said.

"I'm not sure what you think we can do. You were warned to make sure you had financial gain from John's accident. We warned you. We learned from Lydia's case that you need to have it all in hand and know that you're better off with no husband than maintaining a marriage. We told you *all* of this, Eve. Twice. You were given every opportunity to listen but you heard only what you wanted to hear." Alice smirked at me. "You see, Eve Good, you don't know everything and cannot control everything. I'm quite enjoying thinking that your life is falling apart around your ears. John Good will be rolling around his grave laughing at you now."

I hated the sound and sight of her.

"I refuse to leave."

"John himself had suspicions about you. He even told me, a total stranger, about his odd, plain wife who had a vicious temper and not a lot of Christianity. A manipulator he called you. How right poor John Good was!" She sat tall in the seat. "The Sinful Roses was not made for the likes of you. It has a higher purpose. You use and abuse it. It was founded to protect women from evil, not to shield the evil in women."

"You and your posh words and fancy clobber! You're no better than me, glamour-puss. You're a murderer too."

"But, Eve, you didn't kill anyone, remember? Have you forgotten? You're an innocent, timid creature. *John fell.*" She mimicked my voice: "*I'm lost. My darling John fell!*"

"I have murdered people!" I said. "How dare you laugh at me! I'm better than *all* of you silly Roses! I'm a real killer and they may be found soon and I need you to get the others here so we can discuss what's going to happen next."

"I cannot do that. That's not how it works. Go home and we'll contact you."

"I have no home. It has burned down."

"For the love of God!"

"Luckily it didn't spread to the other house in the cul-de-sac. Thankfully Marjorie wasn't hurt by the fire." I thought about mentioning Frank Hockley but I didn't. All of that was too precious to spill into reality. "I set the fire though. That's why I'm here. I'm going to need some advice, I imagine – either that or I'll need some help to disappear. Can you see now that this is urgent?"

"You didn't tell anyone about Lydia, us or the Sinful Roses? No one at all? You never discussed it with anyone?"

"You said yourself I have no one to tell." I shook my head and told myself that Tilly was gone and even if she was still alive, she would never speak of the Sinful Roses.

There was little need for me to read the newspapers Lydia had brought with her. The headlines were big like Lydia's annoyance.

"She killed your friend Cedric," Alice told Lydia. "That's his body they've found under the stairs. You'll need whiskey. Eve here says she needs our help. I know, Lydia. The colour of you says it all. But I did warn you. Cedric wanted his rent paid. That's all I can figure out that he did wrong." Alice flung the newspaper at me. "You are such an ass! Remains are found in a house where another man died only a few months ago!"

The papers were not very fair in their accounts of my sins. Murdering their owner and their respected boss was a bad move. John, of course, was getting glowing references from his superiors and colleagues. He was the best husband in the world to a hysterical, bad wife. They were all having a great time making my life even more miserable.

"You spoke of us. *I know you did*. You'll pay for doing that," Alice said.

Lydia left in a flurry.

Alice reached into her handbag – out came the barrel of a pistol. She was trying to unnerve me. "Lydia has given her orders and they were very clear. Lord love her, she is troubled about this. Tell me now, Eve – one woman to another – John's death – was it really an accident?"

I sighed. She was still trying to scare me. "He fell, I tell you – he fell."

She didn't even try to muffle the noise of the gun. The trigger was pulled and a pressure of heat hit me. The pain pierced me once in the arm and then a second time in the breast.

She shot me. *The bitch shot me! Twice!* I really didn't think she was capable of it – until then.

My eyes blinked and the burning was unbearable. My knees slumped off the chair and thumped the hard floor. I gulped the pain down into my throat. I backed away from her on my behind, slithering painfully against the wall.

Alice leaned over me, her perfume strong. I clung to my heart.

"We told you that there was no going back, no turning back of the clock. This should have been done months ago. There are consequences when people talk about us. I told you that I would kill you before I let you drag us down."

"I'm … innocent," I panted. Shallow slight breaths were all I could manage.

My lungs – fierce – pain – taste blood – Alice's face – her lips – talking.

"Can you hear me, Eve? This is what happens to those who let us down. You deserve this. The Sinful Roses' justice has been served. Die well. You were never one of us. You were *never* a Sinful Rose."

Next thing I knew I was in a hospital bed. I'd been dumped on the side of a main road like an animal. Left to bleed into the ditch! Tossed out of her car no doubt! There were no witnesses to say how I got there. Luckily, I was soon spotted.

Alice can say whatever she likes but I never wanted to be a Sinful Rose. I never needed any of them. I don't care if my testimony to you gets them into trouble. Eve Good will win in the end!

# Chapter 31

## Laurie Davenport

Eve's words shouldn't have shocked us but we both sit in the chairs dumbstruck.

"It's high time we questioned this Eve Good with no nonsense taken," I announce assuredly after a long and laboured silence.

It seems that Eve has managed to shock the unshockable Norah.

She moves over by the bookshelves and the morning sun is warm. I feel sticky and sickly. She replies after a while with an edge to her voice. "If these Sinful Roses exist at all it will be only a matter of time until I find a Ravenscairn 'location' in England and make contact with them. Eve Good is not going to help us much further, as she has never met Charlotte."

"I want to ask her things," I say with a begging tone I wish would go away. "I've made a list." I touch my temple. "In here."

"Ah, the great mind of a detective," Norah mocks.

On another day I might have chuckled at that, but I feel she's being sarcastic.

I know I'm finding women hard to understand but Norah's moods move like the wind. Why does she not want me to question Eve?

"I'm a man who finishes his tasks," I start and then touch my scars and realise I didn't finish my time in the war. I abandoned other men at the front. I was injured but I was glad to leave that mission incomplete. That failure stops me in my tracks and my headache worsens. "No, that's not true – I left good men behind me to die – but I sure as hell am not going to stop until I know there is no such thing as these cursed Roses."

"I have some new information," she says and seems to hesitate. "Fredrick thinks Charlotte disappeared to get money from either you or her father or both. Her father is denying getting a ransom note but it is known that he did. Servants talk."

I gulp back anger. "Charlotte knows I've no money to speak of these days. There you have it, Norah. A broken man in an old house. What is there to love?"

Norah comes and crouches down by my chairs. "Stop this, Laurie," she says softly. "You are mending your life."

"Bring the car around and let's go and talk to Eve. I've had enough of sitting in this chair," I say.

"Let's wait a while," Norah says and touches my knee as she leaves me to sit elsewhere in the room.

"I want to go now!" I demand. It's childlike, bold and sharp. Hearing Eve recount Alice's attempted murder is sinking in.

Norah has been reticent for days now about becoming a Sinful Rose. Even by the way she helps me put on my topcoat and get into the passenger seat, I know she's determined to avoid all retreat on the infiltration of the Roses idea. Her driving is smooth and I can picture her steady gloved hands on the wheel. The day is wet and the wipers are making a creaking sound across the windshield. They need to be looked at but I'm not going to suggest it. What would a woman like her know about windscreen wipers?

"I can almost hear you thinking," she says when we are well on the road home from Thistleforth. "And I know it's risky for me to do this, but we talked the General into it now and it's the best way to get more information. Eve has told us all of her tale. And now we know some of the women at least and what we're dealing with. A dangerous club of women. But – we need proof. Charlotte has been taken in for questioning and dragged over the coals for wasting everyone's time. And Freddie said she's still staying with Lady Dornan. She gave their address. I mean really! They're brazen to still be together, aren't they?"

I shrug. "I feel slightly sorry for her –" I stop for I can sense Norah opening her mouth to protest. I go on, "I know I shouldn't feel anything but contempt for my wife or Eve Good, but they've made me curious about all of it. In a macabre way I want to know more. And before you say anything else, I'm not like Lord Dornan and no, I've not fallen in love with Eve Good. I'm just more and more uncertain about her every day."

"She was still adamant right to the end that John Good fell. Do you believe her? She was truthful about the other things – we hope. Perhaps John Good did just fall and then she didn't think she needed to help the Roses?"

I make a noise in my throat to give myself time to think. I'm not sure about any woman since Charlotte tried to kill me. Since I became blind, Freddie expects me to gain some kind of sixth sense to unravel the Roses mess, but really I have a muddle for a heart and mind.

Norah says, "Laurie, you know that not many women want to murder their husbands? This is all very unusual. Many women are distressed or dissatisfied with their lives, but the number of those who will actually contact the Roses is quite low. Especially now, for their men are at war. At the very least it seems ungrateful and I cannot see many women contacting such an organisation right now. That's why I think I will be successful in being accepted into the ranks."

"Perhaps we should ask Eve how best to go about it all?" I say.

That makes Norah swerve my car. She gasps and I hold on for dear life, hoping her eyes are back on the road.

"It's just she knows the whole thing from the inside too," I say. "And she might have some information of use."

"We won't tell a *soul* about my joining the Roses! *Do you hear me, Laurie?* Other than the General of course. And we definitely won't be telling your pal Eve!"

"Of course, that makes sense," I lie, thinking of Giles' knowledge of the whole thing. "But we can always ask Eve things on the sly? With us being good detectives we should be able to extract information from her?"

"All we've done is listen!" Norah snaps. "We were warned not to try to be professionals about this."

"Says the woman who's going to be going into a den of vipers with no training whatsoever." I don't like the atmosphere between us. I admire Norah but she's getting irritable these days. I know this happens to women every month, but her outbursts are sporadic and unpredictable. Is it that she doesn't want us to become reliant on each other? It is too late for me. I'm totally in awe of her. Hooked and sunk in glorious love with her.

Every time she mentions Freddie and marrying him, I think I might commit murder!

I tilt my head in her direction. "I can always keep the conversation going with Eve while you spend time seducing your new husband."

"That's a *nasty* thing to say. You're in such a bad mood and I'm tired of it," Norah says, swinging the Crossley right around so that it feels like we are heading homewards again.

"I don't like being a passenger when a woman is driving," I say through gritted teeth as she cranks at my gearstick. "And if you're going to be busy with the Sinful Roses, I want to make myself useful and visit Eve alone."

She changes gears and boots us forward. It feels like she's driving far too fast. How I hate not knowing what's going on! She's not mentioned that she's turned the car around. What am I to do now?

Of course, I'm too proud to ask her what's what and instead I keep the tension high and ask, "Have the General and you set a date then?" There's an annoyance between us now that is fiery and I want to blow on the flames. Self-sabotage has always been a strong trait of mine. "A wedding in the snow might be fitting? You'd like that. A fake Christmas wedding."

"Stop being mean," Norah says, sounding decidedly mean herself. "Just because I won't be around to be at your beck and call and be able to give you my full attention, you've been acting like a child for days."

That just puts the tin hat on my annoyance. "Child? Me? For days? You cannot be serious!"

"Ask Giles – he'll tell you that you've become reliant

on me and it's high time that you stop acting like a spoilt schoolboy."

"Might I remind you, Miss Walsh, that I'm your employer," I say slowly. "And I don't take kindly to you being insulted. And leave Giles out of this!"

The thump of the car over a bump almost jolts my stomach into my chest. A woman should never have been allowed to drive an expensive and loved vehicle.

"And might I remind you, Laurie Davenport, that you don't employ me," Norah says haughtily. "And I don't like your tone and manner. I've been nothing but good to you."

"Yes, and you did throw yourself into my arms too. Let's not forget that!"

The car skids to a halt. Bits of my tyres are no doubt in the tarmacadam. I instantly regret what I said but stubbornness refuses to let me apologise. I cross my arms for she is no doubt glaring at me.

"Did you really say that?" Norah whispers. The car door opens. "Do you really think that I'm a trollop? I care for you very much, Laurie, and that has hurt."

"If the cap fits," I say. I'm on a roll that's hard to stop.

"*Fuck you!*" Norah says and the cold winter air blasts into the vehicle for she has opened the door fully. "I kissed you because I felt sorry for you! There now, you have it, you *bastard*!"

The door is slammed. I'm alone and the car is still running. She'll be back.

I wait. There's no sound other than the idling of the engine. No Norah, no footsteps, no door opening. Where are we? Where is Norah? Where am I?

I sit into the driver's seat and cut out the engine. The

silence is truly deafening. I feel the steering wheel under my palms and curl trembling fingers around the warm grooves.

Again the realisation of my injuries hits me. Living is almost worse than being dead. I'm not a man any more. I cannot go where I please or do what I want. Norah did more than slap me when she left me alone in the car. I squint to try to figure out where I am but to no avail. She has left me helpless and that is better than any retort. But she also has told me that she pities me. That stings almost as much as my vulnerability.

I know I deserve a harsh rebuke but the cruelty of abandoning me somewhere on the road home is too much. Tears spring up and I gulp them down.

"A real man doesn't blubber," Charlotte once said.

"Real women should nurture, shouldn't they?" I'd replied. Of course Charlotte was not the nurturing type.

I know nothing about women. I know nothing and can see nothing. I sniff in self-pity and still nothing changes my situation. I lean a very tired forehead against the steering wheel and think about driving into a wall or off a cliff. Anything is better than this existence.

Then I hear something or someone approaching. It could be Norah but the sound is different. Is it someone who means me harm? I hold my breath.

There is a slight tap on the window to my right. Norah has returned.

I shuffle taller in the seat and fix my tie and find the mechanism to roll the window down.

It is Giles for I can smell his hair lacquer.

"Sir, is everything all right? You're not driving, are you, sir?"

"No," I sniff. "I got into the seat to turn off the engine. I miss my old life, Giles. I miss it terribly."

"Where is Norah, sir?"

"I don't know. She just left me here." I rub the back of my hand across my eyes. "Where am I, Giles? How did you happen to find me?"

"You don't know? You're just outside the gates to the house, sir."

I am amazed and confused. So Norah hadn't abandoned me unprotected in the countryside after all. Yet wasn't it cruel of her to make me think she had? I feel utterly humiliated.

"So you didn't see her?" I ask Giles.

"No, sir. Perhaps she went in the servants' entrance to speak with Cook. They're quite good friends now."

"Well, I'm afraid that Norah and I are not good friends. We've had a falling-out."

"A lovers' tiff?" Giles says with a chuckle.

"She pities me," I murmur, knowing he'll still hear me. "And we're definitely not lovers."

"Dear me," Giles says. "It's starting to rain, sir. Let's get you into the house and I'll ask Norah to come and move the car."

Giles has never learned to drive.

He opens the door and leads me, like a child, back to the house. The irony is not lost on me that Norah considers me one and she has made me an infant quite easily.

"Women are unsavoury creatures," I say to Giles while we walk across the gravel. "If I knew we were this close to the house, I could have managed to come home by myself."

"Of course you could have, sir," Giles replies. "It was nasty of her to leave you there."

"I was a little cruel but I was trying to stand up for myself." I sound whiney. Mother would roll her eyes at me bemoaning my lot. I'm regressing in age and maturity far too easily. "I think it is because I'm uncertain about everything. I tend to be snappy. But she is feisty."

"Admirably so," Giles says. "Norah will be putting herself in danger for your benefit, sir."

I'm reminded that Giles is privy to the plan. It makes me feel doubly inadequate. Because of my wife, Norah will be in danger and I'm not a very good detective if I've told our plans to my butler!

"About that, Giles, please don't tell her that I said anything."

"Mum's the word, sir. I would never divulge anything. That goes without saying. I promised discretion."

"Thank you. I had no idea our avenue was so long," I say, panting slightly to keep up.

"Sir, you should speak to Norah and mend things. Shall I look for her after I have settled you down?"

"You think I should apologise to her? But you didn't hear her," I protest. "And she was changing gears constantly. She isn't a good driver."

"Her driving is fine, sir, and you need her," Giles says, patting my arm. "And you should tell Norah that you care for her before it's too late."

"Too late?"

"Before you say something to make her leave the manor for good."

I hold my heart and feel it pound in my chest. There's no way that I want Norah to disappear. It's inconceivable.

"Or before you give her a reason to kill you," Giles says with a chuckle. "Here we are. Home now, sir."

# Chapter 32

## Laurie Davenport

Giles has hit a nerve. Without meaning to he has planted a seed that is hard to uproot. Anxiety floods my thoughts. Lying on my bed does not calm me in the slightest. Maybe Norah is killing me slowly? I've been feeling out of sorts. Emotional and not myself. This is all her doing. I cough and feel my forehead. I'm not feverish but that doesn't mean anything at all. Is it love-sickness or a poisoning? I know nothing about Norah. Well, very little. I do love her but suddenly I also fear her.

When my mind wanders, it seems plausible that Norah is in league with Charlotte and the others.

I'm losing a grip on reality. Every day I'm listening to a woman who murders many and she makes sense of it. My own wife has tried to kill me – what would make Norah any different? It seems that all women are out to get me and the fears magnify when I think of Norah's wish to join the Sinful Roses. What normal woman would care to be in such a position? Unless she's not frightened of them at all? Norah never flinched on listening to Eve's tales. Why not?

Because she is a Sinful Rose herself, that's why! She is slowly poisoning me with tea or whiskey. The fire in Armagh could have been her doing.

My heart almost stops when I think that she wanted to get at Freddie too. I would almost be a practice shot for the General's demise. And of course Norah could disappear easily back to Ireland or wherever she came from. My heart pounds and pounds.

What do I really know about Norah Walsh? What were the abilities Freddie referred to? Why did she not want me talking to Eve alone? It's because I might find out things about Norah's mind, Norah's motivations. It would be easy for Norah to kill me if she had a mind to. She knows Charlotte's failures well.

I might be bumped off any day now. It might happen today. *Now.* She'll not make mistakes – she'll be successful for her women friends. My breathing is laboured. Norah has made herself dependable, and reliable. She even tried to seduce me. She also disappeared when Charlotte and Lady Dornan arrived. They were worried that I would suspect their alliance. A man in love or lust is most definitely blind! Norah knows what she is doing. I'm a total fool. A very-in-love ass of a man!

The knock on the door makes me jump. I ignore it. It comes again.

"Sir?" It's Norah.

I hold my breath for the door is unlocked.

"Laurie?" she says. "I have news. May I come in? That address Eve Good mentioned is indeed Alice Longmire's."

For weeks I've wanted Norah in my bed and now I'm even afraid for her to enter the room. The door creaks open because of my fearful silence.

Norah stops just inside the room. "Are you listening to me, Laurie? I have news."

"Yes," I say, croaking on a dry throat.

"Alice Longmire's husband died following a mugging."

"My goodness," I say quietly.

I can see Norah's shape in the light from the door. She's a blurry shadow. If she lunged now and stuck me like a pig, I might just see it coming.

"I refuse to apologise to you," she says. "We both said things that are regrettable. Let's move on."

I nod for I cannot speak. There's a huge lump in my throat. Disappointment and fear mingle.

"I shouldn't have left you in the car," Norah says. "Giles gave me a good telling-off. You men stick together. But I agree with him. It was not a nice thing to do."

"I'm very tired." I lean back onto the pillows, hoping that she'll leave and not kill me today. "I did get a shock."

"Don't milk it," Norah says. "You're not a weakling and you were only at the gate."

"How was I to know that?" I stand. "I had no idea where I was!"

She shuffles her feet. I hope that she's looking suitably perturbed but I doubt a murdering woman would be in the slightest put out by a helpless blind man playing the victim.

"I'm a little bit sorry," Norah admits. "But you said some terrible things." She's talking quietly but does not seem upset. "I'm not going to apologise for standing up for myself."

"Standing up for yourself? Is that what that was? Leaving a cripple in the middle of nowhere on purpose is standing up for yourself! All this female liberation nonsense has gone to your head if that is what you do to a poor, blind man who depends on you!"

"Poor blind man," Norah scoffs and laughs. It isn't a

cruel laugh but it's a laugh nonetheless. "I left you at the gate of your own house. And I had work to do. Mrs Fellows, for instance. I thought we might speak with her, but I've found that she died just last year. She survived Eve Good's attempted murder but passed away of natural causes in a care home. The poor woman had no family left, God rest her soul."

"Anything from Lady Dornan or Charlotte?"

"Nothing," she replies. "What were you expecting?"

"Perhaps a confession or some sort of proof that they and others are murdering bitches."

"The General's update went well and he has promised to leave Eve in England for the present time and you can visit her soon. He has a few women looking out for the Ravenscairn advertisements. But he specifically asked for you not to mention Charlotte's plots to kill you to anyone. It all seems more implausible than ever now and Charlotte's father is even more influential. Freddie is worried you will step on toes."

"Freddie? Is that what he's called now?" I snap and then think for a second with a finger to my chin. "Oh but wait, you're betrothed. I suppose it's only right that you call him that."

"I refuse to keep arguing," Norah says.

"Giles did warn me that if I wasn't careful you might try to kill me," I say and flop back against the pillows.

There's an eerie silence.

I suddenly feel utterly stupid for saying such a thing. "He was joking, of course, Norah. I was trying to make you laugh."

"That's not funny, Laurie. Not funny in the slightest. I've never given you any reason to say that."

I bend my elbows and thrust my hands behind my head. She could easily stab me now and I sense her eyes are doing just that. Piercing me with dagger stares. I shouldn't think such awful things of the woman who's been so good to me. I could rise, apologise and take her in my arms and kiss her instead. But I don't. The door slams.

I cannot bear that she's so cross with me. She's right. She is nothing like the women I fear. What have I been thinking? There's nothing to even suggest she's like Charlotte and the others. And now I've totally ruined things. Typical Laurie Davenport. Stubborn and stupid fool to the last.

I somehow make a mess of everything. I adored Charlotte and went with her to Belfast and Lady Dornan's house – like a lamb to the slaughter. She said we should look into me expanding my connections in Ireland. It made sense to travel. Even attending the party seemed like a good idea. The best of the best people were there. And everything was modern but tasteful and they knew all the right folk to invite. There were many glamorous women there that evening, but I only had eyes for the stunning Charlotte. She shimmered in a red evening dress. I recall the music we danced to was "Tomorrow is Another Day" by the Dorsey Brothers, a lively tune with cheery lyrics and it was a good omen – or so I thought. "You're enchanting," I said, blushing. Her blue eyes were amused and her hand warm. I wonder now – did she ever tell me the truth, did she ever love me, could any woman ever love me now?

I've got scars and blindness to further burden a personality that drives women to abandon me at best and murder me at worst. I am doomed. Effectively and efficiently doomed.

# Chapter 33

## Eve Good

The nights here are very dark and remind me of Newburn Crescent. There wasn't much street lighting there and when the night fell and I was all alone, I'd listen to the sounds of the house. The creaks and groans of timbers and the sigh of a house settling into its night-time peace.

Thistleforth House sounds larger than usual tonight. I heard some of the guards mention its name. When I close my eyes, other senses do seem heightened. That must be how it is for the blind Mr Davenport. The doors bang and clunk and the echoes get further away. There's a peaceful stillness in knowing you are locked in, but for the past few evenings I've found I'm unsettled. Feeling vulnerable again suddenly, the hairs on my arms stand and a shiver traces down my spine. I'm a sitting duck for the Roses. Miles from any system that might have protected me in the past, across an ocean of water and still in danger.

Laurie Davenport's face smiles at me in my mind. What a pity to see such handsomeness disfigured. He's also lost the swagger a man of his age has. The war has a lot to answer for. The ring on his finger means he's married. To Norah Walsh? I doubt that. She's not of his class and she's Irish. And why would he introduce her by her maiden name? Unless they were trying to conceal the relationship from me? I cannot place what she feels for him. Davenport is weak and she's far from that.

When the grub comes I try to ask the guards about her. I get the sense that she's not trusted by many. It's the way they smirk or raise an eyebrow when I ask about her. It's like she's not one of their own and under suspicion. I don't blame them. She's got an edge to her that reminds me of other women I once knew.

These will be my last instalments. I write quickly as the night-time routine will start soon. I can picture what will happen. I know what is going to come ...

When the place settles down to sleeping here, it's still early. I might not have a clock but I know there's a clearing out of corridors and a blacking out of windows. There's little to do then but sleep. Sometimes I hear planes or engines, or running in the hallways and I day-dream about being far away somewhere exotic and warm. But mostly, I'm left. Forgotten. Abandoned for most of the day and night.

I sit upright on the bed, cock an ear, listen intently but continue to write. Those sounds are new for this hour. Opening of gates, or locks, the clip-clip of a woman's heels in the corridor. That's odd. At this time of night? Guards all wear softer soles. My heart races. The sound of those steps is purposeful.

Then there's no noise for a long time. My breath heaves in my chest. Holding it, I listen hard. Like my life depends on it. Nothing.

I continue to write as quickly as I can, speeding over the page, listening at the same time, straining against the house noises for a sign of where the woman might be now. Nothing but the thumping of my own heart.

233

I pause. The air drains slowly from my lungs as I again strain to hear anything at all.

There are no further footsteps. I must have imagined them. I sometimes do. I know I am not safe. Locks and bolts won't keep the Sinful Roses out.

I write on.

I've always had a vivid imagination and also a gut that screams truths at me. I knew John Good's fall would be the death of me. The bastard toppled to his end to spite me. I laugh to myself. Not for the first time, I snigger at the hand of cards I've been dealt. A murdering harlot lost her good husband to a threadbare piece of carpet on the stairs. And it all led me down a path of destruction. There was no need for the Roses at all. The irony. And now, I cannot get rid of the bitches. Even in here …

What was that?

There's a turning of a key in my door.

They have come.

*"Come on in, you bitches, and let's get this over with!"* I say into the blackness.

And lay down my pen.

# Chapter 34

## Laurie Davenport

The evening rolls into night and Giles and I have dinner together in the kitchen. We're discussing the whole debacle in depth and I'm trying to convince him that all of this murdering wives business is not a possible train of thought any more. It all seems more and more fanciful.

Norah is obviously giving me a wide berth following our falling-out and I'm feeling decidedly sorry for myself. Giles is such good company when I am low and in need of a friend but of course I don't tell him this and find the silences long.

"The reports on the wireless are promising, sir," he says as he sees me to my room. "I know you hate to hear about it, but I do think our chaps are giving Hitler a thrashing. Try to get a good sleep. Tomorrow is another day."

The morning brings with it a clarity. It's time for Laurie Davenport to work on his life. No more wishing my life would return to what it was. No more mooning about over Norah. Whatever is going to happen I need to take it by the throat and give it a good shaking into place. I'm not going to sit about this house, wallowing in self-pity. I dress myself these days and aim to confront my fears head on and sort things out. I start to gingerly make my way downstairs, in case I crash into something else and make a mess. The clock chimes seven o'clock but Norah is in the hallway because she answers the telephone when it rings.

"Good morning, Fredrick. We were just going to have some breakfast and then make our way over to Thistleforth."

She listens.

"*What?*" She gasps. "*No!*"

A silence follows as she listens.

"I'll tell him, sir. He'll take it badly. It's the most terrible news, no matter what she's done in the past. And she was telling us a lot but not relaying much proof of anything. I'll look out for the delivery of her final words. All lies, you say? Suicide. Of course, I want to read what she says and I will take it all with a pinch of salt." A pause. "I'll not let it upset me. Yes, sir. I know I've a lot to learn and this was only to get Laurie back on his feet. But what you are talking about is not possible any more. Please just do as I ask and only send over the last instalment. I know what I'm doing and I think you're being very unfair to me ..." Norah sighs and waits. "I'll speak with Laurie. Although he has been a little hard to manage lately and I don't think he'll take this very well. Goodbye." She clunks down the receiver and curses loudly. Then curses loudly again.

"I was listening," I say for she will see me loitering on the stairs.

"It's fine. He's got some bad news from Thistleforth."

"What's happened?" I ask, moving towards Norah's outline.

"I'm afraid Eve took her own life last night. Slit her throat with metal from the bedstead. Gruesome stuff.

236

And the General feels that we need to come off this investigation. It's leading nowhere."

Failure drips from her and I feel dejected like she does.

"Poor Eve," I say as Norah leads me into the dining room for breakfast. "But why did she kill herself now?"

"She was finished telling us her tale and she knew that she was going to be questioned and holes would be poked in her story. She was worried about going back to prison. That was a bleak place, Laurie. Even for the likes of her, it was grim."

We're mostly silent until the tea arrives on a squealing trolley with Giles in tow.

"Tea," he announces in a cheery way. "Are you two still at loggerheads?"

"No," we both reply together.

"I'm terribly glad that you agree on something," he says, leaving and closing the door.

"This business of looking into the past and the future with fear is not healthy," I say. "Charlotte wants us to get a divorce. If she gets a good settlement it will make her happy." I pause. "And Freddie believes Eve was lying all this time? Was it definitely suicide?"

"Cut her throat herself in her locked room. Looks like it. Yes."

"So what now?" I ask us both.

"She's gone and there's no-one else talking about any Sinful Roses or murdering wives," Norah says. "And there's no other proof of any crimes. It seems it was all fiction. Made-up. Lies. In a way it's a relief,"

The gap Eve is leaving in our lives stretches out in front of me. All of that time spent worrying about her ramblings seems such a waste. Norah will want to leave now too. That makes me heave out a large sigh. I need to find a way of making Norah stay. I need to make her see that being with me will fill all those ambitions of hers. But the reality hits. I am a scarred, almost bankrupt, blind man. What future would an ambitious young woman have with me?

I heave the chair back from table as I've no appetite for kippers and toast.

"I think it's time for me to move on," I say and sink my head in my hands. I should take a drink or something to eat but I feel too weak and fed up to bother. "We've been taken as fools and have failed miserably. I was even starting to doubt our ... connection."

"Doubt our what?" she asks.

"Oh, I don't know. I suppose it's the female sex I don't understand," I sigh. "These criminal women are too much for a man like me. They make me see badness in everyone."

"You're not dealing with normal women though, Laurie. I go over and over it. At least Eve has admitted to her crimes but she doesn't tell us much about anything else. Dropping names like Alice Longmire and information about Lydia Babbington piqued our interest, but she never mentioned your wife."

"I never asked her. I slipped up badly there and now it's too late. But Eve's crimes were many years ago now. Charlotte is too young – she wouldn't have known her surely?"

"Eve possibly only knew Alice and Lydia or read about them in the newspapers."

"She made up the whole thing to have fun?" I ask, incredulous.

238

"It seems that she did," Norah says with a long pause. "I think that it's time we put all of this behind us. I just know too that I can't go back to work for the General. He's an annoying bastard!"

Perhaps Norah is looking for reassurance that all is still fine between us. Our argument and her abandoning me in the avenue won't leave my mind. I vaguely hear her talking as my mind swings back and forth over all that's happened. I hear her mention again that she won't work for Freddie and that she might go home to Ireland. Here and now is possibly where I should ask Norah to stay in Davenport with me – but I don't.

# Chapter 35

## Norah Walsh

The corpse is cold. Eve Good is gone. For good. We Irish are used to rituals and traditions around death and dying. We aren't afraid of a dead body and I shouldn't be too upset by Eve's passing, but a lump sticks in my throat. The marks on her neck are stitched but look fierce bad. Awful bad! Her blonde hair is caked in dried clots and although her face is clean, its paleness and peaceful expression don't add up. Eve Good never looked so serene and yet death has given her a glow of goodness.

Then my eye is drawn back to the gash. How can a woman be driven to do this? I've read Eve's words in Fredrick's office before the orderlies looking after Eve's body took me down here.

Walking back up to his office takes me a long time. Everything blurs as tears sting. What would my mother think of me now?

"Have you been crying?" Fredrick asks when I knock on his door and step back into the office. "You remember her vileness, don't you? Her cruelty? What are you crying for her for?"

"It's just that it's all over," I lie.

"You don't want to leave Davenport?" Fredrick says, lighting a cigar. "Or you're sorry that you've been led a

240

merry dance by Eve Good?"

"Give it a rest," I tell him, gathering my coat and hat from the coatstand near the door. "You can be such an ass, Fredrick. You think you know it all. But you don't. I'm going to prove it to you that I'm more than you think I am."

"All these women wanting to prove their power!" he says, blowing a smoke ring. "I'm far too busy for all of this. Are you going to seduce old Laurie? Or what? The whole purpose of all of this was for him to feel like a man again and for you to do his heart and prick some good. Have you done it? No!"

"I'm going to finish what *I* set out to do," I say, dragging my coat on and buttoning it. "I also know that I need time away from the lot of ye."

"And what about Laurie?" Fredrick asks. "Are you sure that you're not going to tell him what you're trying to do?"

"I'm damn sure that he doesn't need to know," I say. "And you're not going to tell him either!"

I close the door with a determined swing on my way out. I just wish I could stop crying on the walk back to Laurie's car. I'm sure of very little right now but I know that Eve Good's spirit will haunt me until the end of my days.

# Chapter 36

## Laurie Davenport

"Can you read that old newspaper clipping for me again?" I ask Norah.

Even though she has been to identify Eve's corpse, read the writings to me again in full, I cannot let it go. We are going through old material in the files and I'm hoping I get some enlightenment from the process, but Norah is getting impatient with me. She sighs and reads.

"'*Eve Good Shot. Mrs Eve Good, disgraced widow of Sergeant John Good, was found shot on the road from Netterby to Belfast, yesterday evening.*

*Thirty-year-old mother of seven, Mrs Dora Kilbride, noticed her lying in the ditch. "There was a lot of blood," Mrs Kilbride recounts. "Like a stuck pig, she was. There were two big wounds, I'm certain of that." Other onlookers were reluctant to speak and the locality is still in shock following the incidents in Whinpark. Police are tight-lipped, following the burning of the disgraced Eve Good's place of residence in Newburn Crescent. The remains of a body found on the premises has been identified as Mr Cedric Fellows, the beloved proprietor of this very paper. Mr Fellows was also a generous and loving nephew to a Mrs Marjorie Fellows, who the depraved Mrs Eve Good is also accused of attempting to murder. With medications in her system, Mrs Marjorie*

Fellows almost died and says Mrs Good administered these medicines and also put them into her food. Newly promoted Sergeant Irvine said, "There has been much discussion about this woman (Mrs Good) and these tragic events. We must now look at all the facts before speaking further. This is a complex case and we feel there may be people with information who have yet to come forward. With the charred remains of Mr Cedric Fellows found in this victim's place of residence, this is turning into a multiple homicide investigation with many facets.'"

Norah pauses and glances up at me.

I just nod at her to continue.

"'Upon being pressed about the shooting of Mrs Good, Irvine did mention that many lines of enquiry were open to them at this time, and he wished to reassure the public that Scotland Yard are also involved. He also specified the need for the public to come forward with what they know. "We call on the women of the area especially. They are home during the day and hear things that will be relevant." Irvine also went on to add, "The truth will always rise to the surface. Anyone who thinks they will hide from justice is fooling themselves. There will be always be consequences for evil deeds – either in this world or the next." Mrs Marjorie Fellows, now well recovered from her ordeal, has let it be known to the paper that she did indeed witness the death of her beloved nephew Cedric Fellows at the hands of their neighbour, Mrs Eve Good. Following the shooting of Mrs Good, Mrs Marjorie Fellows felt she could now speak of the horrors she witnessed from her own window. "Eve Good brutally murdered my Cedric. She trod on his face and head and drugged him inside the house. Over the time she visited me Eve Good made me take medications and I don't know how she did not murder me too. I'm still not sure how I managed to survive or why I was spared." Mrs Fellows

243

declined to answer if she was glad to hear of Mrs Good's shooting, but said, "Evil walks among us. It can even live beside us and we might never know until it is too late." Back in her elderly brother's residence, Mrs Fellows feels safe at last and is making a speedy recovery from the traumas she suffered.'"

Norah pauses again. "It's just as horrible now as the first time we read it, isn't it?"

"It is," I reply. "A nightmare."

She continues. "'*All of this has thrown light on the accident which supposedly befell Mrs Good's own husband, Mr John Good, November last. Sergeant Good was found at the foot of the stairs, having supposedly fallen or tripped and been unable to save himself. Now it seems that the initial concerns of Sergeant Irvine are proving correct. "We always felt that there was more to John Good's death than met the eye. Once the young mechanic, Tim Harbour, came forward as Mrs Eve Good's lover, we felt we had motive but little evidence to convict her of that also." Irvine refused to comment about the uncovering of a hurriedly buried and butchered corpse of Mrs Eve Good's relative through marriage in Inishowen, Donegal. We have learned however that a Mrs Tilly Hockley, wife of the deceased, is helping police in Donegal with their enquiries. Constable Irvine also did not comment on whether the pressure from the police provoked Mrs Eve Good into further attacks and he would not be drawn on why someone might wish to murder her. He does state however, "The persons who shot Mrs Eve Good are still at large and we will hunt them down. Attempted murder is attempted murder. However, thanks to the valiant efforts of the police force and the morality of good men, this deranged and depraved woman's true nature has been uncovered."'*"

"It seems that she was telling the truth about a lot of her crimes. It all fits with what you've read to me from her transcripts and the newspaper accounts," I say, sipping the cold tea we've been having for the last hour. "Then why lie about the Sinful Roses? Why tell the truth about almost everything else and lie about them?"

"I contacted the women's prison in Armagh," Norah says. "The prison guard who looked after Eve the most was eager to talk with us, now that Eve is gone. Remember her? She said that Eve tried every trick in the book in the prison. They never believed a word she said for she was always making up tales about the other prisoners. She also had faked many suicide attempts that didn't make it into the files."

"Dear Lord."

"The guard spoke to me on the telephone for ages and she's convinced that Eve cut herself the time that got her moved to the infirmary and then to Thistleforth House. She said there was no way anyone would ever try to harm her. None of the other prisoners bothered with her at all. She was in Coventry or ostracised for this and that over the years. Her behaviour was always unpredictable, but she would attempt to lie or harm herself to get out of trouble constantly."

"It sounds like her, doesn't it? Rings true."

"Definitely. She sent out the bait about the Murdering Wives Club. Of course men in authority would be interested in such a thing. Women murdering their husbands would be a worry. Especially in wartime! When people nibbled at her nonsense she grew brazen and made up her story and then we came calling and she was set."

"The fire in the guesthouse?" I ask.

Norah hums. She's thinking.

"Unless it was simply unrelated and we just

happened to be in the wrong place at the wrong time?" I suggest.

"Well, yes," Norah says. "That's a possibility. Marjorie Fellows also reported that Eve read the newspapers from front to back. Over and over again. It was a hobby for her. Lydia Babbington was in the papers for months and Eve would have also read about Alice Longmire's husband getting robbed and stabbed. It was in the papers at the time because there was another woman with him. Scandalous."

"You really think Eve made it all up? Made up all the times she was with Alice and Lydia? Made up such an awful thing as a murdering wives club?"

Norah sighs and I wish I could see her. For she must be beautiful when she is thinking.

"And there have been no sightings of Ravenscairn mentioned in any magazine or newspaper?" I ask. "No sign of an advertisement at all?"

"Not one."

"Mind you, Eve never told us that. It was Tilly her cousin who said that, wasn't it? Maybe the southern Irish papers have references to Ravenscairn in them?"

"Good thinking. But I doubt we will find it even if we can lay our hands on Irish newspapers. I can ask a few relatives to keep an eye out, I suppose."

"I don't know what to believe. In my gut I think she was convinced that these Sinful Roses were trying to kill her. I believed her accounts. Why would she lie about all of that?"

"To get attention. To pass the blame," Norah says.

"She was in prison anyhow and, yes, she wanted to get better surroundings but it was all a bit much for her to come up with just on a whim – wasn't it?"

"I doubt Eve Good ever did anything on a whim. She had plenty of time to think up a tall tale in prison. She was a bad bitch, liable to say whatever would make her life better. The prison guard was convinced that she was a liar and is worried that she still isn't dead. I had to promise her over and over that I went to check the body myself. I could understand her worry. Eve Good is a cat of nine lives when you think about it."

I shudder. "What is it you Irish say, Norah? God rest her soul?"

"Yes. Make she rest in peace now," Norah says. "And may she take her thundering lies with her."

"Does this mean that Charlotte wasn't trying to kill me then?" I muse. "I've thought about this over and over. My whole system was in shock when I came home and Charlotte was never very loving. I shouldn't have expected so much from her. Perhaps my disappointment evolved into accusing her of strange things."

"You were quite sure," Norah says. "But ..."

I pinch the bridge of my nose. "I might have imagined it all?" I don't tell her that I even suspected her of such atrocities. "It seems unlikely that she was out to kill me."

"It does."

"Lady Dornan, though, *is* a murderess," I remember suddenly.

"She's happily married now to a lord and there's no reason to think she is anything sinister. She did her time in prison and I doubt she wants to go back."

"Charlotte mightn't even know of Lady Dornan's past?"

"She might not. And even if she did it adds to the

glamour. It strikes me that Charlotte might like that. Some people like surrounding themselves with criminal people."

Norah moves off the couch and I hear sounds near the gramophone.

"How about a tune?" she asks.

"I have a confession to make," I say towards the shelves of records. "I did worry that you might marry Freddie. I would have missed your company."

She sighs heavily. "We waited and waited on an advertisement. It has been weeks since we started looking and even in the library archives we failed to find any mention of a Ravenscairn. There was no point in marrying a man if there was no Murdering Wives Club to join." Norah laughs at that and I try to join her.

"So, Freddie's bachelorhood was always going to be safe from ruin," I say.

"And in any case I wouldn't have been 'married-married' to him, thank goodness!" Norah confirms. "For General Ashfield is definitely a man that I *would* gladly murder."

She's joking and I enjoy her company, as I always have done. How did I think badly of my Norah? I want to sweep her up into a tight hug and a passionate kiss. I want to whisk her into my arms and tell her how I feel. But I don't move. What if she rejects me again? I'm not sure I could take it. I'm feeling foolish enough. The chances are that she'll tell me what I feel between us is all in my imagination as well. It is better to be safe than sorry.

I scratch at my beard instead and say, "I'm glad that we have made up our differences. I hate when we argue."

"Giles said we were like an old married couple who

bicker." Norah laughs again. "But I'll have to go soon. There's no job for me here now. You've come a long way and are much better and my role here is not necessary anymore, is it?"

I'm going to lose Norah and every muscle freezes. She cannot go, but how do I make her stay? Do I want to make a show of myself and fawn over her and beg like a dog? I could gush undying love or admit that I'm far from ready to deal with my blindness unaided? Should she not say she wants to be here with me?

"I've been looking into getting another job and I may need to get a reference," Norah says.

The time we kissed flashes into my mind. It seems like a lifetime ago. How do I make her stay? How do I mention that glorious time without making it sound like I have ulterior motives? But then I do have less than moral notions. I want Norah Walsh naked and under me so that I can make mad passionate love to her. Now. *Say something, Laurie. For the love of God, man, tell her what you are feeling.*

"Did you hear me, Laurie?" she asks quietly. "I'll need a reference, please. A good one? Even if you don't mean it."

"Of course I'll give you an excellent recommendation," I say with a heavy heart. "I would never have come through all of this without you. But I don't want to give it to you if it means that you'll leave Davenport Manor. Where will you go and what will I do without you?"

"The General said that he would help you come up with something. He also has promised to help me find something suitable. He's not the worst friend, I suppose. In the meantime I want to go home to Ireland. This war is all getting a bit much."

"Home?" I splutter. Norah will be miles and miles away and my heart won't cope. "And can he help you get work there?"

"Good references even from English toffs will help me no matter where I end up," Norah says.

"I thought you never wanted to go home?"

"Whatever gave you that idea?"

"Must have been something you said once upon a time." Hoping we don't start arguing again, I add, "Is there anything I could do to make you stay?"

"Try me with something, Laurie, and we'll see if it works."

I wish instantly that I knew what to say!

# Chapter 37

## Norah Walsh

Poor Laurie couldn't think of anything to make me stay. He simply stared with those lost gorgeous eyes and offered me some more tea. I'm glad he didn't manage to say what he was feeling – if he said he had feelings for me what would I have done?

Catholicism and the oppression I grew up with should have installed a more stoic attitude. But no! I'm a blubbering mess. Crying into handkerchiefs and snivelling into sleeves will only go unnoticed for so long. I stand and look out on the rain battering the gravel as the view from my favourite parlour window is as cloudy as the world seems.

"It's all going well. Do not lose faith now," Alice Longmire promises when we speak on the telephone.

I'm not sure how she considers a dead woman in a locked room in the middle of a military establishment a good thing. I was not an Eve Good supporter, but seeing her lifeless corpse was upsetting though there wasn't any blood when I saw her. I don't do blood very well. Never have! When I was a child I watched pigs get slaughtered and those sights were not nice at all.

"We are glad that you believe in honouring, serving and protecting your own." Alice goes on with the great speech I'm sure she's given many times to those she recruits.

I've always longed to hear about belonging to something powerful, and as she speaks I think of how I've felt drawn to something like the Sinful Roses all my life.

"The greater good," Alice Longmire says.

I can hear how unafraid she is of authority and how self-assuredly she can swear to "sort things once and for all for women everywhere".

I go along with the rhetoric.

"So," she concludes, "we'll be in touch."

*"But when?"* I ask, alarmed. This is not good enough. I have no time to lose. And is she suspicious of me?

"Just wait."

"But why the delay? You'd better remember that I came to the rescue. One good turn deserves another."

"Don't prod the bear while she's sleeping," she says. "We would have found Eve eventually."

"You don't even know what I want from you!"

"Look, we all know that you've found a taste for this work. We are in need of strong leadership now, Norah Walsh. Like some of us you've taken a shine to this way of life. We're not just a murdering wives club. As you can imagine, Norah, we're much more than that. We'll be in touch. Until then, get some rest."

As I put down the receiver, I should be exhilarated and happy, but all that I feel is a pang of love for Laurie Davenport.

Before I leave for London, I return to see Fredrick one last time. He's in good humour and I hope that perhaps he's in the mood to discuss my future in a sensible fashion.

"Suicide. Eve Good committed suicide," he says, puffing on a cigar. "And Charlotte Davenport is back but getting a divorce. No dead husbands apart from the poor blighters on the front. Job done, Norah Walsh. I don't know why you insist on annoying me here though. Have you not had any luck with becoming the wife of Laurie Davenport?"

I feel that there's a tiny hint of jealousy there but I shake my head and put us both out of our misery. "No. I'm leaving Davenport Manor. Now this is all over, the plan is to move on to better things. That is what I was promised."

Fredrick smokes on. "The mission was to seduce Laurie."

"Laurie is a good fellow," I start to explain. "But after Charlotte he needs someone who is his equal and who can … I don't know … be honest with him. I'm not that woman. Anyhow, I've too much to do. Too much ambition."

Fredrick shakes his finger. "No, Norah. No. From the day and hour you walked up to me at Wester's I've told you that you cannot join the women at war here. Even British women with impeccable references and reasons for enlisting in the war effort don't get in. You hate guns, blood and killing. You've not got the stomach for it! *And* you're Irish! I won't hear of it. Anyhow, aren't you enjoying playing detective right here? I'll not lie to Laurie if he asks me questions about what I know. Stop with these silly plans and go back to Laurie and fall into the role of being a good little wife. There's a good girl."

I slam the door on my way out. I want his head to be in the way and bash it, but he calls after me. "You'll be a good wife, Walsh. You'll be back."

I've been used. The bastard never had any intention of letting me better myself. He used my ambition against me.

The only person who hasn't taken advantage of me is Laurie, and I've taken advantage of his good nature. The tears come again. His fears and disability became a way for me to enhance my own situation. And now, he's still in the same chair, in the same parlour and not able to even see his beautiful home. If Eve Good hadn't spoken to us, she too might still be breathing. There's a lot I will have to answer for at the Pearly Gates.

# Chapter 38

## Laurie Davenport

Giles opens the door, places the tea tray on my lap and clicks off the music of Nat King Cole. "I miss Norah," I tell him. "It's been almost a month and not a word from her. I know that you're wonderful to me. But you're not Norah."

"I can try the Irish accent and wear strong perfume?" Giles places my hand on the china cup. "Can you manage from there, sir?"

"Thank you. But you might join me. There's nothing worse than drinking tea alone."

"Cook will have my hide but I'll linger for one cup."

We sip in silence for a time, him in his thoughts, me dreaming of Norah.

"Did Mrs Davenport get the divorce papers yet, sir?" Giles asks.

"Oh yes. Signed and all. We're almost free of one another."

"It took a long time to thrash out all the issues. It's a good thing I'm a bachelor," Giles muses and sips like a gentleman at his tea. "And there's been no mention of your other worries at all now?"

"About her trying to kill me?" I ask. "No. None. How did you put up with me?"

Giles goes still.

"I must have been so hard to live with. Going on and on about her attempts on my life and then all that silly business with the criminal Eve Good, Ravenscairn and the Murdering Wives Club."

"Was it a silly business, sir?" Giles says. "I did worry about you at the time but it was mainly because Mrs Davenport is well capable of all your accused her of. She is well capable of almost anything."

I love that Giles stands up for me. He's a true friend.

I want to tell him that but he adds, "What's this you were saying about Ravenscairn?"

"That Norah and the General's people were waiting to see an advertisement of a 'Ravenscairn location' in London or round about here. Apparently that was how murdering wives could contact the Sinful Roses and learn how to do it properly. Eve Good was a good storyteller. She somehow made the whole thing up so don't trouble yourself about it."

"Rightyo, sir."

I go to put the music back on.

"And you think it was all for nothing?" Giles asks.

"Yes. It seems that way. Eve knew nothing of note."

"What does General Ashfield think?"

"Norah said he was fine about it. Just glad that we're all safe and sound. I think he was glad that he didn't have to get married!"

"*Ha!*" Giles says. "And you were glad too I'd say, sir."

"I was, I am," I admit, picturing Norah lounging across my bed, her full lips ready to be kissed. "I didn't want her to marry anyone else."

"Or put herself in danger," Giles says.

"That's just it, there would have been no danger.

There was no organisation to try to get into," I explain slowly. I'm not sure what record is in my hands and it might be rude to ask Giles to read it for me for we're still talking. I set it down.

"And Mrs Davenport knowing Lady Dornan was just a coincidence?" he asks.

"Yes."

"And what does the General think about that?"

I hear Giles pouring more tea. I should return and sit with the man when he is good enough to keep me company.

"Freddie? I don't know what he's thinking. I've not bothered him since Norah left. Not bothered him for over a month."

"I think you should telephone General Ashfield though. If I were you I would get another man's opinion on all of this."

I sit with a flop. What on earth does he mean?

"I can tell by your face, sir, that you're confused. I just wonder what the General thinks about you giving up on this entirely? You cannot return to your work and I thought you were making great headway even if it was with that godawful criminal woman. I thought maybe you could continue being a detective? You've gone back to your old depressed ways this past month. Perhaps ask for Norah to come back? Or ask for more of that type of work? It gave you a purpose. We all need that."

"Have you forgotten that I'm blind? I had to leave the communication with the General to Norah," I explain. "It's another of my limitations. Calling someone is awkward. Perhaps we might practise."

"Let's do it this very minute."

"Finish your tea," I concede. "I have all day."

I drink and think on Giles' advice. I had made up my mind to make something of my future before Eve Good's suicide, and things then snowballed. Being involved in the investigation helped me and I wasn't bad at it. Perhaps I could ask Freddie to send Norah over, or ask him for seduction tips?

"Of course, I needed Norah to be effective in the work the General gave me. It stands to reason I'd give it up when she isn't available."

"I don't see why, sir."

"I'd need someone to take notes, to help me get about, to make telephone calls and the like ..." I stop and try to quell the sense of panic listing all the things I cannot do brings.

"You can overcome all of that," Giles says. "Look how you move around this room unaided. Who would have thought you could do that? Also, a friend of mine has a son in medical school, and he says that there are many men coming back blinded and they're putting programmes of learning together for them to help them rehabilitate."

"I could try those, I suppose," I say unenthusiastically. "Or I could find out where Norah is?"

"Is she gone for good?" Giles asks. "I ask because you've been listening to your music again and lingering in this chair. I know you have feelings for her and you should really do something to get her back."

How do I describe to him how I fear failing yet again? How do I explain my worry that she'll reject me? I shake my head. "I don't know, Giles. I don't know that I trust my feelings."

"Don't fret about it now. I just wondered what was

what. Making conversation, if you like. You can talk to me, you know. I realise that I'm a servant but I promised your parents to always look after you and ..." his voice shakes, "and with you losing your sight, it has killed a little part of me too. I wish to help you in whatever way I can."

I reach out for his arm and find his hand to squeeze. "Thank you. Norah has gone to see her family in Ireland. I don't know how long for. I don't think she'll ever come back and that does make me very sad. She has asked me for references, but I've not written any. I don't want her to leave."

"You don't want her to go for good." Giles slaps my arm. "That's good news. We'll convince her to come home to Davenport." He grips my hand but lets go of it before we lose sight of the stiff upper lip we have. "You've not finished your tea but let's telephone Fredrick Ashfield. It's still hard to believe that snotty-nosed brat I remember ruining the roses is a general!"

Freddie's secretary puts me through straight away.

"Was wondering when I'd hear from you," he says gruffly, and then whispers, "And how is my fiancée?"

"Norah?"

"Who else?" he asks, fluttering papers near the receiver. "I know she thinks it's all a wasted effort now that that bitch has done herself in and the women she mentioned seem clean as a whistle – but I don't know – I told her something was definitely up there."

I am astonished. "You did? She never told me that."

"Really?"

"You *do* know she's gone to see her family?"

"Yes. She asked. I agreed. Reluctantly. But she'll be back, Laurie. She's not gone for good."

"Did she ask you for a reference?" I ask.

"She's always threatening to leave the job. She and I argue like an old married couple but she never leaves. She has it too good here. Perhaps I'm slightly in love with her?"

"*Really?*" I gasp too loudly.

"I'm joking, Laurie," Freddie says slowly. "I wanted to hear your reaction. You poor old sod. You do have it bad for her, then?"

"I suppose I have." I want him to reiterate his lack of love for her again. I need to be sure he was joking. "I don't know how to be with a woman now."

"I bet you can't, old boy," Freddie whispers. "I look at them all and wonder if they might be one of these Sinful Roses."

"Didn't Norah say to you that we concluded that was all a ruse? That it was all a tall tale from Eve Good's overactive imagination?"

"No. Miss Norah Walsh has said nothing of the sort. For she knows what I would say. Before you started your investigation, something or someone was killing men on home soil. And now it has all stopped."

"Stopped?" I venture. "Since we started questioning Eve?"

"Exactly."

"And you think Eve was telling the truth?"

"You were the people who spent hours reading the woman's words. What do you think?" Freddie sounds impatient and there is noise in the background on his end. People calling him away.

"I believed Eve's accounts," I say, holding the bridge of my nose. "But then I am a soft fool as we both know.

And Eve didn't give us any proof really, did she? And the police didn't believe it?"

"Who do you think sent the case to me!" Freddie says. "They didn't have the manpower to deal with it but they all felt one of their own, Sergeant John Good, was murdered. I think their gut instinct was there was more to it all and that when Eve started singing about the Murdering Wives Club – well, it all made sense to them."

"*Fuck me!*" I say for there is no other way to express this mess. "I got the impression from Norah that she concluded Eve had invented it all for her own purposes!"

Freddie is called harshly by someone. I really hope he stays on the line even though my head is bursting and I don't want to be thinking that my soon-to-be-ex-wife is a killer again.

"Perhaps I should question Charlotte or Lady Dornan?" I say. "By myself? If it is a waste of time, then I'll not look silly in front of Norah. Giles thinks I can do much more things on my own from now on too."

"He's right, the old codger! But going alone to speak to two women you think might be out to get you into a coffin … is *not* a good idea?"

"True … the only other avenue is that we find a Ravenscairn location locally and go watch it or go with Norah's plan."

"Does that mean my freedom is on the chopping-block again?" Freddie asks with a chuckle.

"Without Norah we are both lonesome men," I say, forlorn. Everything is in a complete muddle.

"Ask Giles what he thinks, old boy," Fredrick says. "We men need to stick together at times like these. Listen, I've got to go. Keep up the good work."

"When will Norah be back?" I ask.

"I've no idea. She said that you were in charge now. I laughed and let her go. I think she's running rings around you, Laurie. Pull that woman into line once she gets back. I think it's about time that you show her who's boss."

"Of course I will. I'll show her who's boss," I say.

I'm confident about that reply for all of three seconds.

# Chapter 39

## Laurie Davenport

The morning's post is sitting unopened on the table. It's been a week since Freddie's motivational telephone conversation, but without Norah I'm still at a loss. I am torn. I really doubt that there's any truth to Eve's tales about murdering women, but something niggles in the back of my mind that maybe I'm wrong.

I've opened the briefcase clasp. I've not been able to read the files and I've raked though my memory to find something or anything of note for the Sinful Roses case. Giles has also switched off the music. He doesn't like my taste.

He's still tidying around and I can hear him tutting about something.

"What is it?" I ask.

"Norah has bundles of newspapers and magazines stuffed here and there. They are everywhere!" he says, making a racket of noise with the paper. "I think I'll move them out of here – stack them up on a shelf somewhere."

The telephone rings in the hall and he goes to answer it.

A minute or so later he is back. "That was the General," he says. "He's wondering why you haven't phoned him about the letter he sent over. I knew you should have let me read those letters on the table for you. Freddie wishes you to open them and then telephone him back."

I nod, curious as to what made Freddie contact me.

Giles sits at my desk and rips the first envelope open with my silver letter opener. I hear the slice.

"A bill," he says, and the process goes on. "Papers from the solicitor … Word about your pension – we can deal with that later. Here's the one he means."

There's a slice through paper and an intake of breath.

"Is it Norah?" I ask, on the edge of my seat.

Giles must be reading for he doesn't answer.

"Giles, is it from Norah? Charlotte? Who?"

"It's from Eve Good," Giles says, and he coughs. "Isn't she dead?"

"She's supposed to be."

"Hang on – let me read on and then I'll read it out to you," Giles says. "I'm a slow reader."

I nod agreement but sense he's not taken his eyes off the page. The wait is endless. What on earth is going on? What is Eve writing to me about? And from the grave?

"*Giles!*" I hiss. "Hurry up, for pity's sake!"

"Sweet divine!" Giles says under his breath.

"This not seeing is driving me insane! Giles, read it to me – *now*. I cannot wait any longer."

"We may need brandy," Giles says, "but here goes."

He begins to read.

'"*The Sunny Morning of 8th July 1944*

*My dearest Mr Davenport,*

*I hope this letter finds you well. I asked that it be delivered upstairs and I asked that it be then sent directly to you. I am not stupid and know that despite all of my protestations my other letters go through official channels and are read by others. But I've asked that this be just for you. I wanted to post it but of course I have no address. It is my dying wish and I am* fulfilled now that the truth is out there and written down or shared – I have a sense of achievement. Also, I wanted to thank you for having me brought to this place where it is pleasant and I can see the sunlight.

You are a kind person. I could tell that the day we met. Not many people are. I suppose you have to spend more time listening now that you cannot see. It makes you patient and understanding. I've spent hours with my eyes closed and I cannot imagine how it is for you full-time. I rarely care about how life is for others, but I made an exception for the handsome, blind man with the scars and nice suit that doesn't fit him. There is something special about you, Mr Davenport. I did find your injuries ugly but I didn't pity you because there is nothing worse than pity. Am I right?

Back to the full purpose of this correspondence. I've been told that you will not visit me here. This saddens me as yet again fate will not let us speak. I suspect, Mr Davenport, that it will not be long until I am sent back to the gaol. My tale is told and I will be cast aside or will be thrust amongst the other bitches in Armagh. I'm not a criminal like the rest in there. I am nothing like them. I worry too that I've been brought here so that I can be murdered in my prison by the Sinful Roses for speaking about them. This is unacceptable. I cannot stomach the thought of the Sinful Roses winning. I simply cannot have that. In reflecting on all that has happened, my greatest fear has surfaced. I wonder did this happen to you on the battlefield? Did you get a glimpse of the one regret, the one fear you had when you were close to death? I've uncovered my fear and it is that you don't believe me. I laughed for a long time at that. But it's true I'm worried that you changed your mind about me and my account of things. If no-one knows of my brilliance, then my life will have been for nothing. That would just be the most awful thing. I must admit that I did lie to you a little. I think deep down, in the case of John, it was just the killing which interested me, rather than killing him in particular. Then, Frank Hockley made me see red on more than one occasion. He really was a vile man! But it was for no great purpose or reason. I just wanted to do it and it thrills me still to think of it. Isn't that terrible?

I hope you got to hear all of my exploits in my other letters. However, I've not heard from you and I've told you everything and suddenly I feel very vulnerable and uneasy. I'm worried that either you aren't aware of the other letters, or that you think I am deranged? I also am worried that you don't believe women are capable of such thoughts and deeds? I fear that is why the Sinful Roses have stayed hidden for so long. There is no consideration given to the depravity of the female mind and heart. Perhaps it is a good thing that we are considered above men in such matters? But then, the Sinful Roses would win, and I cannot have that! It is all true. All of it! The Sinful Roses have always been on this earth and will always be amongst us. I'm far from perfect. I'm far from Good, but I rarely lie.

I also want to say this, Laurie. I swear it with all my heart. John Good FELL down those stairs. I owe the Roses nothing. I just wanted to walk away then from all of the urges I had, but they were not happy. I firmly believe it was they who drove me to those other crimes. They put pressure me and then, to silence me, they tried to kill me. They will do so again. If they hear I am alive they will not rest. I promise you that too. Lydia Dornan and Alice Longmire are Sinful Roses. Every Rose knows that death is the only reason for being a Sinful Rose and is also the only way to leave.

By the way, I never liked that Norah. If it is she who is reading this then she will learn how I feel about her. But I don't *care. She possibly won't read you this next bit, but I pray that by some stroke of luck it is someone else reading these words for you. You couldn't see the way Norah looked at me. I closed my eyes to her because I thought she'd kill me with her looks alone. If she is not a Sinful Rose, then I'll eat my hat! I saw that you wore a wedding ring and that she didn't. You called her Miss Walsh, but I hope that you're not thinking of marrying her? I could tell that you have a fondness for each other. I only hope that Norah is not your fiancée.*

*I hope that somehow you get to hear my words. I pray that you listen. You should worry about women killing men. Look at me. We exist.*

*I don't want to die alone. My spirit will always watch out for you, because you were respectful. But, Mr Davenport, I am depending on you to bring this to a happy or at least satisfactory conclusion. I trust in you as I hope you trust in me,*

*Your friend in life and death,*
*Eve Kanaster*

Giles throws the letter on the table.

I breathe deeply. The birds in the garden sound very loud.

# Chapter 40

## Norah Walsh

I've at last been summoned by the Sinful Roses. In my initial 'application' I wrote that I'm unmarried and with no reason to hurt anyone, and my need for them is sheer ambition to learn and find purpose in my life. Several phone conversations with Alice Longmire followed as she vetted me. She sounded positive but she didn't commit to taking me on.

The whole process made me nervous. But they still want me because a second summons has just arrived.

*Attend Sinful Roses meeting 11th August 1944. Eleven o'clock. At 208 Kensington High St, Kensington, London.*

There's a nice feeling behind the terrifying one. Finally, I'm accepted. The scary thoughts come from the fact that there'll be no going back now. I will just have to go and meet with them.

Like others before me I'm looking for something greater than myself. I need to be more than a wife and mother lingering in a kitchen. Lady of a Manor isn't even enough! Leaving Ireland, I knew I'd find it hard if not impossible to return to the place of my birth. I have outgrown Meath. This is more like the place I saw myself. In charge, in control and making something meaningful happen in my life.

"Too big for her boots," the women outside Mass in Ireland would say. "She's got notions about herself."

That would be exactly right. I want this more than anything.

I look at the swirling handwritten note and think on Eve's first description about going to Ravenscairn to meet with the murdering wives. She was bored, she wanted to belong and she saw the Sinful Roses as an exciting diversion to her mundane life.

Right now, I understand that. I'm sinking and the Roses feel like a life-raft. I'm no longer in Davenport Manor, or in the arms of a lord or a general. The poky flat I'm in smells of damp and the bombs come closer and closer. The sirens screech through the night and the fearful time in the Underground is just giving me time to dream of a way out of being a terrified woman alone.

I'm tired of trying to thrive in a man's world. Let's see how it goes being in a woman's one. With the Roses, how will my life be? The curiosity is killing me. What will they expect of me?

What was it Alice Longmire said? *"We all know that you've found a taste for this work. Like some of us you've taken a shine to the thrill of it all. The Roses need good leaders now, Norah Walsh."*

Being a leader of like-minded women sounds good to me. I'll go where I'm wanted the most. Turning my back on my own is what I do, but something tells me that ignoring the Roses is not a sensible thing to do.

Laurie's handsome smile is in my mind as I put on my lipstick in the mirror and dab the last of my perfume between my breasts. In going to meet with these women, I might also find out if Laurie is still on their list. If I could steer their wrath elsewhere, it would be a good thing. Learning all I can about them will help me keep Laurie safe. This is what I tell myself as I put on my coat and fix my hat.

I cross the road to catch the bus. What is it I heard my mother say when I was a little girl? "Say what you like about those Sinful Roses, but they have my respect. They've got power and isn't that just what we all need? And may God Himself grant them all that they need to help others."

I could pretend that I'm on this bus to help Laurie and other needy men and women but, to be honest, it is the word 'power' that's ringing in my ears. For once, just once, Norah Walsh would like to be the most powerful person in a room.

# Chapter 41

## Laurie Davenport

"Sir, I've just noticed something. The word *Ravenscairn*. It's circled on this newspaper – one of the papers Norah had. The ones I removed from this room."

"*What?*" I gasp.

"I was having a look through them and I spotted it."

My emotions flicker and fade.

"Read it," I say.

"Very well, sir. It says: '*Friends of the Sinful Roses be advised that a Ravenscairn House is open. Send personal details to c/o Sinful Roses PO Box 77 at 208 Kensington High St, Kensington, London. Appointments will be given if investigations establish need.*'"

I am stunned. She has deceived me.

"We must go there, Giles. We must go there now."

"How, sir? How do we get there? And why are we going?"

"We watch and wait. Well, you watch and I wait." I get to my feet and head for the door. "Call us a hire car and perhaps we should call Freddie."

Freddie doesn't come to the phone but I press his secretary to let me speak with him. "It's urgent. A matter of life and death."

"Is this about Eve's letter?" he asks when he comes on

the line. "Isn't it worrying? When you made enquiries I sent it on so that you might be wary again for your safety. I told Norah that we shouldn't have kept it from you."

"She wanted to keep it from me?" I say as my heart sinks to my feet. "Freddie, Giles found Norah has circled the very thing she told me she couldn't find. The Ravenscairn location that exists in London. She lied to me that there was no mention of it in the papers! Do you think ... I cannot believe that she has anything to do with the Sinful Roses. Please tell me that she's not kept anything more from me?"

"Women cannot be trusted. Why do you think I'm single at my age? But I trust Norah implicitly. Sit tight, my good man. I promise you that all will be well. I know Norah and she may be hiding secrets but she has her reasons. Just tell Giles to get that pistol out from under his pillow and listen out for intruders. Be vigilant. All should be all right."

"Sometimes all right just isn't good enough," I say, exhausted. "I want my sight back and I need to stop getting teary at everything."

Freddie coughs – he's not wishing to talk about emotions. "It looks like your friend, Eve Kanaster, was worried you wouldn't believe her. She was quite taken with you, Laurie. One good thing is that you still seem to have a way with the ladies!"

"I seem to be a soft touch for criminal women, you mean!"

"Ah now, Laurie, that is the old nonsense talk returning. You've made great progress with Eve Good and finding a new role for yourself."

"Yes, even before the letter, I was finding it hard to

think of Eve dying alone in her room. I've thought of suicide, Freddie, but I never could have gone through with it."

"Good, good." Freddie sounds distant, like he has heard too much from me.

"Before you go, Freddie, why would Norah not tell me about the advertisement? She knew I couldn't read the papers. She knows I cannot see and would possibly never know about it. I am devastated, Freddie. I feel cheated. More than that. I am betrayed."

"I'm not the man to talk to about all of this. All I know is, Laurie, you're going to be all right. You just have to give all of this time and trust Norah."

"Time?"

"And patience! Please just wait and have faith. Now, I really must go. I hope that you'll consider writing all of this out for my reports when Norah comes back."

"Eve would like that," I whisper, for as odd as it sounds I miss her. "She respected me and didn't pity me. Eve Good trusted me and told me the truth. Every other woman in my life since this blasted war has let me down in some way."

I hang up the phone without waiting on Freddie to speak.

"Giles, get our coats and hire a car, for we are going to Ravenscairn."

We get to the address and Giles watches the front door like a hawk. Nothing of note is happening and his impatience with me is making me even more nervous.

"What's happening now?" I ask.

"Nothing has changed and the driver has taken off for a walk as he's had enough of sitting outside an abandoned house for hours at a time!" Giles replies. "I don't blame him. This is pointless."

We've tried to keep explanations to a minimum and are paying him handsomely.

Rain comes and goes and nothing happens.

I think of some help from my morphine. "A slippery slope," Norah would say. "You don't want to depend on these things."

I can understand Eve's anger and total rebellion. I want to do the total opposite of what Norah would wish me to do. On purpose I want to hurt her, the way she's hurt me.

"I don't know what to think any more," I say to Giles as I tap my cane off the back of the seat in thought. I'm on edge. "Something's not right. I can feel it. You know when you just know? I might be blind but I know there's more to this."

"The letter was simply awful," Giles says. "You've taken to blaming yourself for things that are out of your control again. Cook has sent sandwiches and I can smell the egg and onion."

"Have one," I say and even though my stomach growls I cannot face one. "I'm not hungry."

"Sweet Lord," Giles says suddenly. "That lady looks like she's going in and her so prim and proper. Oh no. She's just looking, she has walked on."

"And they definitely cannot see us here?" I hiss. "They don't know we are watching the house?"

"I cannot see how they would," Giles says.

"What does it look like? The house, I mean?"

"For the fifth time. It's an ordinary terraced Georgian house on an ordinary street with nothing distinguishing about it."

"And there is no-one at the windows? Going inside? Nothing happening?"

"No. Nothing. Absolutely nothing. This is a waste of time."

I let out a long and bitter sigh. I don't want to think about what we are doing here at all. I want to go back to the time when I had peace of mind, believing that these Sinful Roses were the figment of a madwoman's imagination. When I was safe, when I was almost normal again.

"Wait, there is movement by the front door," Giles says. "Two women have gone inside. What will we do now?" He dithers in the seat, moving and screeching across the leather. "Let's call the police!"

"And say what?" I snap. "We must follow them inside."

"We can't do that!" Giles says, highly incredulous. "What if they see us?"

"We've got to do something!" I say, fumbling for the door handle. "We need to find out what they're doing. What good are we sitting here?"

"We are alive by staying right here," Giles says. "And it's lashing rain. Let's wait out this shower. It's torrential. Can't you hear it on the roof?"

"For the love of God, man, we are detectives. We're men on an important case. A spot of rain shouldn't bother us. Does a tiny spot of rain stop our fighting heroes from doing their duty?" I'm most annoyed at his lacklustre reaction to the situation. "Get a move on, my good man, and help me out of this vehicle."

"I have no umbrella! We'll be soaked!"

"For pity's sake!"

Giles has no idea what a real wetting is like. As a Royal Engineer in the heart of an Italian winter, I know what it is to be cold and bitterly soaked through with snow, mud and blood. "Help me get across the road, this instant!" I order like an officer.

Getting out of the automobile onto a footpath streaming with rain takes us far too long. Giles is unused to helping me and I stumble and catch the tail of my coat in the door. It's farcical and we're thoroughly drenched before we start on the small expedition of walking across a road. Being arm in arm with a man feels odd and my cheeks flush despite the rain and cold day. We must look a queer sight.

My feet squelch for Giles walked me into the drain. But we make it up the path and steps quietly. I motion for Giles to go inside and he falters for a second until I elbow him. The knob turns and he stands in and drags me after him. There is a pleasant smell from the air and I realise it is perfume. A mixture of a few scents.

The voices take us to the right and then Giles draws me by the elbow until I am facing a wall. I see a large lighter space to our left and guess it is a doorway. Voices emerge.

Giles' whisper is no more than a breath close to my ear. "Stay still, sir. But if anyone begins to come out or in from outside, I will pull you quickly to our right under a stairway where we will be hidden. It is dark out here in the hallway."

I nod and strain to listen.

# Chapter 42

## Norah Walsh

Alice has just finished arranging wooden chairs in a room illuminated only by some weak ceiling lightbulbs. The blackout blinds are closed tight, letting in – or out – not a chink of light. With my help she has also placed a table and two chairs on a podium at the top of the room – for the chairwoman and the secretary, she says.

Now that everything is fixed to her satisfaction, she lights up a cigarette in a long holder and lights a cigarette.

She takes a long hard look at me and points to a chair. "Sit yourself down. Don't look so nervous. Everything is under control. Eve Good is no more. Though we may have to go to ground for a while."

I nod, longing for a smoke or drink to settle my nerves.

"But eventually we'll be able to come out of the shadows and meet again."

I want to query everything, from her own motivations to her ambitions. But she's like a stern headmistress the way she's standing, taking a puff from her cigarette in its long holder and then folding her arms again.

"I like the sounds old houses make," she says. "Do you hear that? The creaks and groans of timbers and the sigh of a house settling into its own peace. Makes me feel safe. Thistleforth is a fine house. Not like this dump. But Eve wasn't safe where she was at all – was she?" Her eyes look murderous in this gloomy room. "Nowhere is safe from the Sinful Roses."

The hairs on my arms stand on end and a shiver traces down my spine. She wants to talk about it. The very thing I want to forget and move on from – she wants to relive it!

"It was thanks to you that she was taken miles from any system that might have protected her in the past. She was dragged across an ocean right into my clutches." She laughs. "Everything went so smoothly! Like clockwork. The clearing of the desks and corridors, the blacking out of windows happened right on time – just as our inside source had informed us. Then the activity settled down, almost all lights went out, and there was nothing but silence. And I moved in, with my keys and my map of the layout. I was so eager to get to her corridor. I wanted her to be awake. I wanted her to know I was coming for her, to hear the opening of gates, and locks, the sound of a woman's heels in the corridor – not sounding like the normal guards. And she did. That makes me so happy."

There's a pause in her remembering where I could ask her to stop but I don't. I even smile, encouraging her to confess the awfulness to me.

"I was excited – as you can imagine. I'd waited years to get that bitch. But I hid and waited for another ten minutes to make sure it was all possible without witnesses."

My breath heaves in my chest. Holding it, I listen hard. Like my life depends on it. There is nothing to do but listen.

"No mistakes with knives or weapons she shouldn't have. I fashioned a spring into a sort of weapon," she says, looking at her hand as if her fingers were curling around it. "The sharp end looked like it might cut me if I lashed out carelessly because the metal turned back against my fist but nothing was going to stop the Roses this time. I turned the key in the lock of the door carefully but it creaked as it turned. It felt like it echoed over the corridor and I gripped my weapon and waited. The bed inside squeaked. *"Come on in, you bitches, and let's get this over with!"* Eve said into the blackness. I almost laughed at her fake bravery. She was alone and scared. I stepped in and closed the door behind me without a word. She threatened to scream but she didn't."

Alice stops and looks at me.

"Do you know, I think she lost her voice then. She just seemed to freeze."

I fumble to open a button in my blouse because I need air. Imagining how Eve was feeling is not difficult. It is nightmarish. But Alice needs to tell me this. Her success needs praise.

"Go on," I say with a fear that she'll do this to me someday and I'd better know what to expect. I swallow hard and hold my breath.

"She said words like 'please' and 'don't' but they came out as a whisper. She pissed herself. I could smell it."

I gasp.

Alice enjoys shocking me. She smiles broad and long.

"Relax. Her back was to the wall then and I touched the foot of the bed and didn't say a thing. It was dark and I had to squint to see her fully. She rabbited on about not knowing anything at all. Not letting the Roses down.

The whites of her eyes were bright. The flash of her teeth. But I was as quick as lightning. I held her arms rigid and she crumpled downwards so I could kneel on her chest. She was winded and barely able to breathe. She was angry, agitated and very scared."

She stops. I meet her gaze with my own then, even though I can hardly bear to look at her enjoyment as she talks. She's about to tell me how she killed another human being and, although it should disgust me, I'm enthralled.

When Alice is sure that I'm listening, she continues, "I bent and pressed my nose against her cheek. She smelt clean. She tried to toss me off but I held firm. I was devil-like!" She blew a smoke-ring. "She begged me to stop but I didn't. I was so angry for all she'd put us through. I was spitting in temper when I told her how I'd found her and how I'd kill her."

I gulp back the anguish in my chest. This is worse than reading Eve's accounts. It's much worse and yet I smile.

"No matter how hard she struggled, I had her!" Alice says. "Then the bitch tried to bite me. Like a dog she snapped her teeth but I was quick and she didn't catch my skin. But that made me thump her hard over and over. She said your name. She blamed you for it all."

"Unlike Eve Good, I know where my loyalties should lie," I say in a shaky voice. "I promised to help and I did. I kept you well informed."

"I hurt her good and proper for cursing you," Alice says, pointing her cigarette at me. "She squirmed when I hurt her. I held that cold metal against the soft side of her neck. Near her ear. Here." She points to her own throat. "The spring was sharp. The slicing sensation almost felt like it wasn't happening for a second and then I pierced through the skin with the movement of the cut. Warmth flowed out onto my hands and she struggled and gagged but the instrument was deep. It was lodged and stuck somewhere under her chin. The coil of the spring was slick and slippery but she managed to get a grip on it somehow. I had to move off her but once she wrenched the metal out I could see she was done for. There was blood everywhere. We had won, Norah. Thanks to you, Eve Good lay in her own blood and piss and I told her that we had won. It was a fucking good feeling."

I grip my hands in my lap to stop them from trembling and I'm about to speak when the door at the far corner of the room opens and in marches Lydia Dornan and Charlotte Davenport.

# Chapter 43

## Laurie Davenport

I cannot see Giles and I cannot move. What in God's name have we just heard? A woman recounting Eve's murder? And was that Norah's voice? It cannot be! Everything inside me curls up and almost dies. Whatever hope I had left is scrunched up in the knots forming in my gut.

Suddenly Giles hauls me to the right, pushes my head down and pulls me into a very dark space. We are under the stairs he mentioned.

Voices and the clicking of heels on tiles signal the arrival of the Sinful Roses. This goes on intermittently for quite a while and the volume of voices in the meeting room rises all the time. At last there is a sudden hush and then a loud authoritative voice begins to speak. We stay where we are until we feel no other Roses are likely to arrive. Then Giles draws me out of our hiding place by the elbow and we return to our previous position to the right of the doorway.

I want so badly to see what is happening, but then in other ways I don't want to. We have come inside this den of sin, like Eve did, and I almost feel her at my other elbow, holding me in place to witness what she wants me to hear.

The voice is still speaking.

"We won't dilly-dally with this," says Lady Dornan. "Our Sinful Roses' informant was right to plan this meeting. It was necessary. We have to make plans for the future. Now that the whole world almost fell in around our ears, we must agree on a way forward for the future. Thank you for coming all this way, Alice. This is a very dangerous time. But then, when did women like us shirk from danger? However, we must do so now. We must protect each other and ourselves at all costs. The fact that we are being investigated is a terrible shock and we need to stop any further bother landing on our doorsteps."

Giles' breathing is heavy. The noise of our hearts must be audible.

"There will be no more Sinful Roses for now and we'll have to change the advertisement and house names in the future," she continues with authority. "This has been done before in our history so don't lose heart. I have to tell you though that this is the last time we will meet for a long time. I know it is a sad day for us and I understand that it will make people unhappy. If we are not careful we run the risk of being found out. The amount of applications is low presently and this is a good time for us to pack things away. We must protect ourselves."

There are disapproving murmurs. My stomach heaves. She sounds very much in charge.

"I warned you all that the killing of too many military men was not a good idea," comes Alice's voice. "And it was I who never wanted Eve Good involved. Can I please have that noted, yet again? Eve Good was not one of us, and never was. We should have known better. But she blinded us with her sob-story."

"And there have been far too many problems recently," Lady Dornan says. "There will always be those who are unstable but Eve's legacy has plagued us for many years. Of course, there are women who cannot go through with the deed but Eve was determined from the beginning to be a rotten egg. Charlotte, you are not like Eve Good. Please don't look so worried. You have stayed the course, my dear."

I sway against Giles and he grips my arm.

"Despite being under pressure from us all, the police, and your husband, you have been loyal to the Sinful Roses. I want it noted that Charlotte Davenport has stepped up to the mark with regards to her work for the last six months. She has done all that was asked of her and never uttered a word about us to anyone. Charlotte Davenport, we're relieving you of your duty to us tonight. Thank you for the loyalty and support you have given to us. Yes, it is your case that is causing the problems we are facing, but it is not your fault, Charlotte dear. We all want to thank you."

I almost sink to my knees. I cannot take much more of this eavesdropping. Giles' grip tightens.

I hear Charlotte say, "Thank you for your kind words, Lydia. But I do think it's appropriate now to thank the one who came out of nowhere to help and guide us. Writing to warn us and helping us with this evening and other important tasks recently."

There is a round of applause.

"I, for one, would have been lost without her help and support," says Charlotte.

"Yes, Charlotte," Lydia says loudly. "Of course Norah Walsh's work should be acknowledged here today."

I shudder. Giles puts a supportive arm about me and I lean against him.

"You steered Charlotte's husband away from me and the Roses. We understand that it cannot have been easy listening to Eve talk about us. We also appreciate the danger you put yourself in to expose all of this to us. We are forever in your debt, Norah. Thank you for being an honourable woman."

Tears fall from my chin. I don't want to listen any more.

"And for bringing us news of the definite death of Eve Good," another voice says. "Now that bitch is what nearly sunk us. And it was sheer luck that someone blind, with no confidence or training was working on the case."

"Your being there every step of the way helped steer things, Norah," Charlotte says.

I wipe the droplets off but Giles must see them. What an utter fool I've been. I sniffle and Giles stiffens. It was louder than I anticipated. There's a lull in conversation in the room. I hold my breath.

"And you convinced the cripple that all of this was a lie and in his head!" Lady Dornan adds. "What a clever girl you are!"

I cannot breathe. All this time Norah was a Sinful Rose! My feet move by themselves and I reverse into what was space behind me when we came in. Giles guides me out and when the air hits my nostrils I suck it in and lean on my knees.

"We need to keep moving," Giles says, pulling me on. "I fear they heard us and we need to get to a telephone."

# Chapter 44

## Norah Walsh

"What an unholy effing mess!" I say to Fredrick's grin through the bars at the police station. "Get me out of here."

"You'll have to wait, just like any ordinary murdering whore," he replies with a gleam to his eye. "And giving me evil stares like that isn't going to help prove your innocence."

"I am innocent!" I hiss at him, making the grip on the cold steel tighter. "I went there to catch them – not be one of them."

"That's your story," he teases. "It's a pity Laurie ruined your work as a double agent."

"How is he?" I ask, breathing heavily. "He must've got a terrible shock."

"Fine. Angry no doubt," Fredrick says, fixing one of his brass buttons and picking fluff off his jacket sleeve.

"And what about you? What do you think?" I ask cautiously. "It was you who gave me this assignment in the first place. This is all your fault, you know. What are Lydia and Charlotte saying?"

"Nothing. They know better than to spout about another Sinful Rose. They'll be worried about their own throats."

"Fredrick, stop it! You know I'm not one of them. Stop teasing me and get me out of here!" My heart is thumping that hard I can feel it hopping about in my chest but I breathe deeply. There's little proof of any wrongdoing on any of our parts. Lydia has done her time in prison and Charlotte's husband is sitting in Davenport Manor. There's no solid evidence that Alice Longmire even knew Eve Good, never mind killed her. Much as I'm anxious, my brain is settling into the hope that this is almost over and there's nothing men can do against us all.

I take to smiling at Fredrick like I want to seduce him if he opens the locked gates that are keeping me from my freedom. I'd do damn near anything to get out of here, that's for sure and he knows it. What is Laurie thinking? There's a stab to my guilty heart to think of him. Again, Laurie is a casualty of circumstance.

"I was just at a meeting. We've committed no crimes. What does Laurie think?" I ask, sinking backwards into the cold cell and onto the thin mattress on the low bed. My hands go into my hair. "We caught Charlotte and Lydia, I suppose. But we don't have much proof. Other than our testimonies of what we heard them admit to. But there's not much else is there? Laurie has ruined my work."

"Exactly," Fredrick says. "It was my fault. I sent him Eve's letter as he asked me what I thought. I always felt he should know about it and so I sent it. My fault, I know. I've explained this to him on the telephone and told him there's nothing to be done now. I'd advise you both to let these women off to do whatever they do. Unless we get proof of their direct involvement in murders, our hands are tied – for now at least. We must walk away."

"And …" I say, "when you say for now, does this mean you will let me continue this work?"

Fredrick comes closer to the bars and says, "Someone has to keep an eye on these dangerous women. Does that make you happy, Norah? I thought you'd be running home to Ireland and to safety."

"You really mean it? You really mean that I'll have a role at Thistleforth House?" I ask, peering at Fredrick. "You'll let me stay on the case of the Sinful Roses? Be a detective for you? Really?"

"Well, let's see if there's a need for all that. There'll probably be no more about it after we've scared them sufficiently. I'd say there'll be no more of that silly rabble in the future. I cannot see them bothering us further."

"But I'll be consulted if they show up again? Please say yes, Fredrick? Go on!"

"I'm sure that's the last we'll hear of this murdering wives club! But ... I do know somewhere where you can do a good job." He raises his eyebrow and adds, "You need to get back to Davenport Manor as soon as possible. You'll go, won't you? Laurie will want you back once he knows the truth. I'm sure of it."

"Let me out of here!" I snap and try not to leap into his arms in gratitude when the gate is opened. I look around the great walls and small space and thank God for my release.

It seems that Giles and Laurie were not privy to all of the meeting. They didn't hear the first few minutes where I made an oath to be a Sinful Rose forever more. If they did, I'd never be allowed back in Davenport Manor.

My mouth is dry and I feel weak as water. Walking out towards the front door, I realise that I've had a lucky escape. But, as the cold air hits me, something tells me that I'm far from being a free woman. Much as Fredrick thinks they've all gone away, I know damn well that I'm a Sinful Rose now. And death, in one way or another, is my only escape.

"Does Laurie want to see me?" I ask, worrying myself sick.

"We'll have to explain things to him. Talk him around a bit," Fredrick says, marching for the main door to the street. "But there's no better woman to do that now, is there?" He winks and slightly taps my arse.

I stretch to put on my coat and breathe a deep sigh of relief when I hear Fredrick suggest, "How about I just take you home to Davenport and we take it from there?"

# Chapter 45

## Laurie Davenport

I'm by the window in Davenport Manor, letting the sun warm my knees, when Giles comes in with the jingling china teacups on the trolley. It seems that an aging Giles doesn't trust himself to carry a tray any more. I feel for him. We are all falling apart in so many ways. Time and life itself is cruel. What is the point of anything?

Despite all of Freddie's protestations about what went on in Kensington, his words have not sunk in. He taps my knee again to waken me from my wide-awake nightmare.

"Are you there, Laurie?" he asks, all joyful. "We unmarried or divorced fellows must stick together, eh? You too, Giles. Bachelors should be given medals for stamina in the face of pressure to marry!" He snorts and Giles chuckles. "Thank you for the tea, ol' boy. It might help the mood in this room. It's like a funeral in here. Laurie, you do know that you are safe now? And this whole sorry thing is sorted once and for all? Mission completed!"

*"Fuck you, Freddie!"* I snap. He knows full well that I did sweet damn all to rescue myself or the situation. "I did nothing and well you know it. And you just let those women walk free." I gesture widely with my arms, wondering where I might land a good hard thump on someone to ease this aggravation.

"Don't be so cross," Freddie groans. "All of this would have gone unnoticed had you not been so adamant that Charlotte tried to kill you. You were right and I never doubted that. Not once and you don't give me one bit of credit for being the best friend in the world to you, old boy! Not one bit of credit do you give!" He flips his fingers off my arm in a playful way. I long to punch him good and proper. "You're not to blame yourself for any of this, Laurie. It has all worked out fine. Like I promised. Didn't I tell you it would all be fine?"

"Fine?" I say, breathless. "How in the name of God is any of this fine?"

"Not one man was murdered," Freddie jokes. "It's always a good day when no-one we know dies."

"Stop being foolish! And if you had trusted me through all of this, I would look a lot less foolish too," I say, holding back some threatening tears.

"I know Norah and I should have told you the truth, Laurie. But really you aren't detective material, are you, old chap? If you had stayed on at the Ravenscairn house you would have seen the police raid the place. They took Charlotte, Lady Dornan and Alice Longmire away. Norah did amazing work to get them all there at the one time. It tooks weeks of preparation. Which you almost destroyed, I might add. But thankfully, they know what's what now."

"I should have known what you were both doing!" I say. "You should have told me. And nothing happened to those women! Not a thing. Their names aren't even in the paper. It's a disgrace!"

"Now, Laurie, even I didn't know exactly what Norah had planned. That was the whole point. The fewer people who knew the better. Especially you. You're not good at keeping secrets."

"Giles and I heard Alice Longmire admit to the most heinous of crimes. I mean really! Walking free? Murdering women. Is there no justice!"

"For justice there must be a proven crime."

"Stop talking, Freddie. I am seething!"

"Well, that's good news. Shows you are still with us and well in body and spirit."

"Dear God, I really want to break your nose, Freddie! And you sent Norah here under false pretences."

"Norah being here in Davenport Manor and infiltrating the Roses meant I knew you were safe and also what those bitches were up to," Freddie says. "But there's little we can do to them without solid proof. Norah did her damnedest – but such is life."

"You toy about with people's lives," I say, spittle leaving with the words.

"We just thought it for the best that you weren't involved at the very end. That's all."

"*All?*" I start shouting. "*All!* Norah convinced me it was all in my head. She tricked me! I cared for her and she lied to me constantly."

"She didn't lie to you constantly, Laurie. That's most unfair! When she left she just didn't tell you where she was going. That was for the best. You couldn't have gone to the Ravenscairn house with her anyhow. Stop making a mountain out of this tiny molehill."

"Molehill!"

"And what would you have done there? You almost ruined all of her hard work. You should not have been there! It's a Murdering Wives Club, Laurie, and the last time I looked you're not someone's wife."

"Neither is Norah."

"She had the brainwave to write them a warning letter and say she would keep them informed. She built trust."

*"She's good at that!"* I shout again. *"How long was she playing with me? From the beginning?"*

Freddie coughs.

Giles hands me a teacup and says, "Sir, I think Norah was always building trust with everyone. Including me. Don't annoy yourself unduly. I think at heart Norah is a good woman."

"Is that supposed to make me feel better? Am I supposed to feel better that you were fooled by her too? Am I not supposed to worry that I fell for a woman who was not what I thought she was? *Again!*"

"Laurie, you really are making a bigger deal of this than it is, my good man," Freddie says with an annoying chuckle. "Norah spent time communicating secretly with both Charlotte and Lydia since they came here to Davenport Manor. That was all that was hidden from you. It was something that might or might not have worked."

"And there was no point in burdening the blind idiot!"

"We weren't keen on Norah becoming a Sinful Rose as we thought she needed a husband to be one. But it seems that wasn't altogether necessary. She kept me in the dark too, old boy, until she was about ready to pounce on them all. I could take umbrage too about that, but I don't. Because I see that she was right and got the job done."

*"Huh!"* I set down the tea with a jolt and spill it over my hand. I refuse to squirm with the heat. Anger is

bubbling and I'm determined that I shan't get upset. A man is better to be angry than crying and I cannot be any less of a man right now. "There's nothing done. They are walking about. Free to kill again!"

"They are exposed. Laid bare as it were. There'll be nothing from those bitches for some time."

"And you know that for a fact? Eve Good painted a very scary picture of what these women are capable of."

"I sent you Eve's letter just so you were on your guard again and that all of this was less of a shock. However, you weren't supposed to go to that house and you weren't supposed to get it into your soft head that Norah was a Sinful Rose. That was a little unfortunate."

"And you're totally sure about Norah now? Are you sure that she isn't manipulating you too? Are you one-hundred-per-cent sure she is telling the truth?"

Freddie sounds shocked and says, "Norah Walsh is a great detective. And, yes, I know she's a woman, and it has surprised me too that she's good at it – but there you have it. She is one of the best. I aim to keep her employed in some shape or form. I've promised her that I'll not forget all she's achieved here. And our Norah also got you back on your feet. Don't forget that."

"General," Giles says and pauses. "Shall I …?"

"Just a moment, Giles," says Freddie abruptly. He claps a grip around my sleeve and whispers, "You care for Norah. If you want to be lonely and bitter for the rest of your life, that's fine by me. But don't forget that you care for the woman who got you through all of this. Don't be a stubborn ass and ruin a good thing. Yes, Giles, go and show Norah in."

Norah! I want to see her and don't want to

simultaneously. My mind and heart are in a muddle and I'm on the verge of fearful, angry tears. Freddie cannot witness that and I cough back emotion and find the teacup to sip at. It's a man's job to care and protect his wife, his woman, and here I sit wondering who is friend or foe.

There's a slight creak of the door and Norah's scent enters. I don't know where to cast my eyes and start blinking and fumbling. I don't know what to do with my hands or my feelings.

"Laurie?" she says.

Freddie and Giles' footsteps retreat and hers come closer.

"May I talk with you?"

"No."

She drags the chair over like she used to when we were Sherlock and Watson and deep in conversation. I hate that she lied and that I was fooled over and over again. I loathe that I want her close to me despite all that's been hidden between us.

"I'm sorry," she whispers. "I didn't want to have to leave without telling you that we were so close to finding the truth. It might not have worked and –"

"Please don't justify it. I was a fool. Blind Laurie, the fool. Don't keep the lies going. You don't care what I think. It's a man's job to protect his woman and here I sit, unable to do it. You don't respect me."

"You're a wonderful man," she says, attempting to take my hand, but I pull away. "You're the best man I know. I hope that you can still care for me the way that I care for you?"

Soft skin touches my wrist and I let her take my fingers in hers. I want her so very much. Every ounce of bitterness and resentment fades as she tightly holds my hands in hers. I need her by my side.

"Forget everything else. We're a good team," she purrs. "I didn't lie. I may have led you down a path but I didn't deceive you too badly. I found the advertisement and sent them a letter. It took a long time to work on getting them all together. And then of course I had to go into the Ravenscairn location alone."

"Why take me at all on this process in the first place? Why bother with me, the burdensome idiot?"

"I came here to keep you safe and to keep an eye on Charlotte. Then Eve Good would only talk with a man and you needed all of this to realise life was worth living. You needed it."

"I came to only need you." It's the truth and that's all that swims in my mind now. I cling to her arms and pull her closer still. "I only need you."

"Oh Laurie, that's so sweet. I'm sorry you feel hurt."

"I wish I could see you," I tell her. "I want to know if your eyes are genuine. I don't know what to believe."

"Believe in us. You'll know the truth when you feel this." The palm of a hand leans against my cheek and slides around my good ear and pulls my head down. Norah's sweet breath tickles and she whispers, "I'll be your Watson, Sherlock. Let's start again."

Her lips meet mine. It is simply glorious. There'll be no more talk of the Sinful Roses and, even though my world is full of shadows, I can see shards of sunlight dancing.

## THE END

Printed in Great Britain
by Amazon